The Baron Who Never Danced

BARBARA RUSSELL

OLIVERHEBERBOOKS

Cover art by Dar Albert at Wicked Smart Designs

Published by Oliver-Heber Books

0 9 8 7 6 5 4 3 2 1

one
Theatre Royal, 1887

THE MORE ROYSTON knew human beings, the more he appreciated animals.

He'd been a footman at the service of Lord Stephen Dunn, Earl of Havisham, for two years now, but His Lordship's attitude still surprised him, and not always in a good fashion.

Royston stood at attention in the plush, private opera box of the earl, feeling a bit out of place in his footman uniform. The box looked like a giant jewellery case. Velvet everywhere, golden stucco, and polished wood.

"My lord, I'm afraid I didn't understand," he said.

Lord Havisham brushed an invisible speck of dust from his shiny evening suit. "It's all very simple. I'm going to receive a lady here tonight."

Of course he was. If a competition in adultery existed, the earl would be the champion.

"Mrs. Haywood will come with her daughter, Miss Haywood." Lord Havisham cast a bored glance at the seats in the auditorium that slowly filled with people before the beginning of the performance. "Do you follow me so far?"

"I do, my lord." Royston had understood that part even the

first time the earl had explained it. It was the second part that wasn't clear.

"I want you to keep Miss Haywood out of my box." The earl pointed at the box door for extra clarity.

"Yes, my lord, but what if Miss Haywood wishes to leave? And where should I keep her? In the hallway? For how long? The play is about two hours long."

The earl's request was ridiculous. Soon the play would start, and he was supposed to prevent a woman from watching it.

Lord Havisham huffed. "I don't care where you keep Miss Haywood. Rest assured, I'll let her in at a certain point. I want to be alone with her mother for a while."

The fact the earl was interested in the mother was a comfort of sorts, since he had the tendency to favour young women.

Royston bowed, still full of doubts. "My lord."

"Don't listen to what Miss Haywood says in case she protests. She won't get in here with her mother unless I say so."

Miss Haywood didn't know it yet, but she was going to be upset. Royston bowed again. There was a lot of bowing to perform around aristocrats.

Lord Havisham sat down on the stuffed chair, his features softening. "I know you disapprove, but Mrs. Haywood is the widow of a gentleman who died years ago. A robbery, I think. Anyway, I didn't want to meet her in my house, for personal reasons."

When Lord Havisham talked about meeting a woman for 'personal reasons,' he meant he was looking for a new mistress.

"Needless to say," Lord Havisham said, "no one should know I'm seeing her here tonight."

Royston didn't say anything. The only comment he wanted to voice was, 'You're a bloody idiot and should be ashamed of yourself.' His mother had been a prostitute in a brothel in Clerkenwell. He knew all about lords' mistresses and other dirty secrets.

"Of course, my lord. I know my place. But I must speak my mind."

"Pray, do." Lord Havisham sounded bored.

"My lord, what if Miss Haywood wants to leave the theatre? Once she realises she can't enter the box, she won't have any reason to stay here. Not to mention she'll get upset."

That gave the earl something to ponder. "Hmm... no, don't let her leave for any reason. I don't know for how long I need to be alone with Mrs. Haywood. Just don't let her leave the hallway."

Ridiculous.

Lord Havisham waved him out. "That's all, Royston. You may wait outside."

Royston bowed one last time before leaving the opera box. The things he did for a salary. But the alternative was to return to being a cat burglar, risking being thrown in prison at any moment, or starving in a dank alleyway. Both options weren't appealing in the least.

He stood in the hallway next to the door as the other members of the audience walked to their boxes. Perhaps he complained too much. As someone who had grown up in a brothel, become a professional thief, and narrowly escaped from the peelers more times than he'd care to count, having been hired as an earl's footman was a huge improvement. A regular salary, a warm and dry room, and proper meals.

Two years ago, he'd stopped a rival thief from robbing the earl, not out of goodness, but because he'd wanted to rob Lord Havisham himself. But in an ironic twist of fate, Lord Havisham had misunderstood Royston's action and thanked him for his help. Then he'd offered Royston a position as a footman.

He couldn't judge others. Despite Lord Havisham's questionable morals when it came to his wedding vows, Royston had to admit the earl had been nothing but kind and generous to him. He enjoyed a level of freedom other footmen didn't have, a higher salary than average, and even paid medical bills. His past wasn't a secret to the earl, and as long as Royston didn't steal again, the earl wouldn't give him the sack.

But if he was going to be honest, he didn't enjoy having to cover for His Lordship's philandering, or keep a young woman separated from her mother only because the earl had to dirty-puzzle in his box.

Well, at least tonight, the job was easy. Surely, he wouldn't have any problem keeping Miss Haywood in the hallway.

~

ANGELINE HAD ALWAYS WANTED to go with her mother on one of her elegant nights out. Theatre premiers, operas, concerts, soirées. Mama had never taken Angeline with her until that night.

She admired the way Mama commanded everyone's attention whenever she entered a room, even though she didn't hold any titles. Or how the gentlemen— no matter their age, marital status, or peerage —seemed enthralled by her with just one glance. It wasn't a matter of beauty because Angeline had never managed to tear a smile from anyone, despite the fact she'd inherited her mother's looks. Same raven hair and black eyes, same pillow-like lips, and same curves. Yet no one noticed her.

Not that she minded. In fact, being at the centre of attention wasn't her first aspiration. But she wondered how it would feel to have the same uncanny power of charming people as Mama had.

Every head turned towards Angeline's mother as they crossed the busy lobby of the Theatre Royal. Ladies and gentlemen in their finest clothes waited for the play, *The Romany Rye*, to begin. A few gentlemen were so intimidated by her beauty that they fidgeted and blushed. Oddly enough, others pretended not to see her, even though Mama gave them a graceful bow of her head. How rude.

Mama's blue silk gown hugged her body, exalting her hourglass figure, and showed only a hint of her decolletage. Angeline wondered if her mauve gown had the same effect on her. Not likely, judging from the almost pitiful glances tossed in her direction. Some gentlemen looked at her as if to say, 'Poor creature.'

She paused to admire the high-vaulted ceiling, the frescoes, and the large windows. She could get used to going out with her mama.

"Did you do some research, as I asked you?" Mama asked, climbing the sweeping stairs, her chin up.

"Of course." Angeline hurried up to walk next to her. "*The Romany Rye* is the story of two half-brothers and the jealousy tearing them apart."

"Goodness me." Mama stopped at the top of the stairs. The lights from the chandelier played with her diamond necklace. "I don't mean the play. We aren't here to enjoy the performance. We have a mission."

Actually, Angeline would love to watch the play although her first official appearance in society was more important. Alas, when she'd been the age to be a debutante, Mama hadn't enough money to bring her out. Thank goodness their finances were in order now. More than in order, as the diamond necklace proved.

"Come here, darling," Mama said.

She followed her mother to a quiet, dimly lit corner in the hallway.

Mama lowered her voice. "I'm going to introduce you to an earl. I hope you studied *The Ladies' Book of Etiquette, and Manual of Politeness* as I asked you to do. This meeting is very important."

Well, Angeline had read the book, but remembering it was another matter. "I did read the manual."

Mama narrowed her gaze. "I don't mind you spending time riding or practising with the bow. A lady needs to spend time outdoors, and physical activities are good for the body, but you shouldn't neglect your etiquette studies just because you want to shoot arrows at a hay target."

A target at two hundred yards, something Angeline was proud of and that required a lot of practice.

"We must think about your future." Mama touched Angeline's cheek. "I haven't cared enough about that so far. But I promise you'll have a more comfortable life than I did. You won't make the same mistakes I did."

Angeline held Mama's hand. "Not every man is like Father."

Her father had been a drunk and violent man, who had disappeared one day when Angeline had been a child, leaving them full of debt and in a decrepit house. She had to thank her mother for all the sacrifices Mama had made and for never giving up to keep her daughter alive. Mama had gone into service and worked hard until she'd been able to leave service and establish herself as a respectable lady.

Angeline had briefly worked as a maid as well, but Mama was the one who had improved their lives drastically with her ability to make money. Angeline didn't exactly understand all the intricacies of Mama's financial enterprises— she invested her money in different businesses and stock markets — but she was well-connected in society. An earl had invited her into his box, after all. Mama was London's darling at the moment.

Angeline watched a family of three heading to their box. The girl had to be around fifteen, pretty in a pale-yellow gown. They smiled at each other, looking so happy. A happy family with a proper husband and father was possible. Having a happy family of her own was her mission to prove to her father how wrong he'd been to leave them.

"You worry too much, Mama. I'm sure I'll find a lovely husband and have a house full of children and love."

Instead of smiling at the idea of seeing her daughter settled and happy, Mama's expression tightened. "There's still time to marry. I'm not in a hurry to become a grandmother."

"Time? Mama I'm practically a spinster."

Mama waved dismissively. "A husband can wait."

Angeline didn't argue. Husbands were a delicate topic. After Mama had been abandoned and mistreated by her husband, she didn't respect marriage. But...

"Why am I meeting this earl then? I thought tonight's introduction was the first step to find me a suitor."

"Absolutely not." Mama's cheeks flushed under the rouge. "What I want for you is Lord Havisham's connections."

Connections? What did that mean? Connections for what? Anyway. She was at the theatre and would enjoy herself. Yes, sir, she would.

Footmen and theatre hosts ushered ladies and gentlemen to their boxes. The air was thick with the scent of different expensive perfumes. Mama stopped in front of box number twelve, where a quite imposing man stood as if guarding it.

Goodness. If the man was a footman, he worked in the wrong trade. With his massive body and brooding gaze, he should be a highwayman or a pugilist. Footmen, in her mind, were supposed to be elegant. The man looked like a war machine ready to tramp everything in his path. His dress livery was impeccable and freshly pressed, but the hard hazel eyes were those of a murderer.

Mama stepped back from the imposing footman. "Good evening. I believe Lord Havisham is waiting for us."

The footman cast a long, assessing glance over them as if pondering how long it'd take him to wrestle both of them to the ground. Not much, judging by how quickly he dismissed them. Angeline felt that stare patting her down. She glared back, hoping he noticed her disapproval.

"Who are you, madam?" Even the voice sounded dangerous, as sharp as a knife.

"Mrs. Haywood and my daughter, Angeline." Mama pointed her fan at the door. "His Lordship is waiting for us, and the play is about to start. So please move aside, fella."

Without a word, the footman slid inside the box and shut the door.

"How insolent," Angeline said. "Leaving us here without a word, and he demanded we introduce ourselves" She'd learnt something from that etiquette book, after all.

"Patience." Mama patted her perfect chignon. "The first rule to gain a man's favour is to let him believe he has the upper hand."

"Do you want to gain that footman's favour?"

"You never know whom you might need one day. It's better to keep friends with everyone, just in case."

"Isn't that manipulation?"

"No, it's survival."

The footman came out only to shut the door behind him. "His Lordship will welcome you now." He held the door open for Mama, but after she entered the box, he blocked Angeline. "His Lordship specifically required only Mrs. Haywood's presence."

"Excuse me?" Mama said.

Angeline didn't step back this time. "But we're together. Mama?"

"Wait a moment, darling. I'll have a word with Lord Havisham." Mama closed the door, leaving her alone with the highwayman.

"I'm sure the earl wants to see me as well," she said.

He didn't grace her with a comment.

"I don't understand why I have to wait here."

He didn't say anything.

"You could say something."

"Is 'please wait here' enough?"

She scoffed. "How rude."

"I said please," he pointed out.

Never mind. She waited for the longest minute in her life. When Mama came out of the box, she was flustered and tense.

She shot a glare at the footman. "I'm sorry, darling, but the earl and I must discuss some business."

"In the opera box?"

Mama tapped her fan against her palm. "It's a long story. The earl wants you to wait here. Perhaps at the end of the first act, he'll allow you in."

"I won't be able to follow the play."

"You already know the plot, don't you?" Mama patted Angeline's cheek. "I'll see you later, darling."

"What about the play?" Angeline craned her neck to talk with her mother, but the rudest footman in history shut the door. "I'm sorry!"

He gave her a quick nod. "Consider your apology accepted, miss."

two

ANGELINE HUFFED AS the doors to the boxes lining the hallway were shut, signalling the play was about to begin. "What am I supposed to do here for an hour?" she asked the footman.

"The same as I do. Obey the earl. There's nothing we can do about the situation." He regarded her from underneath bronzed eyelashes.

"The earl isn't my master. I have no intention of staying here and doing nothing."

She'd take a hansom cab home. She should ask for a reimbursement of her ticket at the box office since she couldn't enjoy the play. Or ask the blasted earl to reimburse it. She went to open the door to the box to tell her mother she was leaving, but the footman blocked her, having the audacity to hold her wrist.

"No. The earl's orders are clear. He must not be disturbed."

"Goodness, let me go."

He did as told without hesitation and without an apology.

"Then you'll do me the favour of informing my mother that I returned home." She started to leave when the cheeky man stepped in front of her and blocked her path.

"Miss," he hissed. "Don't make this more difficult than neces-sary. I'm afraid you have to stay here. His Lordship's orders."

"Oh, really?" She lifted her chin, mostly to be able to stare at him in the eyes rather than show him defiance. "Thank goodness I don't have to follow His Lordship's orders." She tried to sidestep the giant, but he mirrored her moves.

"Thank goodness my job is to make sure His Lordship's orders are followed." His tone didn't have an ounce of humour.

"I want to leave. I'm not going to wait here for an hour, hoping your master will show me mercy and let me in."

His luscious chestnut curls bounced over his sharp jaw as he shook his head. If he weren't so intense and menacing, he'd pass for a handsome man. Frightening, but handsome.

"Staying here is in your interest as well, miss. It's late. A lady shouldn't take a hansom cab alone at this hour of the night. It's a matter of safety."

No, it was a matter of principle. Who was this earl who could decide how she was supposed to spend her night?

"I am not staying. Sir. I apologise if my decision upsets you."

She didn't ride and practise with a bow every day to have some hulk of a man bully her. He towered over her and had enough muscles in his little finger to knock her out, but she was light, agile, and quick. If she confused him with quick footwork and was fast enough, he wouldn't catch her.

Besides, she didn't need to go past him. She could run in the opposite direction and leave the theatre using the secondary exit. She had never been at the Theatre Royal, but every theatre had a secondary exit for the performers and staff. The other exit should open to a side alleyway. His Lordship would scold him for not having held her. Served him right.

The man exhaled, his chest lowering. "Miss, I must—"

She feinted a dash to the left. He followed her move, but she spun on her heels and ran towards the other side of the corridor, and goodbye hunky footman.

Ha! It'd been easier than she'd thought. The heavy skirt and petticoats hindered her movements, but she was used to running with them. The secondary hallway leading to the rear was so narrow her skirt skimmed both walls. She didn't dare glance behind her as she sped down the service stairs. The silence bothered her, though. Too quiet for anything good. Midway down, she paused and checked behind her. No one. The loyal footman wasn't so loyal after all. He must have decided that catching her was too much of an effort for his salary.

Pity. She enjoyed a nice chase. Leaving him behind had been too easy. Obviously, the man wasn't as athletic as he seemed. Never mind.

She resumed going down the stairs at a leisurely pace. Mama would be all right. She was a resourceful, indomitable woman. If anything, the earl had to be careful because when Mama set her mind on a venture, nothing could stop her. No one knew the stock market better than she did. Her investments were always a success.

At the end of the stairs, Angeline hurried along the wide corridor towards a set of double doors. She pulled them open. A large figure loomed over her. She screamed.

"Surprised, miss?" The footman filled the space in the doorframe with his bulk.

She stepped back. "How?"

"I guess I know this theatre better than you do. Shall we return to the earl's box after this pointless exercise?" He stretched out an arm towards the stairs. "Ladies first."

"Brutes before beauty."

His eyebrows lowered over his hazel eyes. "Very funny, miss, but I'm tired of jokes. Please go upstairs, or I'll be forced to drag you."

She balled a fist on her hip. "You wouldn't dare."

"Challenging me is a very bad idea."

"I do challenge you, sir. Now step aside and let me go."

"I told you it was a bad idea." He took her waist and lifted her as if she were a doll. His large hands covered her ribcage while her feet dangled over the floor. "You forced me, miss."

"Put me down. This is most undignified."

"I'll put you down, but not here." He went up the stairs flawlessly, despite the fact she wriggled and struggled in his firm grip.

She tried everything— shoving him, moving side to side like a snake to ease his grip, and squeezing herself out of his hands, but the man trapped her. He didn't let her go, not even when they were in the upstairs hallway.

"What is happening?" A theatre host stared at them in horror. "Unhand the lady immediately."

"He kidnapped me." Angeline shrugged herself free from the man's steely grip. Or rather, the brute let her go.

"I have orders," the brute said. "His Lordship, the Earl of Havisham, ordered me to make sure this lady waits outside of his box. I'm only doing my job, sir."

Oh, no. The theatre host lost his outraged air. Just hearing the name of an earl had been enough to change his demeanour.

"Well, in that case." The theatre host moved out of the way. "Continue."

"I can't believe it." The rest of her protest was cut off by the brute grabbing her by the waist again. "This is utterly... I can't... I can't..."

"Say something that makes sense?" Too much amusement rang in his voice.

"You're incredibly rude."

"You're breaking my heart, miss." He clicked his tongue. "You ran. What was I supposed to do? London is dangerous at night. You can't leave unchaperoned."

She scoffed once he put her down in front of His Blasted Lordship's door. She folded her arms over her chest. "And now?"

He stood next to her, silent.

She paced around. "You wouldn't have caught me if you hadn't cheated. Obviously, I'm faster. You're too big to be quick."

He shot her a questioning gaze.

"People with a lot of muscles are slower than petite people. It's science."

He pinched the bridge of his nose.

"This is unfair. Only because a capricious earl gives an order, I must stay here with you."

For the first time, his features softened a tiny fraction. "Those who hold the power can command us. I don't make the rules. You don't make the rules. Time will go faster if you accept this simple truth."

"Absurd. Anyhow, in a fair race I'd beat you." Her mouth twitched as a pungent smell like that of burning paint and fabric reached her nostrils.

He straightened, staring at a point over her head. "Run."

"Do you want to chase me again? I'm game."

"No, run. Fire." He wrapped his arms around her again and moved away from the door before shoving it open. "Fire!" He let her go and disappeared inside.

Heavens. He was right. Dark smoke crept from the service stairs they'd just come from. Her eyes watered as the air turned acrid and grey.

"Mama!" She didn't have time to enter the darn box before her mama rushed out of it.

"What is it?" Mama screamed. Bright orange flames roared from the other side.

"Quick." The brute came out of the box, shoving a tall blond man in an elegant suit.

The shout '*fire*' echoed from every corner of the theatre. The roar of the blaze was unmistakable now. A stream of people shoving each other clogged the corridor. Angeline groaned when someone's elbow hit her ribs and someone else's foot caused her to trip.

"Order! Form a proper queue!" a theatre host yelled, waving his arms.

No one paid him the slightest bit of attention. Smoke saturated the air, and people pressed against Angeline from every side. She was shoved right and left, back and forth, almost losing her footing. Breathing was a chore. Her lungs hurt because, every time she inhaled, it was like gulping acid. Her head spun with the smoke and the chaos.

There was a loud crack coming from the ceiling before a flaming log dropped in a flare of red sparks. People screamed. The log thudded against the stairs, shedding flames in its wake. She gasped when the people in the middle of the stairs disappeared underneath the blaze, the smoke, and the log.

A searing pain slashed her arm as a burning piece of a log fell on her. The silk glove caught fire. She screamed and swatted the flames, tears blurring her vision. She didn't have time to assess the damage as another piece of the ceiling fell behind the smoke.

Panic ensued. Some people pushed her to go down, others to go up. She didn't know where the exit was. Her head hurt, her arm throbbed, and her eyes watered.

"Mama?" She searched around. Mama, the brute, and the earl were nowhere to be seen. She had no idea where or when she'd lost them. "Mama?"

She struggled to walk against the flow of the crowd. Shoves and jabs hit her, and the pain nearly caused her to pass out. She panted, then coughed from the smoke The air turned scorching, and the frightening noise of the fire crackling and eating the walls froze her. The people seemed to be frozen as well because everyone was moving and shoving others out of the way, but no one seemed to be going anywhere. The ceiling tilted. A buzzing noise rang in her ears.

"Miss!" The brute's blackened face swept into view. "What are you doing here?" He hauled her up before she could say anything.

This time, she didn't protest. Her head hurt, and the air was too heavy to breathe properly, never mind talking. She wrapped her good arm around the brute's neck and clung to him as he shoved people aside none-too-gently, making his way against the flow.

"Don't worry, miss," he said among pants. "Your mother is safe outside."

"How did you find me?" she said among coughs.

"I told you I knew this place better than you."

She took a deep breath to thank him, but another coughing fit cut her off. Smoke stung her eyes, and the sizzling noise of the fire scared her to death. She gripped him with all her strength, feeling his hard muscles under her arm. Tears welled in her eyes because of the irritation and the pain.

She and the man reached a part of the theatre less crowded although she couldn't tell where they were. The air was cleaner, but she kept coughing.

"Almost there." He rushed down a dark corridor before barging through a set of double doors. "Here we are." He put her down gently on something hard and cold. His face wrinkled in concern filled her vision. "You're hurt." He sounded desolate.

"A burned—" She couldn't finish the sentence.

"Don't talk. Take deep breaths and spit the ash if you need to."

"Angeline." Mama came from somewhere and hugged her, smelling of smoke and burned silk. "Darling. You disappeared. I was so scared."

"My arm," she stammered.

Mama's eyes flared wide as she cradled Angeline's arm gently. "Do not worry. We'll take care of it." She started sobbing. "It'll be all right."

The earl sat next to her, coughing so hard he shook. Ash blackened his face. The tips of his coattails were burned, and thick tears streamed down his face.

"I'll be right back." The brute... well, she couldn't call him that now, not anymore. The man rushed back into the inferno.

"Royston, don't!" The earl bent over, coughing. "It's an order."

But Royston didn't listen.

From the outside, the theatre was even scarier. Angeline gazed at the building. What once had been the sparkling white walls of the Theatre Royal were spitting fire from every window. The orange glow seemingly coming from every corner created a halo against the backdrop of the night sky. It was an inferno, and Royston had jumped straight into it.

"What is he doing?" Angeline's throat burned with the effort of talking.

"Being a bloody fool." The earl wiped his face with a hand-kerchief.

Sirens pealed. The fire brigade worked around the building with tall sprays of water from the hydraulic pumps, but she doubted any part of the theatre could be saved. Other survivors around her coughed and shivered. Some showed nasty burns on the face and neck. At least she wasn't seriously injured, thanks to Royston. She doubted she would have lasted long without his help.

A collective gasp rose from the crowd as another part of the roof collapsed. She clamped a hand over her mouth. Where was Royston?

"Oh, no." Mama hugged her. "That poor man."

The earl hung his head, running a hand through his dishev-elled hair.

Angeline exhaled when Royston came out of the door, carrying an unconscious young man. A small entourage of people, all coughing and crying, thanked the footman, calling him a hero. He deposited the young man on the kerb next to the others before rushing back inside.

"No!" she shouted at the same time as the earl said, "Stay here. It's an order."

But Royston didn't listen.

When the roof collapsed completely, she regretted not having had the opportunity to thank him.

three

R OYSTON WOULD PROBABLY spit ash and dust for the rest of his life, and his eyes would never stop burning.

Sitting on a bench at the Royal Waterloo Hospital, he wiped the tears that kept streaming down his stinging face. No matter how much water he drank or how many times he washed his skin, his eyes burned, his nostrils singed, and his throat seemed filled with scratching sand. He couldn't complain, though. Aside from the ash and a minor cut on his hand, he was fine. The same thing couldn't be said about those people who had died in the fire. Others, who had been transported to the hospital, wouldn't likely survive their wounds. Too many people had been hurt if the frenetic activity in the hospital was an indication of the seriousness of the incident.

He'd lost sight of Lord Havisham after he'd been sent to the hospital. He'd lost sight of Miss Angeline Haywood as well, but she should be all right although that burn on her arm might get infected. Speaking of which, she walked over to him. Or at least, he thought it was her. His teary, swollen eyes offered only a blurred vision, but he recognised her pretty mauve dress and her petite frame. He remembered she smelled like wild roses, but right now, she could smell like horse dung and he wouldn't notice it.

"Mr. Alexander?" She sat next to him. "It's me, Miss Angeline Haywood."

He recognised her sweet voice as well. When she'd accused him of being rude, it hadn't been so sweet. Also, somehow she knew his family name.

"Miss," he croaked out, coughing in the handkerchief that had once been white.

"How are you?"

"Alive. How's your wound?"

She was a giant mauve blur, but he spotted a movement of her arm. "They applied a poultice to the burn, bandaged my arm, and gave me some laudanum for the pain." Her voice was strained.

"I'm sorry." He coughed.

"Thank you, but it's nothing compared to what other people suffered."

He coughed again. Bloody hell.

"Let me help you," she said.

"You're hurt."

"As is everyone, and I'm not in extreme pain now." She hooked her arm through his. "Come with me. The nurses have set up a room for those patients who need to wash and clean their eyes. Eye and throat problems seem to be common conditions."

Since he didn't have the energy to breathe, talking required too much effort. He let her guide him through the crowd of white-coated medics and nurses to a bright white room. He couldn't make out anything else about the place, just a giant, blurred white thing and other blurred objects. Blinking didn't help to clear his vision.

"There." She helped him to a chair. Then the slosh of water came.

He wiped his eyes again but no luck.

"Let me." She passed a wet cloth over his face several times, wringing it now and then.

A faint scent wafted from the cloth as she patiently removed the ash. Her gentle touch was soothing.

"It's rose and chamomile water," she said. "It's good for the eyes. You might need to see a doctor anyway and make sure there isn't any damage, but the water will help."

He said nothing. With his eyes closed, he focused on breathing. The smell of burning wood would forever remain in his nostrils.

"I didn't thank you," she said. Her soft breath fanned on his cheek. "You saved my life and that of many others. You were so brave. Everyone is singing the praise of the earl of Havisham's brave footman who dared the fire."

Another coughing fit racked him. The cough was so strong that he felt as if red-hot claws were scratching his lungs. "No need to thank me," he said in a raspy voice.

"I beg to differ. Especially since I called you a brute."

"I don't care about that."

She washed his eyes many times until he smelled of something else other than smoke and his eyes burned less, but his sight was still blurred.

"Better?" she asked.

From what he could see, she was staring at him with an intensity he didn't find pleasant.

"Yes." He swallowed more water, but each sip scratched his throat. "Miss, I thank you for your help, but if you need to go to your mother, I understand." He'd rather be weak and sick without a witness. Thank you.

"My mother is all right." She paused before whispering, "You came back for me."

"What was I supposed to do? Let you die? Besides, to be honest, I wasn't thinking at that moment. All I knew was that I wasn't injured and that I could help." He rubbed his eyes. Bad choice. They burned tenfold.

"Don't rub. You'll make it worse."

He jolted when she took his injured hand and cleaned the cut with another cloth. His first instinct was to protest, but her soft fingers on his skin had a calming effect. There was something enchanting in the way she held his big hand in hers.

"How do you know my family name is Alexander?"

"Lord Havisham told me. He's here. A doctor is visiting him. My mother is here as well. She keeps coughing, but aside from that, she's fine."

"His Lordship will need me. Where is he?"

Her grip on his hand hardened. "His Lordship is all right. You're definitely in a more serious condition."

Sod his duty. She was right. He would sit there and enjoy the moment of calm as Miss Haywood tended to his wound.

"The earl is coming," she said, releasing his hand.

"Royston." A big black spot that had to be Lord Havisham stood in front of him.

"My lord." Royston rose.

Lord Havisham put a hand on his shoulder and pushed him down. "No need to stand up. You need to take care of yourself. You did something extraordinary tonight." There was too much excitement in his voice for a man who had risked his life an hour ago. "The young man you saved before the theatre collapsed is the queen's grandson," he added in a whisper.

"Good gracious," Miss Haywood said. "Is he all right?"

"He'll stay here for the night because he can't breathe properly, but he should recover well." Lord Havisham dipped his head, or at least that was what Royston saw. "You're the man of the hour."

He'd saved a royal lad. And? When he'd snatched the half-unconscious young man from a box filled with smoke, he hadn't had any idea who the lad might have been. The small group of people surrounding him should have been a clue, though. Surely, the lad's servants had been with him. If anything, if the royal grandson died, Royston would be blamed.

Having saved a royal didn't seem something he should be happy about. He was glad the royal grandson was alive, but he couldn't care less about who the lad was.

Again, he chose to stay silent.

"Miss Haywood," Lord Havisham said, "thank you for taking care of my footman. Royston is a loyal servant, and loyalty is always repaid."

Royston had no idea what His Lordship meant by that.

He bowed his head. "Thank you, my lord."

"I'll have my personal physician visit you." Lord Havisham took his arm and helped him up. "If you can walk, we'll go home and make sure you are well cared for. I want this hero to receive the treatment he deserves."

"Have a speedy recovery, Mr. Alexander," Miss Haywood said.

Royston wanted to say something, but an ache pounded in his head and a sudden exhaustion caught him. He bowed his head and followed Lord Havisham.

THE WATER in the bathtub was the colour of ink by the time Angeline had finished taking a bath.

So much ash had blackened her hair and skin that she was surprised she hadn't burned. She wiggled the fingers of her injured arm and grimaced. The poultice the nurse had applied helped, but her whole arm throbbed. As the physician had said, the burn would leave a big scar. She wasn't looking forward to changing the bandage every day. The wound was going to hurt.

"Are you all right, love?" Mama helped her out of the bathtub.

"Sore and tired."

"I know. I know." Mama shook. "I'll braid your hair."

Wrapped in a fresh dressing gown, Angeline sat at the vanity and avoided looking at her tired reflection in the mirror.

Mama didn't look better. Her paleness was concerning. She hadn't spoken a word from the moment they'd left the hospital. Fatigue bruised her eyes, and her lips were pressed into a flat line.

"Mama." Angeline caressed her bandaged arm. "I was thinking of visiting Mr. Alexander to know how he's faring in the next few days."

Mama gave a brusque nod.

"How are you? Sit here." Angeline patted the stool next to her. "Why are you so quiet? I'm worried."

Mama did as told. "I'm all right." She rearranged the pots of cream and rouge.

"You're in shock. The fire scared me, too." She held her mother's hand. "But we're alive."

Mama shook her head. "It's not the fire. I mean... what happened today was awful, but it made me think about our lives. You got injured."

"It's nothing."

"I beg to differ. The wound might get infected, but don't worry. I'll use all my knowledge of medicinal herbs to make sure you heal properly." Unshed tears shone in her eyes.

"I trust you, Mama."

Her mother wiped a tear quickly. "If you'd died today—"

"Don't say that." Angeline squeezed her mother's hands.

"I couldn't have borne it." She sobbed. "I can't go on without you."

"But I'm here."

Mama didn't seem to listen. "And if I'd died today, you would have been alone, unprotected, vulnerable."

"But you're here." Angeline hugged her mother, inhaling the familiar lavender scent.

"You don't understand." Mama disentangled from the

embrace. "There are things you don't know about me, about what I do. Things that will put you in danger."

She easily believed that. Statistics and probabilities weren't her forte. She wouldn't last five minutes handling the stock market. But danger? "I don't understand anything about the stock market. Only you can invest money so successfully."

"Darling." Mama's black eyes turned darker. "I don't invest any money in the stock market. I don't understand finance better than you do. In fact, I hate statistics."

"What are you talking about? You're a genius." Besides, why were they discussing the stock market instead of the trauma of the fire? "You have a talent for numbers I don't possess. We have a lovely house and food on our table, thanks to your business skills."

"No." Mama gripped Angeline's shoulders. "I lied to you. For years. The money I earn is from..." She took a shuddering breath.

"Yes?" Angeline stretched out her good arm, ready to catch her mother if she fainted. Mama paled further, and her eyes grew wider by the minute. "What is it?"

"You are going to hate me."

Angeline let out a nervous laugh. "Don't be ridiculous. I could never hate you. Tell me the truth. You're scaring me."

"I have tumbles with rich gentlemen," she said all in one breath.

Angeline tilted her head. "Would you say that again?"

"Our money comes from the tumbles I have with gentlemen." Mama shot each word as if they were bullets.

The world shifted on its axis. It was a good thing Angeline was sitting because she would have fallen to the floor.

"You have tumbles in exchange for money?" Goodness. Considering they lived a comfortable life, Mama had to have a string of clients. But it couldn't be possible.

"It's worse than that." Mama rose and poured herself a glass of water from the pitcher. "These men don't only pay me for the tumble." She drank the whole glass. "I become their mistress, their dirty secret. Meanwhile, I collect material on them."

"Material?" Angeline propped an elbow on the vanity, needing support. The pain in her arm was almost forgotten.

"Compromising letters and paid bills because they take me out to dinner or to fancy hotels. Sometimes they rent a room for me in a fancy area. I also take photographs of them and me together when they're too drunk to understand what's happening. Sometimes they're daft enough to agree to have their photographs taken."

"I need a moment to think." Angeline rubbed her aching forehead. The revelation was too much.

"I know, love." Mama stroked Angeline's shoulder. "It's all true. There's no stock market."

"But for what purpose would you collect— oh, goodness." She breathed hard, and her throat ached all over again. "You blackmail them."

Her mother nodded. "Not all of them. Only those who deserve it. No one cares if a gentleman has a mistress as long as the relationship is kept quiet. The nastier the gentleman, the more eager he is to keep his dirty secrets quiet."

The shock caused Angeline to pause for a long moment. Mama had spoiled her since she was a child. Even when Angeline had worked as a waitress, she couldn't say her life had been harsh. She lived in a nice house, and food filled her table. But blackmailing people wasn't her idea of leading a happy life. Not to mention that she wanted a husband and a family. If Mama's scandalous life came out, she and Angeline would never recover. They would be shunned and might end up in prison.

"Mama." She licked her dry lips. "What you do isn't simply illegal. It's wrong."

"Wrong? Who's worse, those men who don't hesitate to be unfaithful or me? Do you think I would let those pigs put their dirty paws on me without having them pay the consequences?

They deserve it. I tried to live only on the fares they gave me, but it wasn't enough to provide an education for you."

Oh, no. Angeline pressed a finger to her temple as guilt lifted its nasty head. Her mother had solicited herself so that Angeline could study.

"What if what you do comes out? Tricks and plots like blackmailing people have the tendency to be discovered. What would happen to us? We might be arrested or, at the very least, become outcasts, and no man would touch me with a barge pole. I'll never get married."

Mama's eyes narrowed to slits. "And? It wouldn't be a loss. You can't trust men. Do you think that just because a man marries you, he's going to love you and care about you? He'll discard you as soon as he grows tired of you and will find someone else younger and fresher."

"Just because Father was a scoundrel, it doesn't mean every man is like him." Although the word scoundrel was a too-nice word for her father. Felon or crook was a more appropriate term.

Mama was officially the widow of a gentleman. The truth was that no one knew where Angeline's father was. He'd left when she'd been a toddler. Likely, being a criminal, a drunk, and addicted to opium, he had died in an opium den. Angeline didn't care. She felt guilty sometimes about her lack of care, but she didn't remember anything about him, and he hadn't shown himself in over twenty years.

Mama sat again on the stool, her shoulders stooping. "I don't want you to make the same mistake as I did. Marrying, that is."

"Right, because blackmailing people isn't a mistake." Angeline didn't want to discuss the value of marriage now. That was unimportant compared to the monumental revelation Mama had dropped over her shoulders.

She took another moment to digest the news. "Lord Havisham? Does he know that you are a... a..."

"Harlot? You can say it. I don't care."

No, Angeline wouldn't use that word for her mother. "Are you his mistress? Is this why he didn't want to see me in his box?"

She gave a reluctant nod. "I haven't been with him yet, but tonight was the opportunity to plan our first meeting. He offered two tickets for the play, inviting you although I told him clearly you weren't to be touched or informed of my probable liaison with him. Initially, he agreed to everything. He said we would have a normal night at the theatre and pretend to be only business partners as long as you were present. I thought he wanted to talk to me during the intermission, but he had other ideas. He told me he wanted a taste of what I could offer. Hence, you had to stay out of his box."

"What?" Angeline put a fluttering hand on her chest. "That's awful."

Mama didn't flinch. "No, it's normal."

"Why did you take me with you tonight of all nights?"

"I didn't know he would have prevented you from entering the box. I wanted you to have a proper night out and enjoy the play. But then the fire broke out, and you disappeared, and the thought of losing you was too much." A sob shook her. "I had to tell you the truth, make you understand why I've never taken you with me, and if something had happened to me, tonight, you would have been all alone with all the horrible things I did. The thought of those men I blackmailed coming after you because of me scared me to death. Without me to protect you, they would hurt you..." She sobbed harder. "I can't even think of what they would do to you."

"Heavens." Angeline's throat tightened, but not because of the fire. "You're alive and well. But you must stop this blackmail business. It's dangerous."

"It's our livelihood."

"We don't need more money," she whispered. "We have enough in our account to live decently for a few years."

"And after those years have passed?" She regained some colour. "What I do—"

"It's dangerous."

"It isn't only about money, but power. Power I would never have if I had a husband." Mama wiped her eyes and regained her composure quickly as if reluctant to show her fragility. "Once you get married, you become your husband's property. You lose your freedom."

If freedom was having tumbles for money and blackmailing people, Angeline wasn't sure she'd like that type of freedom.

"I hold all the power in my relationships. That's what matters."

Angeline disagreed. It seemed those men used her mother. "Sooner or later, a gentleman will want to avenge himself or simply call the police."

"I don't care what happens to me." Mama lost her determined expression, sagging on the stool. "But today made me understand you could have been left alone with my mistakes."

"No more blackmailing. Please," Angeline said.

"I can't stop now." Her bottom lip quivered, and she started crying again.

Angeline hugged her. What Mama did was wrong from many points of view. But she was Mama, and Angeline's heart broke at hearing her cry. Mama must have spent many nights doing things she hadn't wanted to do. The thought was like a vine tightening around Angeline's throat. She'd help her mother get out of that life.

<h1>four</h1>

ROYSTON SCRATCHED THE skin around the thick, tight bandage that covered his eyes and wrapped around his head. The physician had ordered him to keep his eyes closed and protected from the sunlight and dust to help them recover quickly. His coming and going in and out of the inferno in the theatre had caused a serious eye inflammation that had temporarily blinded him.

Lord Havisham had confined Royston to his bedroom, relieving him of all his duties until he healed completely. At first, Royston hadn't minded, but after a week of being in his bedroom doing nothing and not seeing anything, the inactivity bothered him. Also, his face itched, even though the physician came once a day to remove the bandage and wash his eyes. He suspected Lord Havisham's kindness had little to do with his good heart and everything to do with the royal lad. The earl was going to exploit every ounce of Royston's popularity.

Royston shouldn't complain about his condition, especially since more than a hundred people had died. Many had been trampled to death by the panicked mob. Others had died in the hospital. His injury shouldn't be permanent; the physician was optimistic. But he wouldn't mind some company.

A soft knock came from the door. "Mr. Alexander? It's me, Miss Haywood. May I come in?"

Miss Haywood? He sat up on the bed, wondering if he was decent. "Come in."

The hinges screeched, and light footsteps sounded. Only one pair of footsteps. He stood up, putting a hand on the wall for support.

"Miss Haywood. Your visit is unexpected."

"Mr. Alexander, please sit down. I'm glad to see you again..." A pause. "Sorry, I didn't mean to make a silly joke."

"Not at all. Why are you here?" He wished he could see where she was. He hoped he wasn't talking with the chair.

"I meant to come earlier, but the butler told me your physician forbade any visits for the first few days of your recovery, and I was in pain as well." The swish of fabric came.

"How's your arm?"

"My mother prepared a special poultice to numb the flesh and protect it from infection. I have to say it works. I'm much better now."

"Great. So you are here because...?" Did he sound rude? He couldn't tell anymore.

He was grumpy on a good day. After a week trapped in his bedroom with an itchy bandage around his face, he was allowed to be even grumpier, wasn't he?

"I'm here to keep you company." The noise of paper shuffling came. "I've brought some newspapers and magazines to read to you. But if you'd rather stay alone, I'll leave immediately."

Being alone or spending some time with the spirited Miss Haywood? Very spirited. Not really a choice, and he was desperate for company.

"Please stay, Miss Haywood. I appreciate your company."

"Thank you, Mr. Alexander." There was the scraping of wood. "You may sit down. I'm sitting on the chair."

"Great." He plopped himself on the bed. He should have tidied up a bit. He had no idea if there were undergarments or dirty socks around.

"I have the *Herald* unless you want me to read something else."

He shifted his position, trying to straighten the bed covers. "The latest issue of *Uppercut* should be on the table. I'd like you to start with that."

"*Uppercut*?" Papers rustled. "What is it? A sewing and knitting magazine? Oh, a boxing one. I didn't know there were boxing periodicals."

"That's my favourite, and I'm eager to know who won the last match."

"Very well."

Twenty minutes later, Miss Haywood's voice dropped to a flat, boring monotone.

"*... and Ed the Beast smashed a powerful hook against Gorgeous Ross...* I'm sorry, but who gave these names to these pugilists? They're ridiculous."

"Would you mind keeping going? I'd like to know who won," he said, literally on the edge of his seat.

"But it's so boring and violent. Can't I read something else?"

"Just tell me who won."

"All right. Let me skim this very long and convoluted article, full of blood and violence. So... the Beast was hit... Gorgeous won the third round... blood, blood, blood... punch, punch, punch, someone lost a tooth, goodness, so brutal!"

"Miss Haywood, please." He shifted again.

"Fine. It's the Beast. He won. Happy?"

He sagged. "No. I bet a quid on Gorgeous."

"May I read something else? Does this magazine have at least a horoscope column?"

"The horoscope? That nonsense about the planets? Please no."

She huffed. "Why not? It's all the rage in American newspapers and magazines. Some newspapers here have started including them. They're exciting. Let's see... no, of course there isn't anything remotely entertaining in this magazine, not even a comment on the weather. Of course, it's a matter of taste. I appreciate you finding *Uppercut* very entertaining."

If she was making faces at him, he would never know.

"Let's see the *Herald*. Gossip column," she said brightly.

"I'd rather read the horoscope."

"But there's an article about you. *The brave and selfless Mr. Royston Alexander, a footman at the employment of Lord Havisham, was praised for his heroic acts by the queen herself.* That's good, isn't it? *Since Mr. Alexander disappeared from the public to take care of his injuries, we interviewed a few acquaintances of his and learnt that the proclaimed hero...*" She coughed. "I've changed my mind. I want to read more about Gorgeous Ross. The poor thing lost the match. He must be distraught."

He turned in the direction of her voice. "Miss Haywood, tell me what the article says."

"It's all silly things you don't need to hear."

"I do. Please?"

"But why would you... oh, fine." She cleared her throat. "*We learnt that the glorified hero of the terrible Theatre Royal fire is the son of a fallen woman. He grew up in a house of ill repute without a father...*" A muffled noise rose. "Please, I don't want to read this. I'd rather read about hooks and uppercuts."

He acknowledged the sting of sorrow in his chest. "What they say is true though. I was born in a brothel. The girls who lived there helped my mother raise me. When I was a lad, I learnt to box from one of the nice jockeys. I kept the girls safe by kicking violent jockeys out of the brothel. One of the girls taught me how to play the piano. Another one how to play chess. Another one taught me how to..."

No, he didn't want to talk about dancing. About that rich jockey who had forced his mother to dance, using a whip, torturing her while the music had kept going until his mother had died. She'd suffered from a heart condition, and the forced dancing had been too much for her frail body. Just thinking about dancing made him sick to his stomach. A bitter taste soured his mouth. He scratched his face again, only to feel the sting of the pain and think of something else.

"Oh, I understand that, Mr. Alexander." Her embarrassment slipped into her voice.

"I didn't mean *that* sort of thing, miss. I was referring to something else."

"Those years must have been difficult for you."

He opened and closed his fists. He usually didn't talk about his past to anyone but having been blindfolded for a week made him a little desperate for company. He wanted to talk now, maybe because, with the darkness surrounding him, it was as if he were alone or in a confessional. Or maybe he was simply tired of keeping his story to himself, and he liked Miss Haywood.

"It wasn't that bad," he said. "I had a warm and safe place where to sleep. When the jockeys arrived, my mother would send me to sleep in a separate bedroom on the other side of the brothel. Despite that, I understood quite quickly what was going on in the other rooms. The girls spoiled me and took good care of me. I can't say my childhood was horrible. There were bad moments, of course. A man, in particular, was very cruel to my mother. He used the whip..." No, he couldn't go on.

A gasp came from her. "Heavens. I'm so sorry."

"I'll spare you the details. I apologise for having brought that up. It's not something you want to hear, miss."

He jolted when Miss Haywood touched his hand briefly.

"If you need to talk, I'll be happy to listen."

"No, it's all right," he said.

Minutes of silence stretched. He was glad she didn't fill it with senseless chatter.

He touched the bandage again and scratched his skin. "I didn't ask if you have other problems aside from the burn."

"I'm all right. I stopped coughing quickly after the incident, thanks to a syrup my mother prepared for me. She's a little shocked though." Her voice lowered. "She hasn't been the same since."

"None of us will be the same."

"You're right." A long pause filled by her soft breathing. "Thank you again for saving my life. I'm sure I'd be dead if you hadn't found me."

"You don't have to thank me." But he'd like it if she returned to read to him. If only he were bold enough to ask her.

"I should go." The swish of fabric came. "I'll be back tomorrow if you agree."

Thank goodness she brought that up.

"I'd appreciate it."

"See you tomorrow— drat. I'm sorry."

He laughed, and the laughter relieved him of the heaviness of his sorrows. "Don't worry."

"Good evening, Mr. Alexander."

After she left, a delicate trail of her rose scent lingered in the air.

ANGELINE KNOCKED on Mr. Alexander's door, acknowledging the odd flutter in her belly. Her excitement might be due simply to her gratitude towards him and a sense of guilt that didn't want to leave her. She'd called him names before he'd saved her life, risking his own. She still found him a little rough, but his kindness and good heart were undeniable.

"Come in." His voice thundered from the other side.

"Good afternoon, Mr. Alexander." She slid inside the small room in Lord Havisham's townhouse.

The shirts and trousers that had been scattered around during her previous visit had been neatly folded in a pile. His bandage was gone, but his eyes were still red and puffy.

He blinked a few times. The stubble suited him. It enhanced his strong jaw. "Miss Haywood. Are you wearing green or blue?"

"Neither. It's a dark-red dress. Why aren't you wearing the bandage?"

He shuffled around, touching the walls and the table as he went. "The physician said I could remove it, but my sight is still blurred. It should improve in a couple of days, he said. How are you?"

She flexed out the fingers of her bandaged hand. The skin itched and tugged at the edges. "On the mend. The wound itches, but thanks to my mother's potions, there's no infection."

"I'm glad to hear that."

"I've brought a chessboard if you'd care to play." She sat at the table. "Since you told me you know how to play, I thought you might enjoy a game."

He walked to the chair and sat down with tentative movements. "I can't see the chess pieces well. It's all a blurred black-and-white thing."

She set the pieces on the chessboard. "You'll have to trust me then."

He blinked, and goodness, his eyelashes were thick and golden at the tips. Quite pretty. "I trust you, miss."

A sudden flush warmed her face. She hadn't realised his trust meant so much to her until that moment. "Let's start."

An hour later, she'd lost her bishop, knight, queen, and countless pawns. How annoying. She should cheat before he destroyed all her pieces and won.

"Knight in D five," he said.

She followed his instruction, already glowering at him. The knight was dangerously close to her king.

"And I think this is a checkmate," he said with too much amusement, rubbing his hands.

She rested her chin on her fist. "I hate you, Mr. Alexander."

He barked out a laugh that made her laugh as well. It was the second time she'd heard him laughing. She liked it. He had a deep, rumbling laugh that filled the room.

"I appreciate the fact you didn't take advantage of my condition," he said.

"I thought about it a few times though. Before this game, I considered myself a decent player." She collected the pieces, but he did the same thing, and their hands touched over the king.

A little shock of sensations went up her arm. She should remove her hand, but the contact with his rough skin was shockingly too pleasant.

A blush crept over his face, exalting the rich colour of his chestnut hair and hazel eyes.

He withdrew his hand. "Apologies."

"It's all right." She worked quickly, stashing the pieces inside the drawers under the chessboard. "Are you going to resume your work soon?"

"I'm eager to do something, anything. This forced inactivity is wearing me down."

"I read in the *Evening Standard* about a formal ceremony to celebrate your heroic acts."

He shot his gaze towards the ceiling. "I'd rather get punched by Ross the Gross."

She chuckled. "You deserved recognition."

"That's not important. They should question the engineer who designed the Theatre Royal. The disaster could have been avoided if the theatre had been better designed. All the exits were crammed. People didn't have enough space to run. And they gathered all in the same corridor. That's why I managed to come and go a few times because there was almost no one in the lateral exit."

"I don't think you'll be able to escape the glory." She set the chessboard aside. A beautiful waltz music came from the upper floor. "What is it?"

He huffed. "Lord Havisham is organising a ball, which I'm afraid is in my honour. I guess the musicians are rehearsing."

Would she be too bold if she asked him to dance? Who cared? She'd risked her life and discovered her mother blackmailed people. Seize the day. "That's your opportunity to make amends after you so completely destroyed me at chess. What about a dance? I love dancing."

He stiffened, opening and closing his hands. "I can't see properly."

"We'll be careful. I'll make sure you don't hurt yourself."

"No."

"Just a count of eight."

"I said no!"

She fell silent. Heavens, he was angry. His eyes seemed sharper, and his voice deepened.

She smoothed down her skirt. "All right. I didn't mean to upset you."

He frowned, still stiff and tense.

She rose. "I..." She didn't know what to say. His outburst had been unusual. He was grumpy, but not short-tempered.

He stood up as well. "Thank you for your company." The words were polite, but the tone was not.

"You're welcome. I'll be back tomorrow." She waited for him to say yes.

"Actually, the physician will be here tomorrow."

She'd truly upset him. "Send a word if you want me to come."

"Thank you."

She left the room and headed for the servants' entrance since the butler had told her not to use the main entrance. Why had he raised his voice? Obviously, he didn't like dancing, or maybe he was upset because of his eyes, or maybe she'd been too bold. Never mind. His tone had hurt her, though.

She walked past the busy kitchen, from where steam and the smell of spices came, and exited through the back door. A woman and a man were playing cricket with a child in the park opposite the townhouse. They cheered when the child performed a good delivery.

"Come and kiss Mama." The woman opened her arms, and the child rushed to her, laughing.

The man kissed the child's head, and a squeaking "Papa" came out of the child.

They laughed together.

Beautiful. The feeling of being surrounded by love and of building something so precious with someone she deeply loved had to be the best in the world. No matter what Mama said, building a family was Angeline's dream.

She wanted to be as happy as that woman. She wanted to have a family and grow old with the man she loved. Mama might think that dream was silly, but Angeline's heart thudded faster whenever she saw happy families. Maybe because she'd never had one. She loved her mother despite everything, but a big family was another thing.

While every other young woman had to deal with matchmaking mamas who pushed one possible suitor after another towards their daughters, Angeline had the completely opposite problem. Her mama considered marriage the worst thing that ever happened to humankind after the invention of crinolines. A free woman held more power than a wife was her motto.

Shaking her head, she took the side alleyway that would take her to the main street when her mother came from the other direction, head down and quick feet.

"Mama?"

Her mother jolted. Her large hat hid her face, and her long

cloak covered her from chin to ankle. "Angeline. Thank goodness." She took Angeline's good hand and led her to a dark corner. "I was looking for you."

"Is something the matter?" Angeline was almost scared of asking.

Her mother panted, glancing around. "Do you trust me?"

"That's a tricky question after your latest confession. Tell me what is going on. No lies, please."

Mama exhaled. "We must leave London for a while."

"What? Don't tell me one of the lords you blackmailed wants revenge."

"Shush!" Mama gazed around. "It's complicated. See, I've been meeting with a prominent physician—"

"You blackmail even doctors now. What's next? Vicars? Judges of the peace?"

"No, it's not what you think. This physician is helping me with medicinal herbs... never mind. It's a long story." Mama exhaled through her teeth. "Please go home, pack a few essential things, and wait for me. I'll be with you as soon as possible, but you must be ready to leave when I come back."

"Where are you going? To see Lord Havisham?"

"No, I would never meet a lover in his own house." Mama inched closer and lowered her voice. "Please do as I say and be quick. Don't talk to anyone. Don't stop to buy anything. Just go home and get ready."

A combination of frustration and worry itched along her skin. "See what a mess we are in? You promised to stop."

Mama jabbed a finger at her. "No, I didn't do such a thing. *You* ordered me to stop. I've never said I would."

"Goodness, Mama." Angeline rubbed the ache on her forehead. "You'll send us to prison."

"Not if we're careful." Mama ushered Angeline towards the other side of the alleyway. "We don't have time to discuss. This is a serious matter."

"Who is chasing us?"

"It's better if you don't know for now."

"Mama," Angeline half-whispered, half-hissed. "This business of yours must stop."

Mama seized her good arm. "Too late now. Go home and wait for me. Now." She hurried away, leaving Angeline in the company of too many questions.

And the worst thing was that she wouldn't see Mr. Alexander any time soon.

five
Two years later

TWO YEARS HAD passed since the tragic Theatre Royal incident, and what had changed in Angeline's life? Almost nothing.

She still lived in London in the same house, she was still a spinster, and her mama was still the dirty secret of many, many rich and powerful men. After many promises, broken promises, many '*this is the last time I blackmail someone, I swear it*,' and several nervous breakdowns, Mama's blackmailing enterprise was still up and running.

Two years ago, Angeline and her mother had been forced to leave London in a hurry after Mama had bedded and blackmailed the wrong man. What His Grace Dimitri Gruzinsky, Grand Duke of all the Russias, lacked in sense of humour, he made up for in absolute rage. Not at all intimidated by Mama's compromising photographs, damning documents, and threats to expose him to his Grand Duchess, he'd gone berserk and sworn to kill Mama and Angeline, burn down their house, curse their souls to hell, and declare war on Britain.

Now she understood why Napoleon had so miserably failed to conquer Great Mother Russia. He had all her sympathy.

And to think she'd considered Mr. Alexander to be short-tempered. He was an amateur compared to the Grand Duke.

After Angeline's last visit to Mr. Alexander, she and her mother had left London at night like thieves and hadn't returned until His Disgrace had grown tired of searching for them and returned to his gilded palace in Saint Petersburg.

Angeline had hoped that such a close brush with death and months spent running from one small town to another would have prompted Mama to change. But no. The only change was that Mama had taken to studying medicinal herbs and potions with more passion, becoming a true expert. She'd also become close friends with an Austrian physician, a Dr. Karl Bauer, who had taught her everything about medicinal plants from all around the world.

But that was the only significant change in her mother's routine. Angeline started to believe Mama was addicted to her paid tumbles and blackmail business. She also suspected Mama couldn't stop lying.

On top of everything else, she hadn't seen Mr. Alexander since their last chess game. Busy hiding from the deranged grand duke, she hadn't dared send a message to Mr. Alexander for fear it could fall into the wrong hands.

The only thing she knew about him was that his eyes had healed. Aside from that, she had no idea where he was and what he was doing since the newspapers had stopped talking about him. No, she knew something else. He didn't work for Lord Havisham anymore.

For some reason, she missed him. He'd dragged her out of the burning theatre, and she hadn't been able to see him again. Worse, he likely believed her sudden absence was due to their last encounter when she'd asked him to dance and he'd raised his voice. But between angry Russian aristocrats and Mama's intrigues, she'd lost contact with London's society for a while.

Since they'd returned, Mama had been determined to make up

for the lost time by attending every party, afternoon tea, and soirée, no matter how small or insignificant.

Sitting in the carriage that was taking her to Lady Redvers's house, Angeline tugged at the neckline of her silk gown. The devil kept slipping lower, even though she breathed slowly. If she sneezed, she'd undress herself. Her gloves, instead, were particularly long and thick. The burn had left an ugly, bumpy scar on her arm too many people found revolting. If she was going to be honest, she found it revolting, too. It'd taken her months to get used to the feel of the rough skin under her fingers whenever she'd touched the scar. It looked like a snake had sunbathed for too long.

"Stop fiddling with your neckline." Mama swatted her hand.

"I'm practically naked. I might as well remove the bodice altogether."

"Don't be silly." Mama tightened the silk sash around her shoulders. She shifted on the seat, glanced out of the window, shifted again, and glanced outside the other window.

Angeline had seen that circumspect behaviour during the days of the Russian incident, and she didn't like it.

"Tell me the truth," she said. "Are we being followed? Is it the grand duke again?"

Mama let out a nervous chuckle. "No, no. Silly you. Everything is fine."

"No, it's not. Tell me the truth, or I won't come with you to Lady Redvers's ball. Oh goodness. Did you blackmail Lord Redvers? Is he one of your gentlemen?"

"Heavens, no. I didn't do business with him. It was his brother. Very nice man. I mean he's nice for a man. Anyway, it's thanks to him that we've been invited."

Business was a nice way to call blackmail.

"What is it, then?" she asked.

Mama smoothed a crease on her skirt. "I'm afraid you'll be angry with me."

"Tell me," she gritted out. "Every conversation that starts with that line leads to a disaster."

Mama took her time, keeping her gaze low. "There's a gentleman I want you to meet."

Angeline held her breath in surprise. A suitor? Had Mama finally agreed to help her find a husband? Could she finally think of settling down with a family of her own?

On impulse, she grabbed Mama's hand. "I'm so glad you changed your mind about my search for a husband. There's nothing, nothing I want more than to become a wife and a mother, take care of my family, and be surrounded by love. Oh, I'd love to have a couple of dogs as well, and a cat, of course. Cats are such clever animals."

"Stop it." Mama arched a single eyebrow. "I might cast up my accounts."

"Well, you have your tastes. I have mine. But I'm looking forward to meeting potential suitors."

"Angeline—"

"I want to marry for love. I want a husband I truly love and who loves me back. No marriage of convenience. And someone who wants children. I'd love a big family."

"Angeline!" Mama raised her voice. "Mr. Oscar North, the man I want to introduce you to, isn't and will never, ever be your suitor, not as long as I breathe, and if I were dead, I'd become a ghost and haunt his house to prevent him from courting you."

"Do you have to be so dramatic?" Angeline scoffed. "I don't understand."

"He saw you a few days ago walking in the park with me. He didn't stop to chat because he was in a hurry, but your beauty struck him."

It was Angeline's turn to arch her eyebrow. She didn't consider herself unattractive, but a man who got struck by her beauty with one passing glance at her sounded suspicious, to say the least. Not to mention that even those men who'd shown an interest in her had quickly changed their minds when they'd seen her scar on her arm left by the burn. Comments like 'What's that thing? Is it contagious? Can't you take it off?' still echoed in her ears.

Angeline stared at her mother. "Is he one of your gentlemen?"

"Since you ask, yes. I've never blackmailed him, though, and our liaison is over."

"That's a relief. So he glanced at me. And?" she asked.

"He wants to meet you." Mama shrugged.

"And?" she prompted.

"If he likes you, he proposes to..." The rest of the sentence was gibberish so quickly her mother spoke.

Angeline didn't understand a single word. "What? Speak English. Please."

Mama released a long breath. "He would like you to become his mistress."

She couldn't have heard that correctly. "Mistress?"

"For one night only. Don't worry." Mama waved a hand as if what she'd said didn't matter.

"Don't worry?" Angeline shouted. "What have you done? What did you tell him? I swear I'll throw myself out of this carriage right this instant if you made a deal with Mr. North about my body."

Mama opened her mouth, but she was cut off.

"Madam?" the driver said from the box. "Is everything all right?"

"Lower your voice." Mama turned towards the window. "All fine, thank you, Smith."

"Nothing is fine. How could you?" She was so angry she couldn't talk without stuttering. "You sold me. My virginity."

"Now, who's being dramatic? Stop it, for goodness's sake," Mama hissed.

"I can't breathe." She gasped, a hand on her heaving chest. Even her sight darkened at the edges.

"You ninny. Stop this nonsense and listen to me before you

have a fit." Mama sat next to her and gave her a light slap on the back. As if selling her daughter's virginity to a stranger weren't enough.

The slap wasn't strong, but Angeline had to admit she breathed a little better. Her wrath was intact though. She shook with outrage.

Mama soothed the spot she'd slapped. "I don't want that man's dirty hands on you, and I swear on my honour—"

"Choose something else to swear on."

"He won't have a tumble with you, not him, not anyone else you don't choose," Mama said with a fierceness that was too honest not to be taken seriously. "Unless you fancy him, of course. In that case, it's your choice."

A headache bothered her. "If you don't want me to have a tumble with this Mr. North, then why meet him?"

Mama leant closer and whispered, "In case Mr. North decides he wants a more carnal meeting with you, I'll organise everything so that he'll *only* believe he had a tumble with you, but it'll be an illusion, a magic trick. Still, he'll be absolutely convinced he spent a night with you, and he'll pay a hefty sum for the honour. In fact, I've never spent a night in bed with him. He believes he did, but it's not true."

"How?" She was so shocked she didn't think straight anymore because she wanted to know what Mama had in mind.

"Dr. Bauer developed a few drugs to cure the maladies of the mind, a so-called alienist, and I learnt from him. With the right mixture of drugs, the right technique, and the right dosage, I can make Mr. North believe he's the queen. Hallucinogens are powerful allies." Mama raised her eyebrows.

"Somehow, I don't feel reassured. In fact, I might throw up."

"Darling." Mama took her chin. "I know what I'm doing. The whole procedure has been tested, tried, and perfected several times."

"Good Lord." Angeline put a shivering hand on her cheek.

"You've been drugging unaware people to test Dr. Bauer's drugs. Those people could have died. Honestly, every time I think you've reached the lowest of the low, you surprise me."

"Tosh. Dr. Bauer supervised the dosage. In fact, we have a prolific partnership. He teaches me about the latest developments in the drug field, and I test the potions. Everything has always gone beautifully. The drug mixture has always worked to perfection... alas, with one notable exception."

"The grand duke," they said together.

Mama exhaled dramatically as if she were the wronged one. "The mixture of drugs, Dr. Bauer called it poly, quite unoriginal if you ask me. Anyway, the poly didn't do anything to that blasted duke. What a pain in the neck. I had to really lie in bed with him. Not that he was a terrible lover. He had great technique."

"Mama, please."

"But I've never met a more unbearable man." Mama shook her head.

Angeline sighed. "That's true. He was such a— you're distracting me. I have no intention of drugging and blackmailing Mr. North."

"There won't be any blackmailing, only the drugging," Mama said in an outraged tone as if Angeline had said something offensive. "He has only to believe he was with you. That's all."

"No."

"At least meet him."

"I don't think it's a good idea."

"His income of fifty thousand pounds per year is a very good idea." Mama fixed a wayward curl of Angeline's hair. "Mr. North is a bumbling idiot, easily manipulated, the best kind of man. All you have to do is smile, bat your eyelashes, and he'll fall at your feet. Also, he's rather handsome, and as I said, you won't have to do anything. He'll pay a hefty sum for the fake privilege of being with you, and you two will go separate ways without him being any the wiser."

"What if he tries to touch me tonight?" Getting out of the carriage was an idea that didn't lose its appeal.

"Well, it's up to you, of course. But he might want to touch you a little bit, be more intimate. Of course, you won't allow him to do anything too improper." For once, Mama's tone sounded like that of a proper, match-making mama.

"Good heaven." Angeline rubbed a tight spot between her eyebrows. "You promised you would stop. Instead, you simply changed your brand."

Mama smiled. "Thank you. Every good business evolves."

"It wasn't a compliment."

The carriage jolted to a stop, and a flare of panic caused her to still. Now she had to leave the carriage, enter Lady Redvers's brilliantly illuminated house, and be in the same room as Mr. North.

She touched her scarred arm. "I can't do this, Mama. I absolutely can't do it. It's wrong. I won't discuss the matter further."

The footman opened the door. "Madam, miss, Lady Redvers's residence."

Mama snatched Angeline's hand and turned towards the footman. "Shut the door. We'll be ready in a few moments."

The startled man did as told.

"I love you, darling. I really do. That's why I'm sparing you from a gruesome, hard life. When I became the mistress of several lords, I didn't have any potion to help me out on long nights. I had to lie in bed with them even when they disgusted me." Her cheeks flushed. "I did it for you, for us, to feed you, clothe you, and keep a roof over our heads. You won't have to endure the smelly breath of a heavy man on top of you or experience the humiliation of being treated like nothing. Never. I don't want that for you. I have never have. I'll personally kill anyone who dares to hurt you. But you must help me. You must sacrifice a piece of your integrity to lead a life of safety and leisure."

Angeline's heart broke. Her mama had endured a miserable life all alone. First, her husband had hurt and abandoned her. Then she'd sold herself to earn money and keep her daughter alive. What really hurt Angeline was the fact Mama hadn't told her anything. If it hadn't been for the darned fire, Mama would have kept lying.

Yes, things hadn't changed much since Mama's confession, but at least now Angeline was aware of all the horrible things Mama had done for her. Guilt bugged her like a noisy fly. For years, she'd enjoyed a happy, carefree life without having the foggiest idea of what Mama did. But Mama didn't have to keep doing anything. Angeline was an adult. She would work, beg, and do anything to keep Mama out of the clutches of men who wanted to pay to spend a night with her.

A sickening lump crawled into Angeline's throat. "We've been going in circles about your idea of safety many times. We have enough money to leave this life of lies behind."

"No, we don't. Why do I need to hire a footman and a coachman for one night? Because we can't afford to pay them regularly. We'd be broke in a matter of months."

"I don't care." She couldn't completely remove the frustration from her voice. "We don't need a footman. We only need a place to live and food. I can work."

Besides, being aware that everything she owned— from the gown she was wearing to her umbrella —came from Mama's illegal money was a constant burden.

"Twaddle." Mama scoffed. "How do you think I lasted this long in this business? I never demand huge sums for my silence when I blackmail my prey. If I didn't do that, they would turn against me. Instead, I'm never greedy. I ask for an affordable payment, nothing that would be too conspicuous. The downside is that I must keep going, and I'm not getting any younger. And if you think it's easy for a woman to find a proper job, think again. I tried and failed."

"I don't want to spend my life like that." She sounded ungrateful.

Her mama had made unthinkable sacrifices to stay alive. Angeline had received a good education and had always enjoyed the freedom to do whatever she wanted, from learning to use the bow to riding and attending concerts. But the path Mama offered was a miserable one.

Mama continued. "As I said, trust me. My poly potion really works. When the moment comes, Mr. North will believe he had a tumble with you."

"No." She was growing tired of saying it.

"At least talk and meet him. Who knows? You might like him. Don't humiliate me by refusing to even talk to him." Mama opened the door. "We're ready," she said to the footman.

No, Angeline wasn't.

six

TWO YEARS HAD passed since Royston had been awarded a title, and he'd learnt something important. A title and some nice clothes hadn't changed him.

Deep down, he was still the same man from the gutter who had grown up in a brothel and made a living as a cat burglar. Also, his new peers had taken enthusiastically to the fact the queen had bestowed upon him the title of Baron Wharton, a title he'd never wanted but had to admit was convenient. Most of the time.

Invitations to the opera, dinners, and balls flooded his letter tray. Invitations he mostly declined, which, instead of discouraging the peers from inviting him, made them even more insistent. That night, he'd accepted Lady and Lord Redvers's invitation because they'd been particularly insistent, especially the lady.

He suspected his large fortune, granted as a reward for his courage, the queen's praise, and his successful steel factory had something to do with his popularity.

He paced in the fancy parlour of Lady Redvers's house. The room, with its rich brown colours and the grand piano, had a soothing effect on his nerves, but his pulse didn't want to slow down. Being among aristocratic people as a supposed equal and not as a servant was something he hadn't got used to. At least he didn't feel the urge to rob anyone, which was good, he guessed.

The clock on the mantelpiece informed him that Havisham was late. The earl had requested a quiet meeting at the ball with urgency. Royston wouldn't stay here all evening. If Havisham didn't appear in five minutes, he'd leave. He wasn't the earl's footman anymore.

As if on cue, the door swung inwards, and Havisham slid inside. "Wharton, apologies. I was delayed."

"Havisham." He bowed his head.

Havisham clapped his shoulder. "Thank you for agreeing to this meeting."

Royston glanced at Havisham's hand on his shoulder. When he'd been in Havisham's service, no one had given him pats on the shoulder, and he preferred it that way.

"What did you want?"

Havisham's expression darkened. "I'm afraid I need your help for a rather delicate matter."

Royston waited for Havisham to add more, but when the earl didn't say anything, he prompted with, "Yes?"

Havisham checked the corridor and shut the door. "Do you remember Mrs. Haywood, the woman who was with me the night of the fire?"

Actually, he remembered Miss Haywood better. Her deep, large black eyes were hard to forget, her kindness had left a mark on him, and her sense of humour still made him smile. Miss Haywood had kept him company during his recovery until he'd behaved appallingly with her when she'd asked him to dance with him. After that, she'd vanished.

At first, he'd believed she'd been avoiding him, but even her mother had disappeared, which made him think they'd moved out of London.

There had been rumours about a foreign count, or someone similar, wanting to marry Mrs. Haywood. No one knew for sure.

Anyway, in the past two years, he'd received his damn title, had a pompous ceremony at Buckingham Palace, and hadn't seen Miss Haywood since their last horrible encounter.

"I do remember Mrs. Haywood, Havisham," he said.

"I guess you also remember why I met her at the Theatre Royal." Havisham arched his brow.

Royston exhaled. "I do."

"In the days after the fire, I met her. A few times. Many times. Until she left London."

He shifted his weight. As Havisham had said at the theatre, he'd wanted Mrs. Haywood as his mistress. "I see."

"A few months ago, Mrs. Haywood returned to London."

"Did she?" Royston hid his surprise. So Miss Haywood might be in London as well.

"Yes, but the point is that she isn't the woman I thought she was. We started our relationship again. Everything seemed normal, until we argued." He waved a hand. "Nothing important, but that was the moment when I learnt she'd deceived me. She collected some evidence of our relationship." Havisham lowered his gaze as distress tightened his features.

"What sort of evidence?"

Havisham raked a hand through his hair. "Hard to say for sure. I'm aware she's in possession of letters and a few compromising photographs we took together during a particularly wild night. She was eager to take those damn photographs."

Hell. Havisham's wife was the daughter of a duke. The earl wouldn't recover from a scandal easily, and the countess was a vindictive woman.

"Is Mrs. Haywood blackmailing you?" Royston asked.

Havisham worked his jaw. "Indeed. She's never asked for a large sum, which makes the situation easier for me. But I'm concerned. I can't keep living with the constant threat of having my secret exposed." He paced, shaking his head. "Bloody hell, I want it over."

"I'm sorry to hear about your troubles," Royston said. Although if Havisham didn't tup every skirt he liked, he wouldn't be in this situation. "But what do I have to do with this?"

Havisham pressed a few keys on the piano, trying to play something. Then he faced Royston. "I'd be grateful to you if you could recover the compromising material Mrs. Haywood possesses about our relationship."

"What do you mean?" He tilted his head.

Havisham didn't flinch. "You have a... past. You must know how to deal with a problem like mine."

Royston's pulse beat a war tempo in his ears. "I beg your pardon."

"Now, now, Wharton. Before coming to my employment, you were a thief, a pugilist in an illegal ring, and a member of a gang. I'm not judging you. I'm simply saying that you have skills I desperately need."

No, Royston couldn't change his past, but he could decide what to do with his future, and resuming his life of crime, even for a short time, wasn't what he wanted. He wasn't proud of what he'd done, but not ashamed either. His past crimes had been a matter of survival, not greed.

"I won't do it, Havisham. I have no intention of using my former criminal skills to steal from a lady."

"Lady? What lady? Mrs. Haywood is a blackmailer."

Royston lifted a shoulder. "And you're an adulterer."

For a moment, he thought Havisham was going to punch him. But since the lord knew Royston's past so well, he should be aware that Royston was a good boxer and would dodge the punch easily.

"I'll help you so that you won't need to break into her house," Havisham said. "I'll think of something, an invitation perhaps. I'll make sure she organises a party in her house and that you're invited. No breaking and entering."

"No."

"I will pay you any sum," the earl insisted.

If there was one thing he didn't need, it was money. "I can't do it. I don't want to be involved in this."

"Mrs. Haywood will be here tonight. You might want to talk to her and see for yourself that she's a disgraceful woman. You're good at understanding people."

Royston ignored the quick flutter in his chest at the possibility of meeting Miss Haywood again. "I gave you my answer."

Havisham came closer. "I can make a conspicuous investment in your steel factory. I heard you often employ people with a troubled past to help them. I'll be more than happy to finance your charitable enterprise."

Seriously? Then why hadn't the earl done that before?

He opened his mouth to say, 'no' again, but Havisham cut him off.

"Listen, don't answer now." Havisham opened the door. "Please think about it. You'd do a great service to society by fighting against that blackmailer. She has ruined more than one life."

Royston clenched his fists when he was alone. Sod Havisham. He was an adult who could solve his own problems, and Royston was free to make his own choices.

He sat at the piano and started to play.

Angeline's mother was right. Mr. North was a handsome man, no doubt about that. With his straight, bouncy strawberry-blond hair and pale green eyes, he looked like an angel jumped out of an oil painting. If only he would keep his mouth shut.

His good looks didn't change the fact she had no intention of talking to him. She wouldn't sell her body to a stranger, and drugging the man was plain wrong.

"Miss Haywood, you're a vision." Mr. North took her hand

and kissed it, showing a lopsided smile that caused his face to lose some of its beauty.

Angeline withdrew her hand, gazing around the busy ballroom. If he knew what was underneath the glove, he'd be horrified. "Thank you, sir."

Lady Redvers was a viscountess, and some of her guests were high-ranking nobles. Who knew how many of those so-called gentlemen had been or currently were Mama's lovers or victims?

"Miss Haywood?" Mr. North dipped his head, filling her field of vision. He let out one of his high-pitched, convulsive laughs that made her fear he might collapse with a fit. "For a moment, I had the impression you weren't listening to a single word I said."

Oh, goodness. "Mr. North, let me be frank."

"Darling," Mama said in her fake, sweet voice. "Perhaps you want to talk to Mr. North in private."

"No, what I have to say can be said here in the safety of the ballroom."

Mr. North sniggered again, and she wanted to shout at him to stop laughing because there was nothing to laugh about and because he had a terrible laugh. She'd never been an aggressive person, but between her mama's persistence and Mr. North's obtusity, her nerves were fraying like the threads of a worn hessian carpet.

He offered her his arm. "Come now, Miss Haywood. I'm sure you'll agree with me about the intimate nature of our conversation." He arched his eyebrows.

Her anger reached a boiling point.

"We don't have anything to discuss, intimate or otherwise." She wielded the fan as if it were a dagger.

Mama poked her with an elbow. "Angeline, do it for me. At least hear what the gentleman has to say."

What gentleman?

Mr. North grabbed her hand and tugged at it. "Please?"

"Fine. Let's talk." She'd have the opportunity to tell Mr. North to go find another woman, or even better, she'd show him her ugly scar to scare him off. And Mama would stop searching for people to drug.

And that would be the end of it.

Surely. Most definitely. The end.

seven

IT WAS AMAZING what an unmarried woman was allowed to do with her mother's approval.

If Angeline had been a normal person and her mother had been just like any other mamas, she wouldn't be allowed to be alone with an unmarried man.

The worst thing was that other young women would give their best pearl necklaces to have Angeline's freedom. But she was boiling. She wished her mother would have helped her search for a husband and not for a lover to be drugged.

On the other hand, the best way to convince Mr. North to leave her alone was to have a chat with him. She would be firm and honest, and he would stop pestering her. And Mama would understand Angeline didn't want to be part of criminal games.

"Don't be nervous, Angeline." Mr. North sat next to her on the Chesterfield sofa in a small sitting room quite far from the ballroom. The music couldn't be heard, which meant that if she screamed, no one would come.

"It's Miss Haywood." She inched away from him, wondering if she could jump through the window, land in the garden, and run home.

The sitting room was not on the first floor though, and she might break an ankle. "Mr. North!" She swatted his hand away from her knee. "Stop it."

"Don't be shy. Your mother must have told you what I want from you." He coiled one of her curls around his finger. "We're here merely to discuss the details. Do not fear. I'll be gentle." He snickered, that high-pitched, hiccupping snickering as pleasant as a fork scratching a porcelain plate.

She removed his hand from her hair. "What you discussed with my mother does not matter. I'm not going to spend a night with you."

"I seriously doubt you wouldn't be interested in three thousand pounds." He raised his eyebrows again.

Good Lord. She forced herself to stay calm.

"Excuse me?" She turned towards him quickly enough to wrinkle her dress. The darn neckline dropped a few inches, attracting the full attention of Mr. North's impolite gaze.

"That's the sum I offer. Three thousand pounds for the pleasure of lying with you." He brushed his fingers over the top of her breasts.

Three thousand pounds was the price of her virginity. The man thought he could buy her. She was an article on a shelf. Nothing more.

She removed his hand. "Does my mother know about your offer?"

"No. I wanted to discuss it with you as a matter of respect." He kissed her hand.

"How kind of you."

"Thank you." He wasn't fluent in sarcasm.

She slid her hand out of his. At least Mama hadn't negotiated the price.

"I'm not usually attracted to women like you," he said, caressing her knuckles.

"What do you mean by that?"

"Black hair and eyes, those huge lips that look like a wasp just stung them... I prefer women with fair hair, taller than you are, and who don't have your angular features. But you possess a certain *je ne sais quoi* that has its allure. Yes, I'm convinced that three thousand pounds is an appropriate sum. I would offer twice that amount if you had blonde hair."

"Would you like to inspect my teeth?"

He laughed. "You could wear a wig."

Enough. "Thank you for this speech, Mr. North, because now I'm even less interested in you than I was before, which I didn't think was possible." She rose, but the scoundrel had the audacity to grab her wrist and pull her down onto the sofa again.

"I like a chase, but you're starting to annoy me with your hostile attitude."

She shrugged her arm free. "Oh, I'm devastated. Goodbye." She stood up again, and he dragged her down.

He took her chin between his strong fingers. He could bruise her if he wanted to. "You leave when I say so. My offer is generous because I assumed you'd be cooperative." He put his greedy hand on her breast.

Anger and shock were never a good combination. Angeline acted on sheer instinct. She seized the vase behind her and poured the water in it over Mr. North's glorious strawberry-blond hair—roses, thorns, and all. He froze in shock, his mouth hanging open and drops dripping from his hair.

She shot up to her feet and strode towards the door.

Her hand was over the knob when he roared.

She pulled the door, but it didn't budge. He must have locked it after they'd entered the room. She fumbled with the key until the door opened, but he marched towards her, leaving a trail of drops.

"You aren't going to leave this room." His upper lip curled up in a snarl.

"Try me."

She rushed out of the room, trying to remember where the ballroom was. The big house was a maze of identical corridors, shiny floors, and hidden stairs, and when she'd allowed Mr. North to the parlour, she'd been too angry to pay attention.

"Angeline." His voice boomed from behind her. For a tall man with long legs, he wasn't fast. Not that she complained about that.

No sound of voices reached her. The ballroom had to be on the other side of the corridor. But any room with a solid door would do for now.

The doors she tried were all locked, and the stairs leading downstairs didn't look familiar at all. Piano music drifted from a room at the end of the corridor, and she made a dash for it for no reason other than where there was piano music, there was a pianist. Hopefully, a sympathetic pianist.

"When I catch you, I'm going to rip that pretty blue dress off you," he said.

Well, that was a further incentive for her not to be caught. She barged into the pianist's room, glad the door wasn't locked. Breathless, she stopped in the middle of a cosy sitting room where a man was playing a beautiful piece, bathed in the golden light from the chandelier. The peaceful sight and the lovely music were a stark contrast to the scene she'd escaped from.

The pianist gazed up from the keys and frowned at her. His intense hazel eyes widened in recognition, likely as hers did.

Goodness. It was Mr. Royston Alexander. For a moment, surprise made her forget about the angry scoundrel chasing her.

"Mr. Alexander," she said.

"Miss Haywood." He paused playing and stood up.

Mr. North strode into the room, fists clenched and utterly wet. "I win, Angeline. You're going to regret your abominable behaviour."

Mr. Alexander moved so fast Angeline saw only a dark blur

swishing past her. He stepped between Mr. North and her, blocking her view of her chaser with his broad shoulders.

"What is the meaning of this?" he asked in a commanding tone.

Angeline craned her neck to see past him.

Mr. North lost his cocksure expression. The wet hair didn't help give him a menacing effect. "Angeline—"

"It's Miss Haywood," she said.

"—threw a vase full of water over me." Mr. North gestured at his soaked silk waistcoat and dripping hair.

"Miss Haywood must have had a very good reason for doing that." Mr. Alexander mirrored Mr. North's moves as he tried to get past him and reach her.

A surge of gratitude warmed her. He knew her better than she'd thought.

"I did nothing she wasn't prepared for," Mr. North said. "Now, I don't know who you are or how you know Angeline, but I must ask you to remove yourself from this room and leave me alone with her."

"I won't do such a thing." Mr. Alexander folded his arms over his chest. "Unless Miss Haywood asks me to."

"Not likely," she said.

Mr. North scoffed. "Who the hell are you?"

Mr. Alexander straightened. "I'm Lord Royston Alexander, Baron Wharton."

What? Angeline stepped around him to stare at his face. Not a single facial muscle twitched. If it was a bluff, he was doing a great job hiding it because he sounded extremely serious.

Even Mr. North looked taken aback. As a man who owned a fortune thanks to his family's trade but no title, for business alone he needed to be respectful towards a baron.

"Lord Wharton," he said, slouching his posture. "I wasn't aware of your acquaintance with Angeline."

"Miss Haywood," Mr. Alexander... no, Lord Wharton said, sounding as upset as she was.

"Miss Haywood." Mr. North held up a hand. "I had no idea Miss Haywood knew you."

"I've known His Lordship for quite a long time," she said not without pride. Served Mr. North right.

The scoundrel's eyebrows rose to his hairline as if he'd realised something obvious. "I see. You're my competitor, my lord."

Lord Wharton glanced at her. "Competitor?"

"How much did you offer?" Mr. North asked.

Lord Wharton's frown deepened. "For what?"

"For—"

"Don't." She stepped between Lord Wharton and Mr. North. "It's nothing, a misunderstanding. Mr. North will leave now." She'd rather spend a day on the chair of a dentist than let Lord Wharton know her mother had put her virginity on sale. A fake sale but still a sale.

"What misunderstanding?" Mr. North kept talking unhelpfully. "I'm paying three thousand pounds. However, after tonight's outrageous behaviour, I'll reduce my offer. How much have you offered, my lord?"

Angeline hid her face behind her hands. How she wished to fly away on a carpet like in one of those *Arabian Nights* stories. She was going to die out of sheer embarrassment.

Of all the rooms in the home of Lord and Lady Redvers, she had to choose the one with a man she hadn't seen in two years. The man who'd saved her life was now a baron.

"What are you talking about?" Lord Wharton shifted his gaze from Mr. North to her. Confusion was spelt on his scrunched-up face.

Mr. North nodded towards her. "Ask Miss Haywood."

"Miss Haywood." Lord Wharton stepped closer to her and dipped his head to catch her gaze.

The contact shocked him if the way his eyes became large was any sign. Also, touching his chest was like touching a slab of steel, only warmer.

"Please don't mind Mr. North. Don't listen to what he says."

"I don't understand what's happening here." Mr. North wasn't a great observer since he didn't realise Lord Wharton obviously had no intention of making an offer. "I demand Miss Haywood clarify the situation, especially after she behaved so horribly with me."

Angeline lowered her hands, having no intention of clarifying anything. "Mr. North, please leave. I wish you to leave."

Lord Wharton crossed the room with two long strides. "Miss Haywood was clear." He held the door open and shot a cold, hard glance at Mr. North. "Out. Now." It was an order given with the authority only a man of power possessed.

"The conversation isn't over." With all the outrage of someone who had been deeply wronged, Mr. North left the room.

She sagged in relief as Lord Wharton shut the door. What a mess. What an embarrassment. Perhaps she should take the risk of breaking her ankle and flee through the window.

Lord Wharton drew in a breath that strained the fabric of his waistcoat. "Miss Haywood." It sounded sweet and low.

"Mr. Alexander... I mean, Lord Wharton." She dropped a curtsy. "I didn't know you had acquired a title."

"Sod my title. What was that idiot talking about?" He stretched out an arm in the direction of the door.

"A long story. Rather boring, actually. You are a baron, my lord? Congratulations! How do you like being a lord? Exciting." Her attempt at distracting him from what Mr. North had said was pathetic.

He worked his jaw. She could almost hear his thoughts. Likely, he debated whether to press the subject or let it go.

"You may call me Royston, Miss Haywood."

"That wouldn't be appropriate." She pulled up the neckline of her gown although Lord Wharton wasn't staring at her cleavage. "How did you acquire a title, my lord?"

He glanced at the door again. Hopefully, he'd drop the subject of Mr. North's offer. "I received the title after the Theatre Royal fire. Saving the queen's grandson was enough to make me a baron."

"I didn't hear about it." Because a furious Russian grand duke had chased her mother and her out of London.

"It was in the newspapers. There was a ceremony. I wanted the fuss to be over and done. Not a lot of bruhaha. Somehow, it didn't seem right towards those people who had died in the fire. They lost their lives, and I acquired a title."

"You saved many people that night. Your courage and selflessness deserved to be acknowledged by the queen." She smoothed down her bodice. The chase had caused her muslin sleeves to wrinkle as well. She straightened her skirt too, searching for other excuses not to glance up at him. "Thank you for your help, my lord. We have many things to talk about after two years." Not necessarily tonight's events.

"Did Mr. North hurt you?" A growl reverberated in his voice.

She had no intention of telling him about Mama's scheme, their financial insecurity, the blackmailing, or about Mr. North groping her and his three thousand pounds.

"The man is confused." That, at least, was true.

"My guess is that he attacked you." The gravity in his voice promised a long conversation to come. "You threw a vase at him and escaped from him. You wouldn't have done something like that if he hadn't done something horrible to you."

"Well, yes. He tried to attack me, and I used the contents of the vase to cool down his hot temper." She chuckled nervously, hoping to lighten the heavy atmosphere between them.

A corner of his mouth quirked up. "Clever move. I'll have a word with him if you want, make him understand to stay away from you."

"It's all right. Do not fret, my lord." She fiddled with her hands. "Instead, pray tell me about your new life. I'm eager to hear everything."

"So am I about yours. The last time we saw each other, I wasn't kind to you. I regret having raised my voice."

"I asked you to dance, and you got rather upset." She couldn't completely remove a hint of hurt from her voice because, to this day, she didn't understand his mood change.

"I apologise, Miss Haywood." He bowed.

"Angeline, please."

"Only if you call me Royston."

"Very well, Royston. So, I'm still curious to hear everything about the past two years."

He offered her his arm. "As much as I'd love to chat with you, I believe you should return to the ballroom and to your mother lest someone come here and make assumptions. Let me escort you."

"Thank you." She took his arm, aware she hadn't fooled him. Her attempts to distract him from Mr. North hadn't worked. "You play the piano well."

He checked the corridor before stepping out of the room. "Thank you. Do you play?"

She let out a snigger that sounded disturbingly similar to Mr. North's coarse laugh. He had to be contagious. "We have a piano at home, just because Mama thinks it's fancy, but the only keys I touch are those of my house."

He flashed a lovely boyish smile.

The sounds of footsteps came from the other side of the corridor, and he dragged her behind the heavy brocade curtains covering a bay window.

She nearly tripped on her feet. "What—"

He pressed a finger against his lips.

From the sound of the footfalls, two people were walking toward them. A couple of servants perhaps, although this hallway wasn't in the servants' quarter.

"Miss Haywood is pretty," one man said.

"She is, but have you seen the scar on her arm? I did. It's disgusting. I meant to court her, but after I saw that horrible thing, I changed my mind. I cannot imagine having to see that deformed arm every day. "

Oh, she guessed the second man was Mr. Barnes, a man she'd met during a bow practice session in Hyde Park. Her arm had been uncovered then. He'd voiced his opinion on the scar, so his words shouldn't still hurt, but they did.

Royston squeezed her hand as the footsteps faded. He waited. She stood inches from him. His slow breathing fanned on her neck.

"I think the danger has passed," she said, pretending not to notice his delicious, musky scent.

"I'm sorry you heard that," he whispered.

"It doesn't matter." She cleared her throat.

"It does." He stared at her with too much intensity.

She had to look away from him. "We didn't need to hide."

"Your reputation will be ruined if someone sees us here alone," he whispered.

Ha! If he only knew what Mama had in mind. She would be delighted to know her daughter was hiding behind a curtain with a baron.

"What happened with Mr. North is enough for one night." He moved the curtain aside and checked the corridor. "Come."

The glow from the gas lamps cast deep shadows on his harsh face, giving him the look of a hardened warrior. He hadn't asked further questions about her entanglement with Mr. North, and she was glad for that, but he must have understood the whole sad affair.

More footsteps approached. This time, it seemed that two people were in a hurry. There was a feminine chuckle, followed by a masculine growl.

"Quick." Royston led her behind yet another set of curtains.

She stifled a gasp as she bumped against him in her haste to hide. Her back touched his chest in a more intimate pose than she'd imagined. His arm coiled around her waist and inched her away from the curtain.

"Where are we going?" the woman asked. Judging by her melodious voice, she had to be young.

"Where no one can see us." That was the man. He spoke with a strong voice and had an accent, Cornish perhaps. "And where I can play the piano for you."

Another pianist.

"My mother will look for me soon," the woman said in a sophisticated lilt.

"We'll be quick. I really want to play only for you. Even when I play on stage, I think only of you."

Not simply a pianist but a performer. Not that the information was of any help to Angeline, but she needed to be distracted from Royston's warmth.

She held her breath as the couple walked closer. The footsteps and giggles stopped on the other side of the curtains. Bother. The two lovers had decided to take a breather right there and then. A few inaudible, whispered words were exchanged. Smooching and kissing sounds filled the silence. A little moan came from the woman. The curtains were shoved inwards by elbows and shoulders.

Royston pulled Angeline further back into the nook. The two lovers kept kissing and whispering to each other while inching closer to the curtains. Royston's warmth seeped into Angeline and reached her skin through the layers of fabric separating them.

The hug was lovely. Being held in a protective embrace while feeling his warm, hard body against hers had a calming effect on her heartbeat. A completely different experience from having Mr. North's clammy hands on her.

A hand slid between the curtains, and she stiffened, pressing her body against Royston further.

"Let's go," the woman said, showing more sensibility than her pianist lover. "Anyone can see us here."

Among loud kisses and chuckles, the lovers hurried away.

"Thank goodness." Angeline sagged in relief.

Royston removed his arm. "I apologise for the liberty I took in holding you."

Actually, she enjoyed the hug. "The circumstances were dire." And she hadn't minded.

"Still, I'll be more careful." He checked the corridor again before letting her out of their hiding place. "Quick now. The ballroom is close."

Fortunately, or unfortunately, the rest of their walk to the ballroom was uneventful. No secret lovers. No hiding. No more pianists. No being held by Royston.

She hadn't experienced anything that exciting since she'd won an archery competition years ago.

He paused in a quiet dark corner from where they could see the glittering ballroom. "You go first. If we meet in the ballroom, we'll pretend to have seen each other for the first time this evening. If anyone asks, we've never had that conversation with Mr. North, and you left the ballroom with a lady friend."

She clicked her heels together and gave him a military salute. "Yes, sir."

He frowned. "You aren't taking the situation seriously, Angeline. We're both risking our reputation."

"You as well? Casanovas are usually praised."

His frown deepened. "With due respect, but I don't want to be considered a rakehell who lures beautiful women to have a quick brush with them. Some find a rake admirable. I don't."

"Am I beautiful?"

He pinched the bridge of his nose. "Please, go to the ballroom."

"Thank you again for your kindness." She bobbed a curtsy. "I hope to see you again in different circumstances."

"Angeline?"

"Yes?"

His smile was shy. "You are beautiful." He turned around to walk to the other side of the hallway.

She entered the ballroom, surprised by her high spirits. When she'd left it to follow Mr. North, she'd been a bundle of nerves. She couldn't have imagined she'd come back wishing to spend more time hidden behind a curtain.

eight

ROYSTON WATCHED ANGELINE walk into the ballroom. Her small bustle swayed with each step, enhancing her lovely figure.

Of course, she was beautiful. She was one of the most beautiful women he'd ever seen. Her midnight eyes never failed to hold him captive, not only because they were glossy like obsidian, but also because they kept secrets, like whatever had happened with Mr. North.

She hadn't wanted to tell him anything about that man, and he hadn't pressed her further. But no matter. When she was ready to talk, he'd listen.

He snatched a glass of champagne from the passing tray of a footman, almost missing the days when he was a servant himself. Decent salary, no need to mingle with the crowd, and fewer responsibilities. Because of his past, he did his level best to ignore the dancing couples. They didn't exactly disturb him but didn't please him either. As long as he didn't focus on the dance, he could control the rising darkness.

Lord and Lady Redvers were talking on the other side of the ballroom, and he headed towards them. The second reason he'd come to the ball was to talk to the viscount. Now that the disastrous meeting with Havisham was over, he could focus on what really mattered to him.

"Lord Redvers, Lady Redvers." He offered his best bow. He was about to ask Redvers to have a word with him when the lady cut him off.

"Lord Wharton, finally we have a moment. I shall introduce you to my daughter Georgiana. She's eager to..." Lady Redvers gazed around, waving her fan. "She's here... somewhere. Where's that young lady? She was dancing with Mr. Wright a moment ago then disappeared."

"Mr. Wright?" Royston asked. "The famous pianist at the Opera House?"

Lady Redvers beamed. "The very same, Wharton. He's such a well-mannered man. I shall introduce you to him as well... as soon as I find him." She searched the room again. "People are vanishing right and left. Where is Mr. Wright?"

The mysterious pianist lover must be Mr. Wright. And the girl, Redvers's daughter.

"Since Miss Taylor is temporarily unavailable, I was wondering if I could have a word with you, my lord."

Lord Redvers didn't show the same enthusiasm as his wife, but he said, "By all means, Wharton."

"Thank you. My lady." Royston left with Redvers.

"But..." Lady Redvers kept searching the ballroom.

Royston followed the viscount to an adjoining room where a banquet with refreshments took up half of the space. The music wasn't as loud as in the ballroom, but he'd hoped for a more private place.

"I think I know what you wish to talk about," Lord Redvers said in a grave tone. "News about Parliament's decision on your proposed petition."

Good, so Royston wouldn't waste time. "Precisely, my lord."

The viscount seemed to age ten years in a moment. "Wharton,

the empire has many challenges to deal with right now. Providing public funds for a group of fallen women isn't a priority."

"Many young women need only a chance to improve their lives and to abandon the path of their trade."

Bloody hell. It was infuriating that he couldn't have a seat in the House of Lords since he hadn't inherited his title. If he were among those stuffy peers, he would fight tooth and nail to grant financial help to the girls who wanted to leave a brothel. Girls like his mother.

While everyone was eager to invite him to a ball, none of them wanted to help him when it came to his cause.

The viscount straightened, which didn't give him an impressive change in height. Royston towered over him.

"Wharton, I'm the first to admit your bravery during the fire was unprecedented. You saved our queen's grandson. The empire will always be grateful, and your ability for making money is enviable. But politics is a different beast that requires a different set of skills. I'm telling you this in your interest." Lord Redvers sounded forlorn. "Unfortunately, no one will listen to you. The members of the House of Lords don't believe you know anything about governing the country."

Royston focused on his glass not to let his frustration be shown. "I don't care about being considered one of them, my lord. What I care about are those poor, young, abused women without a home or family. The government should help them leave the trade, find legitimate employment and save their lives."

"I understand," Lord Redvers said. "But even though I'm on your side, I'm afraid that charity for the sake of charity is not going to influence the House. If we start giving money to everyone, no one will want to work."

"I don't believe that."

"You will have trouble convincing others of that," Lord Redvers said. "It's our duty to educate the commoners and guide them towards higher moral standards. Ours is a difficult job involving many hard decisions. But providing homes for them? No one will approve the funds."

Royston's chest tightened. The disinterest in the so-called fallen women was hard to fight. But while the lords debated what was morally appropriate and what wasn't, those women died from diseases, starvation, or even murder. Like his mother.

"Some battles can't be won." Lord Redvers gave a paternal pat on Royston's arm.

He was about to say the battle had barely begun when Lady Redvers swept into view.

"Lord Wharton, finally I can introduce you to my daughter." Lady Redvers gave her daughter's arm a light tug, leading her forwards.

Royston could barely focus on the introduction, catching a glimpse of glossy curls and large, scared eyes. Miss Taylor curtsied and said some pleasantries. He bowed and replied with the same platitudes, his mind still replaying the conversation with Lord Redvers. There had to be something he could do to push for his proposal to be approved. Hell, he'd worked with the best solicitors in town to put it together and make sure it was a strong argument, but no one in Parliament took it seriously.

"You should dance with Lord Wharton," Lady Redvers said.

That got his attention.

Miss Taylor stepped closer to him. The girl looked intimidated by him if the way her eyes flared wide was any indication.

"I'd be delighted, my lord." She sounded anything but.

"Thank you, Miss Taylor, but I don't dance." He got distracted again when he caught a glimpse of Angeline and her mother talking in a corner.

Lady Redvers laughed. "Every gentleman dances, and tonight there are so many of them."

"Yes, but I don't dance."

"But surely you won't refuse a lady," Lady Redvers insisted.

"Mother," Miss Taylor whispered. Her hair was a tad dishevelled now that he noticed that.

"I never dance, my lady." Perhaps rephrasing his statement would let the message sink in.

"A gentleman never refuses a lady's offer." Lady Redvers's pleasant attitude changed into an annoyed one.

But as images of his mother being forced to dance with that man crossed his mind, a cold, sickening shiver crawled down his back. It was as if a file of scorpions marched down his spine.

He almost choked on air. He'd come to the ball only because Lord Havisham had insisted and because he wanted to talk with Lord Redvers; both reasons had proven to be a waste of time.

The evening had been a complete fiasco. Aside from meeting Angeline again. Dancing was out of the question on a good day; it was impossible on a bad one.

He bowed. "Lady and Lord Redvers, Miss Taylor, if you'll excuse me." His voice cracked as cold sweat dampened his neck.

Miss Taylor curtsied while her mother pressed her lips in a hard line. Lady Redvers said something, but a buzzing noise rang in his ears, and he couldn't acknowledge her words.

No, it wasn't simply a noise but the strident music he'd heard that night. That awful music played by an inexperienced violinist to torture his mother. Royston had screamed and begged, but the jockey hadn't listened. He needed a breather.

Deep breaths. Deep breaths. A funny taste poisoned his mouth. Leaving the room, he swallowed a couple of times, feeling as if his tongue had grown in size. Had he been rude to Lady Redvers and her daughter? He had no idea.

He flexed open his hands, reminding himself that, unfortunately, his mother was dead. She'd died that night. Her heart had given up. The jockey had fled in a panic, leaving Royston alone with his dead mother.

There was no reason to torture himself with the scene of her death. It wouldn't bring her back and would only ruin his present.

His logic was solid. Yet those images kept emerging again and again in his mind, unbidden. Although, if he was going to be honest, he felt guilty every time he tried to push them down. It seemed an act of disrespect towards his mother. But how could he live with a ghost that dragged him into a dark pool of memories?

He closed his eyes and focused on his breathing until his pulse returned to normal and the horrible images vanished.

As he staggered along the path in the garden to take some fresh air, he spotted Angeline with her mother and paused. Likely sensing his stare, she turned towards him. Her expression changed from tense to... he dared say happy? Her plush lips curved up in a Mona Lisa smile that he'd gladly spend hours watching and trying to understand the meaning of.

He couldn't help but smile back, which was odd, considering a moment ago, he'd been on the verge of passing out. Yet a small smile from the spirited Angeline washed away his pain.

She raised a hand in greeting. He did the same.

That was the best exchange he'd had that night, and in a long time.

nine

I F MAMA WERE a type of weather, she would thunder and rain over Angeline's head.

After the incident with Mr. North and the pleasurable meeting with Baron Wharton, Angeline had to endure her mother's temper. Not only had Mama given Angeline a piece of her mind at the ball, but also in the carriage, and at home. She'd started her rant all over again in the morning as if Angeline hadn't spent the past eight hours hearing her mother complain.

Your reputation wouldn't be tarnished... it's all a trick... you had only to say yes... it's a lot of money.

She'd heard it all.

"I don't understand how you managed to ruin a perfectly reasonable proposition by Mr. North," Mama half-whispered, half-hissed as they promenaded in Hyde Park the day after the ball. "He was shocked and... wet."

Angeline suspected that the incessant talking and repeating was Mama's strategy to force Angeline to change her mind. Likely, Mama believed that if she repeated the same things over and over, sooner or later they'd sink into her daughter's brain. Good luck with that.

On top of that, Mr. North had had the brilliant idea of paying a morning visit to their residence to complain—again—with Mama about Angeline's appalling and unladylike behaviour. His words, not hers. He'd been as enraged as he'd been at the ball, minus the wet clothes. Mama had nodded her head and apologised, which had made Angeline want to cast up her accounts.

So here she was, walking in the park while her mother scolded her for the umpteenth time for not having let a man discuss selling her body. She was sure other women her age had very different conversations with their mamas.

"You really poured a vase of water over Mr. North." Mama's eyebrows knit together. "I've raised you better than that."

Angeline hoped she didn't have the same menacing expression when she frowned. "Mr. North groped me. He deserved it. And I reacted on impulse. I didn't hurt him. It's not my fault he doesn't understand the meaning of the word no."

"Angeline." Mama came to an abrupt stop in the middle of the gravel path. "I allowed Mr. North to talk to you because he's young, handsome, and rich. Very rich. Less savoury gentlemen might have come forward. All you had to do was endure a conversation with him and then wait for the next part of the deal. I've never asked you to have a tumble under the skirts with him."

"I don't like his attitude. He disrespected me, groped me, and considered me only an item he's buying."

"Welcome into my world, daughter of mine, and lest you get romantic ideas, all men are the same. I had to endure many unpleasant nights to put food on our table."

"And I appreciate it, tarnation!" She regretted her tone when Mama flinched. "I appreciate how difficult it was for you. I understand all the sacrifices you were forced to make to keep us alive. I'm grateful for everything you've done for me, but you seem not to understand a very simple concept." She put her hand on Mama's arm. "Drugging unaware men to make them believe whatever you want is not just against the law, it's wrong."

It was astonishing that Angeline's moral values came from her mother. Those values of honesty and integrity had always been lies. Lies that were corrupting her as well because she couldn't deny the fact she was Mama's accomplice. An unwilling one, but still an accomplice.

Mama pressed her lips in a flat, grim line. "No. It's wrong that a woman, whose husband left her and their child without means to survive, must struggle and humiliate herself for a piece of bread and a place to sleep." Her eyes shone, and her voice cracked. "I've crawled through the mud of this city to survive. I've done horrible things that kept me up at night. I had to change myself to survive because years ago I wasn't the ruthless woman I am today. And if an idiot like Mr. North thinks he can take my beautiful daughter by paying me, then I'm going to trick him and take his money. Serves him right. He deserves nothing less than to be fooled."

Angeline hugged her mother, her heart torn. The pain in her mother's voice touched her deeply, and to be honest, she wasn't sure what she would have done in a similar situation. But she wasn't her mother, and their current situation wasn't catastrophic. There were other options that didn't involve breaking the law, selling herself, or, in general, lying to protect her mama.

"I understand your sentiment," Angeline said, her voice cracking. "I really do. But your revenge on the rich and powerful men won't change the past and won't make a better future."

Mama sniffled but composed herself quickly. "I only care about your future. I don't care about changing the world. The world can go and rot for all I care. I want you to have a secure future in which you have the power to make your own decisions. Everyone else can sod off if you excuse my language."

"We have options though. I can marry. If I find a good match, we don't have to drug or blackmail people anymore." She lowered her voice.

"How is marriage better? What if you end up marrying someone you don't like, but who has a lot of money as happens to half of those eager, giggling debutantes? Will you enjoy his touch? Will you feel free and independent? Your husband will control your expenses, choices, and even your children."

Angeline shuffled her feet. Many women married men they didn't love only for their status and money. But surely, there were people who married because they respected and cared for each other. The world couldn't be as grim as Mama described it.

"And what about your arm?" Mama touched the scarred arm. "Gentlemen don't find your scar appealing. If a man doesn't accept you for who you are, how can he love you?"

"I could find someone I like and who likes me. Someone who doesn't disgust me as much as Mr. North. There are nice men in this world."

Unbidden, Royston's harsh face came into her mind.

He wasn't born a gentleman, but he was a true one. When they'd waved silently goodbye to each other in the garden, a flutter had started in her stomach. Their shared adventure behind the curtains had deepened the bond between them. She missed him. She should send him a note and ask to arrange a visit. That wouldn't be inappropriate, would it?

"Darling." Mama held her hand. "Men are all nasty, conniving creatures."

"You're quite deceitful yourself."

Mama ignored her. "Men will woo you, at first, only to lure you into their beds. They might marry you, but then what? They'll lose interest after you give them your body. Then they'll find a mistress who's younger and prettier than you. Or worse, they'll come to your bedroom when they're drunk and force themselves on you."

"You have a dark vision of the world."

"Because I lived that vision. My tested and tried method—"

"Crime."

"—will give you freedom and dignity. You won't be forced to suffer from a violent husband's hands or his needs on your body.

You'll be able to do everything you want with your money and time. If you find someone you like, you'll be free to take him to bed, but it'll be your choice, and the best thing is that you won't have to marry him."

Both paths Mama described seemed awful. Angeline was spared an answer as Lady Redvers and her maid walked over to her. Angeline tensed. Oh no. If Mr. North had complained to Lady Redvers as well, Angeline would join the first circus in town and leave London not to hear yet another lecture.

"Mrs. Haywood and Miss Haywood." The lady closed her parasol and smiled. "I hoped I would meet you."

Mama and Angeline dropped a curtsy.

"Lady Redvers," Mama said. "Thank you again. Angeline and I had a lovely time."

Almost. Meeting Royston had been great.

The lady's smile faltered. "Half of my guests are here, promenading. It's splendid to have a chat after the ball."

Angeline perked up. Royston could be here then. Or maybe not. He didn't seem the type of man who cared about meeting the guests of a ball the next day.

"Have you met anyone else from last night?" Lady Redvers gazed around.

"Not yet, my lady." Mama's tone was all sweet and kind, not at all like a moment ago when she'd thundered against society.

Lady Redvers leant closer to Mama. "I confess I hope to meet a certain gentleman, someone who would be a good match for my Georgiana." She turned to Angeline. "I'm sure your mother has her eyes on a valid suitor for you as well. You're too old for a Season, if you don't mind my saying, and beauty and youth are fickle friends. You blink, and they're gone. No one wants to be a spinster."

"Er... of course not, my lady." Hopefully, that was the correct answer.

Although Angeline reluctantly agreed with Lady Redvers. She

wanted a family of her own, a man who loved her and children to fill her house. She wanted to take care of her family, and no, being a spinster wasn't the best outcome for her.

Instead, Mama's black eyes became two narrow slits. Nothing like talking about marriage to spoil her mood.

Lady Redvers searched around again. "Mothers always worry about the future of their daughters. With the way the young generation behaves these days and the loss of our values, it's increasingly difficult to find a proper gentleman."

"I absolutely agree, my lady." Mama nodded sagely. "We want only the best for our daughters. That's what I always say to Angeline."

"Yes." Lady Redvers paused, twitching her mouth.

The two mamas had matching fierce expressions although for different reasons without their knowledge. They weren't actual rivals.

"May I ask who the gentleman who caught your eye is, Mrs. Haywood?" the viscountess asked. "We don't want to pursue the same gentleman. That would be rather inconvenient, don't you agree? Although Georgiana is a viscount's daughter. Her opportunities are far wider than your daughter's."

No, she wouldn't intervene. The conversation was all for her tiger mama.

Mama didn't fluster. "I seriously doubt we have in mind the same suitor. I suppose your daughter will find a suitable match among the titled gentlemen. Angeline will more likely be courted by a gentleman of means."

"Excellent." Lady Redvers exhaled.

"Although," Mama continued, "Miss Taylor has a genteel upbringing, and so does my daughter. They're both daughters of gentlemen. They're equal from that point of view."

No, not really.

Even Lady Redvers disagreed, judging by how she stiffened. "But a title is a title."

Mama showed a lopsided smile. "I can't argue with that, my lady."

Oh, goodness. Angeline pretended she didn't find the conversation awkward. Miss Taylor was going to be sold to the highest bidder as well. Maybe Angeline should propose an exchange—Miss Taylor would spend some time with Mama, and Angeline would get Lady Redvers's help to search for a suitable husband.

She followed the flight of a group of sparrows as Mama and Lady Redvers changed the subject and talked about the absolute tragedy of young debutantes wearing yellow that Season. Why not the traditional white? The world was going to the dogs.

A familiar, broad silhouette caught her attention. She must have focused on the man too long because Mama and Lady Redvers stopped talking and followed her gaze.

"Oh, goodness," Lady Redvers said. "It's him."

"Who?" Mama asked, shifting her gaze from Lady Redvers to the new baron.

Royston stopped in front of them and removed his tall hat, letting his luscious curls tumble down his jaw. "Lady Redvers, Mrs. Haywood." He acknowledged the maid before tilting his head towards Angeline and giving her a smile. "Miss Haywood. What a pleasant surprise."

Angeline curtsied, but Mama remained stiff, even cold. "Mr. Alexander? Is that you? My goodness, it's been a while."

Lady Redvers shot her an incendiary glare.

"Mama," Angeline said. "This is Lord Wharton. The queen bestowed a title upon him after his show of bravery during the Theatre Royal fire."

Mama's lips parted. For once, she was speechless. "Apologies, Lord Wharton. I had no idea." She curtsied.

"Apologies accepted, madam." Royston bowed again. "I trust you ladies are having a fine promenade."

"Lovely, my lord," Lady Redvers said in an overly cheerful tone. "Thank you for having come to the ball last night although I was sorry to see you leave early." A strained note crept into her voice.

"I apologise. An urgent matter required my attention." He tensed, tossing a fleeting glance at Angeline. "But believe me, my lady, it was a night I won't forget."

Goodness. Neither would she. So he was as pleased as she was for their secret encounter.

"Such lovely music last night," Mama said. "It's a shame I didn't see you there, my lord. Angeline didn't tell me she'd seen you." She glared at Angeline.

Yes, Angeline hadn't said anything because Mama had been too busy ranting.

"The baron didn't really mingle." Lady Redvers chuckled. "I wonder why you didn't dance, Wharton."

A muscle in Royston's jaw ticked. Angeline couldn't deny her curiosity. Dancing was a sensitive subject for him.

The viscountess continued, "My daughter, Georgiana, would have loved to dance with you. You remember my daughter, don't you, Wharton?"

Royston nodded. "Of course I do. The lady with the red hair and the green gown."

Lady Redvers's smile vanished. "No, Wharton. I believe you're confusing Georgiana with my niece Therese. Georgiana has brown hair like mine and wore a pink gown."

Mama seemed to fight a chuckle.

Royston opened his mouth but didn't say anything.

"Sometimes it's difficult to remember every name and face at a ball, isn't it?" Angeline said to help him.

His crooked smile was worthy of a pirate. "Do not worry, Miss Haywood. I would never forget yours."

A hot flare of excitement crept over her cheeks. "Thank you, my lord."

Every gaze turned towards her— Lady Redvers's angry one, Mama's surprised one, and the Redvers maid's a knowing one.

"I hope to see you soon, Wharton," Lady Redvers said in a less cheerful tone than before. "There are many balls and events to attend at this time of the year. Georgiana will be present as well."

"I'll do my best to attend, but it's a particularly busy moment for me," Royston said. "My newest venture requires much of my time."

"What venture, my lord?" Mama slightly stepped in front of Lady Redvers, almost blocking the viscountess's view.

"I acquired a steel factory, madam."

"Steel is the new gold," Lady Redvers said, excited again.

Mama's gaze sparkled and not in a good fashion.

Royston put his hat back on. "Ladies, I'd better be going. I have an appointment." He smiled at Angeline one last time before bowing and leaving.

The moment he was out of earshot, Lady Redvers angled towards Mama. "Mrs. Haywood, may I ask what game you're playing?"

"What game, my lady?" Mama followed Royston with her gaze with too much interest. "I had no idea Lord Havisham's former footman was a baron now. My daughter didn't inform me." Her tone promised another long conversation later on in the privacy of their home.

"Not simply a baron but a very wealthy man whom the queen likes." Lady Redvers let out a soft huff. "I must be blunt, Mrs. Haywood."

"Please be," Mama said.

Oh dear. Angeline had a hunch about where the conversation was going.

Lady Redvers lifted her chin. "My Georgiana thinks highly of Lord Wharton. She and the baron are clearly interested in each other."

Really? Angeline cast a glance at Royston walking away. He'd seemed pleased by their secret encounter.

Mama smiled. "Forgive me, my lady, but I had the impression

that Lord Wharton couldn't remember your daughter from last night."

Angeline shifted her weight.

Lady Redvers seemed about to stab Mama with her parasol. "I hope Lord Wharton will become Georgiana's suitor."

Mama didn't flinch. "I wish you all the luck but forgive me again if I don't understand. You have me quite confused. Miss Taylor is a viscount's daughter, and Lord Wharton has only recently acquired a title. Yet you consider him a good match for your daughter when you so clearly expressed the reasons why Angeline and Miss Taylor wouldn't have the same suitors."

Angeline lightly poked Mama with her elbow. Mama was over-stepping.

Lady Redvers flushed. "Well, you obviously aren't aware of Lord Wharton's strike of good luck and excellent skill for business. He invested the money and land profits that came with the title into his very successful steel factory. Wharton Steel has grown quickly, and now Lord Wharton has made more than two hundred thousand pounds in just two years. His income is growing each month," she said the sum with awe, and Angeline couldn't blame her.

Mama was speechless again, but Angeline could bet the gears and wheels in her brain worked furiously.

"Goodness me," Mama said.

"Exactly." Lady Redvers leant closer. "Rumour has it, Lord Wharton earns almost as much as the Duke of Devonshire, thanks to his business deals with other countries." She let that information sink in for a while. "So you see, Mrs. Haywood, Lord Wharton is more than a suitable match for my daughter. But he seemed interested in Miss Haywood." Resentment dripped from her voice.

Again, every set of eyes pointed at Angeline.

"You're mistaken, my lady. See, I was in the Theatre Royal

when the fire broke out and Royston... I mean, Lord Wharton helped me get out. He actually saved my life."

Lady Redvers's stern expression didn't change. "I'm glad to know you and Lord Wharton are good acquaintances and nothing more. I hope your relationship with him will remain a good one. Now if you'll excuse me. Good day, Mrs. Haywood and Miss Haywood." She strode off with her maid behind her.

Angeline released a breath. "Heavens. Lady Redvers is like one of those dogs who mark their territory."

Mama laughed, but the sound had an icy quality that left a trail of goosebumps on Angeline's skin. "Perfect. Perfect."

"What's perfect? The comparison between Lady Redvers and dogs?"

"Change of plan, darling." Mama hooked her arm through Angeline's. "Your new target is dear Lord Wharton."

"You must be joking. You heard Lady Redvers. She wants him to be her son-in-law." Which was sad, but she didn't believe Royston was interested in Miss Taylor.

"Who cares about what that hag wants? Two hundred thousand pounds isn't a joke. My dear, you must learn the art of seduction."

"No." Angeline swallowed hard. "I won't drug Royston. He saved my life, for Pete's sake."

"Royston. Very good." A crease appeared on Mama's forehead. "There won't be any need for drugs. You like him, don't you?"

"I... well... I'll admit he's a kind, handsome gentleman." With a hearty scent and a strong body.

"Excellent. You won't need to drug him. Have a nice tumble with him. I'll do the rest, and that will be it."

Angeline exhaled, tired of another argument with her mother. If Royston wanted to pay to spend a night with her, then she wouldn't spend the night with him.

And *that* would be it.

ten

ROYSTON GLANCED BEHIND him as he walked along the Serpentine, heading to the other side of Hyde Park. Angeline and her mother were still in the middle of the path, talking.

Damn. He hadn't expected to meet Angeline so soon. On second thought, it was better that way. He'd already made a *faux pas* by telling Angeline he wouldn't forget her. The remark had come out of his mouth unbidden. He didn't regret his honesty. Lady Redvers and Mrs. Haywood didn't need to know he wished to see Angeline again.

The encounter would have been the perfect excuse to say he would call on them. The more he thought about what had happened last night with North, the more worried he became.

He wanted to ask Angeline what her business with that man was, but he also simply wanted to spend more time with her. She had a fierce spirit he deeply admired. He liked her strength and unconventional attitude. He liked her sense of humour. He liked holding her, too. Her wild rose scent was delicious. And he couldn't care less about her scarred arm. Besides, he had scars on his soul uglier than any burn scars.

When Angeline and her mother disappeared behind a turn, he focused on his next meeting. He crossed the park and exited it, patting the thick envelope in his jacket. Carrying three hundred pounds while walking across London wasn't wise, but he didn't trust anyone.

A thief robbing him today would make a fortune, granted he managed to subdue Royston. He took a series of shortcuts and stopped in a quiet alleyway at Mrs. Walsh's door.

He knocked and waited, gazing around. The alleyway was dark but clean of rubbish or sewage. The houses close by weren't fancy but decent, with recently painted doors and pretty curtains at the windows. The shops were just around the corner. Mrs. Walsh couldn't have found a better location for her women's shelter.

The door swung inwards, and Mrs. Walsh came into view. "Good morning, my lord."

"Madam, good morning." He removed his hat.

Mrs. Walsh smiled, and a few wrinkles appeared around her eyes. "Lord Wharton, thank you for coming here. I didn't think you would come in person."

"I wanted to ask you personally how you were faring. I see you found great accommodation." He moved to enter, but she held up a hand.

"Apologies, my lord, but you must understand I can't let you inside." She stepped out of the house and left the door ajar. "Please don't be angry, but the women I provide lodging for in the house don't wish to see a man in a place where they feel safe."

"I understand. We can arrange for a different type of delivery in the future, but today, I wanted to talk to you." He searched the alley and pulled out the envelope. "I hope this helps. I'll send more as soon."

Mrs. Walsh took the money and curtsied. "Your generosity won't be forgotten, my lord."

"What else do you need?"

Her smile didn't reach her eyes this time. "Nothing. Your

Lordship takes good care of us. I am able to rent this house thanks to you, my lord."

"Mrs. Walsh, I was born in a brothel. My mother would be alive if a place like yours had existed. Please be honest."

She hesitated. "Money helps, my lord, but things need to change from the head. We ask for laws that protect us and give us the opportunity to start afresh."

Ah, yes. Parliament. He didn't tell Mrs. Walsh that the head had no intention of changing.

He put his hat on, caught by a moment of sadness. No, more than sadness, it was a painful sense of impotence. The same sense of impotence he'd experienced when his mother had died. Or rather, when she'd been murdered. He hadn't done anything but watch and cry.

He rubbed an aching spot in his chest, wondering if he would ever overcome that sense of lack of power. He was a baron now, but he didn't feel powerful.

"If you need anything, send for me," he said, controlling the quivering in his voice.

"Thank you, my lord. Really. You do so much for us." She bobbed another curtsy before entering the house.

He wasn't doing enough. Aside from providing money, he couldn't do anything else. His title was useless from this point of view. Or maybe he didn't possess the skills to navigate politics.

A seat in Parliament was his goal when he'd realised that the combination of money and political power would give him the chance to help women like the ones in Mrs. Walsh's house, to do more than hand them money.

If he were in Parliament, he'd fight for those who raised a child on their own after a terrible past of abuse, poverty, or both. Charity could only do so much. And if he failed in the House of Lords, he would fight to raise awareness of the suffering of the fallen women until people would listen.

He walked back to the park, in the company of too many dark thoughts.

His mood didn't allow him to enjoy the sunshine glittering off the Serpentine. His steel factory was his pride, not only because of its impressive success. Many honest men and women from the rookery had found employment at Wharton Steel.

The factory had changed lives for the better, and he was finally doing something useful with his life, instead of stealing or throwing punches in an illegal ring. But Mrs. Walsh was right. Fallen women needed new laws and the government's intervention to change their circumstances. Something more than even a hero baron could offer.

"Wharton, fancy that."

Royston jolted at hearing Havisham's voice. "Havisham."

The earl's reddened face and short breath made Royston think Havisham had run to catch up with him.

Havisham took a few deep breaths, one hand on his hip. "I saw you coming out of an alleyway and called you, but you didn't hear me."

"I was lost in my thoughts."

"I was thinking about asking you for a meeting," Havisham said.

Not another meeting. "For what reason?"

"I understand I didn't make myself clear during our last conversation and that I might have offended you."

Instant tension tightened Royston's neck muscles. "You made yourself very clear. I don't need your money, Havisham, and I don't want to steal from anyone."

Havisham held up a hand. "I respect your decision, and I apologise for having offered you money you obviously don't need. I didn't mean to offend you."

Royston chose his words carefully because he couldn't forget Havisham's kindness. "Also, I'm sorry to say that I find it hard to believe Mrs. Haywood is capable of blackmailing anyone."

"Are you accusing me of lying?" The earl's voice hardened.

"I'm saying you might be mistaken or there's something else going on."

"She's a ruthless blackmailer, trust me. I'm sure she has a string of lovers she regularly blackmails." Havisham hesitated. "I have a new deal to offer."

"Havisham, please."

"My new offer isn't money. It's something more important for you." His icy blue eyes glinted as he came closer. "I offer you a seat in the House of Lords."

Blimey. That caught Royston off guard. "Do you have the power to grant me a seat?"

"I wouldn't have offered it otherwise. I'm the seventh Earl of Havisham and know the House of Lords well. I'll support your case and present it to the lords myself. I can assure my fellow peers will follow me once I support you, and I'll see that a seat will be yours. I just need you to help me."

Dammit. "But to have the seat, I have to retrieve the material Mrs. Haywood has on you."

"Exactly," Lord Havisham said. "I appreciate your moral reservation about taking something from Mrs. Haywood without her consent. I was unfaithful to my wife. I can't deny that. But Mrs. Haywood collected evidence against me and blackmailed me. I've walked away from the life of an adulterer. I want to take care of my children and my wife. Mrs. Haywood threatens to ruin everything my wife and I have built so far. Think about the consequences my family will face if Mrs. Haywood reveals what I did. My wife will be devastated, and her father will destroy me. My family will be torn apart. Please. I need your help and discretion."

Mrs. Haywood was undoubtedly doing something against the law and morally wrong. But Royston didn't believe he could right a wrong with another wrong. Years ago, he wouldn't have hesitated to say yes. Now he wasn't so sure.

"What is more important, Wharton?" Havisham said. "Taking

those bloody photographs or having the opportunity to help people?"

"Why are you offering the seat right now? Why not before?"

"I had no idea you wanted a seat. I spoke with Redvers at the ball. He was sorry because of a conversation he'd had with you and told me he could do nothing to help you." Havisham shrugged. "I assumed a seat held more value than money for you."

It did. "What will you do once you have those documents? What will happen to Mrs. Haywood?" Royston narrowed his gaze.

"Absolutely nothing," Havisham said. "I'm not interested in revenge or destroying her. Besides, she doesn't know I want to cut ties with her. She doesn't suspect anything at the moment. I gave her the last batch of money three days ago and pretended everything was fine. I won't see her again. In fact, I really don't care about what she does. I simply want her to stop blackmailing me. Believe it or not, I don't hate her, but I hate the leash she has on me. I want my life back."

Well, if Mrs. Haywood wouldn't be harmed by Havisham, and if Havisham wanted only to live a quiet life with his wife and family, then retrieving those documents might be worth it. Besides, should Mrs. Haywood find herself in financial trouble because Havisham didn't pay her anymore, Royston would be more than happy to help her.

Also, blackmailing was illegal and morally wrong. But... no. Despite all those valid reasons, he'd left his criminal past behind. He wouldn't become a thief again. He'd get a Parliamentary seat but on his own terms.

He touched the rim of his hat, his shoulders stooping. "I'm sorry, Havisham. I'm not in the trade anymore. I suggest you talk with Mrs. Haywood and find an agreement."

Havisham slouched. "Think about it. We'll talk again soon. "

"I wish you good luck. Good day."

Yet when Royston headed home, he wondered if he'd done the right thing.

THE DAY WAS perfect for Angeline. Sunny weather, blue sky, just enough breeze to be pleasant. And for once, Mama, whose schedule was more busy than the queen's, had taken her to an intriguing social event. This time it was a festival held in Hyde Park with stalls of food, music, and competitions to raise money for charity.

Some important peers of the realm had been specifically invited, but the day was open to anyone who wished to participate in the games and donate money. Rowing, archery— that was interesting —cricket, and games of cards would keep the participants busy for the whole day.

But Mama's goal was to see Royston again and start her matchmaking game to pair him with Angeline. To be honest, Angeline wanted to see him, too. There had been no need to put too much effort into convincing her although she hadn't changed her mind about drugging him. Or accepting his money. Or having a tumble with him only to blackmail him later.

"Keep smiling." Mama twirled her parasol that matched her yellow gown.

"I can't smile for no reason."

"Society is always studying and judging. You must behave like a lady even when no one is watching you."

"Which sounds exhausting." Angeline searched the crowd for Royston.

He might have changed his mind and decided not to come although Mama had told her his presence had been confirmed. He hadn't looked particularly happy at Lady Redvers's ball. Maybe he didn't enjoy social events.

Angeline tilted her parasol to cover her face when she spotted Mr. North. He was heading to the boats on the Serpentine for the rowing race. After all, he had an affinity for water.

"Careful," Mama said. "The viscountess is coming with her plain, forgettable daughter."

Lady Redvers walked straight towards them. Her smile was nothing but a challenge. "We meet again, Mrs. Haywood, Miss Haywood. Such a pleasure."

Angeline curtsied. "Lady Redvers, Miss Taylor."

"Good morning." Miss Georgiana Taylor was a copy of her mother— same glossy brown hair and large brown eyes, but her features were softer and her smile more honest. "Such a lovely day." Even her voice was more musical than her mother's. Quite melodious.

Now that Angeline thought about it, she could swear Miss Taylor sounded exactly like the young lady with her pianist lover.

"My lady." Mama bowed her head gracefully as if her last encounter with the viscountess hadn't been abysmal.

"It's always nice to see some familiar faces." Lady Redvers gestured at the people crowding the meadow. "So many people here have no acquaintances among us peers, like you, Mrs. Haywood."

Miss Taylor and Angeline exchanged a glance.

"Quite the opposite, my lady," Mama said with no small amount of pride. "I have many friends among the peers. You'd be surprised by what I know about some members of the *ton*." She laughed. "I'm joking, of course."

Angeline coughed politely in her fist, silently begging her mother to stay quiet.

"I was wondering whom you know," Lady Redvers said. "Because, pardon me, but you seem to appear at every party and ball."

Oh, Mama knew many of the nobility here at the festival, starting with Lord Havisham. She'd likely blackmailed a few gentlemen there at one point or another. Honestly, whom or how many, Angeline didn't want to know.

"I believe I've never asked what your late husband's trade was."

Lady Redvers was obviously on a mission to discover Mama's secrets.

Well, good luck with that. Not even Angeline knew everything about Mama, and quite frankly, it was better that way.

Mama twirled her parasol with a nervous tweak. The viscountess had struck a nerve. "My dear husband traded in steel, just like Lord Wharton. The baron and I have a lot in common."

Goodness. Mama should inform Angeline of such lies. At least she'd be prepared to answer accordingly.

"Well—" Lady Redvers was interrupted by her daughter.

"Mother, Mr. Wright is going to play a sonata in the gazebo. You promised me we'd listen to his lovely music. Shall we go and see when his performance starts? I don't want to miss it."

Yes, definitely Miss Taylor was the woman behind the curtain, which meant Mr. Wright the pianist would be her lover, perhaps.

"I'll see you later, Mrs. Haywood, Miss Haywood," Lady Redvers said.

After another quick round of curtsies, the two ladies left.

"Talking about steel." Mama tilted her parasol to the side to get closer to Angeline. "Lord Wharton is over there, chatting with Lord Havisham."

"Where?" Angeline searched the meadow through the marquees, stalls, and gazebos and found Royston next to the refreshment table.

"I asked around," Mama said. "Many mothers have set their eyes on Lord Wharton as a possible suitor for their daughters."

"Oh, really?" Angeline scoffed. Ridiculous. Only because he owned a successful factory. No one really cared about who he was.

"He has the reputation of being grumpy."

"He isn't. He just feels uncomfortable among society." He also had a kind heart and gentle hands.

"Some say he isn't even handsome."

"Outrageous." Angeline was upset on his behalf. "He might have a rough type of beauty, but he's very handsome."

Mama laughed. "You like him. Excellent."

"Oh, Mama. You're incorrigible."

"I always do my research, and I'm glad you like him. Because I have plans."

Angeline shot her gaze skywards. "Of course, you have."

"According to my lady friends, Lord Wharton likes well-mannered ladies. Do not show him all your..." Mama waved a hand. "Athletic skills. You're a proper lady, all right?"

"What does that mean? That I can't participate in the archery competition?"

Mama grinned. "Quite the opposite. You will. I insist."

Angeline rubbed an aching spot on her forehead. "I don't understand you."

"I know. That's a problem. See, Lord Wharton signed up for the archery competition."

"Did he? How do you know that?"

"I told you. I do my research. Knowledge is power, my dear. Anyway, you're going to compete against him, and you're going to lose. You'll let Lord Wharton win. Men have big egos. The fastest way to conquer them is to let them believe they're wonderful, amazing achievers."

"I don't think you know the baron at all. He won't be impressed if I let him win, and I doubt he cares about losing."

Mama smiled as Royston tipped his hat at her. "You're wrong, darling. All men are the same. If you win, he'll detest you. If you lose, he'll adore you."

"I don't think so."

Mama's smile faltered. "Between you and me, who knows men the best?"

Dash it. "You, of course. But I know Royston better than you."

Mama's eyes brightened. "I like it when you use his Christian name. Good."

"Mama, please." She exhaled some of her frustration.

"Do you want to prove me wrong? Lose against him, and we'll see what happens."

"No. If I'm going to compete, I'll do my best to win." What a bother. Angeline flexed her fingers to warm them up. "I'm a jolly good archer, and I'll show my skill to everyone."

"Miss Haywood," Lady Redvers said from behind Angeline, causing her to jolt. "I apologise, but I couldn't help but hear what you were saying."

Angeline was sure the lady had eavesdropped on purpose.

"Don't tell me you mean to compete at the archery competition," Lady Redvers said. "Goodness, that would be quite inappropriate. I do hope your mother doesn't encourage you to perform such wild activities."

Mama's eyes became two obsidian blades. "I encourage my daughter to be happy and admired in whichever way she chooses to do that."

Not entirely true, but Angeline appreciated Mama's help.

Lady Redvers ignored her. "Miss Haywood, you're already old enough to be considered a spinster if you don't mind my frankness. You'll ruin your chances of finding a good match by behaving so recklessly. Besides, you'll only make a fool out of yourself." She let out a squeaky laugh that could crack glass.

That did it. Maybe Angeline was too sensitive. Maybe she had a temper; maybe she was a spinster, but she'd show Lady Redvers and everyone watching what she could do with a bow.

eleven

THE ONLY GOOD thing about the day for Royston was the nice weather. The lemonade tasted delicious, too.

He shouldn't have come to the event. From the moment he'd arrived, Havisham had never left his side, asking Royston if he'd changed his mind, Lady Redvers had introduced him to her daughter no less than three times, and Havisham's footmen, who had once been Royston's mates, now treated him like a stranger, which he understood.

Maybe he was a completely different person now that he had money and a title. He still had to decide if becoming a baron and making a lot of money had been a blessing or a curse. For now, it seemed that everyone wanted something from him, but no one wanted to help his cause.

"So this is your last word," Havisham said, sipping a glass of lemonade.

Royston exhaled. "I can't do it, Havisham. If you'll excuse me." He put his empty glass on the table and walked towards the archery field.

The earl nodded sadly, following him. "Listen, I didn't want to do it, but I have some information on Mrs. Haywood that might change your mind."

"I won't change my mind," Royston said.

Havisham took his arm, forcing him to stop. "I didn't want to throw more mud at Mrs. Haywood, but I realise now that you *must* know the truth." He took a deep breath and lowered his voice. "She uses desperate young women for her blackmail scheme. She'd do anything to gather compromising material on rich gentlemen, including abusing fallen women."

Royston's stomach seemed to be filled with ice. He'd heard of some brothel madams who used and abused their girls to blackmail their clients. If what Havisham had said was true, the news struck a deep chord within Royston. Wherever he turned, he found someone who wanted to attack and take advantage of unfortunate women like his mother.

"There's more." Havisham's face hardened. "I paid a private investigator to follow Mrs. Haywood."

"What?" Royston sounded outraged to his own ears.

Havisham looked hurt. "You refused to help me. I wanted to find some information about Mrs. Haywood I could use as leverage to get her off my back. Can you blame me?"

Well, no. "What did the private investigator discover?"

"Mrs. Haywood went to a few women's shelters to recruit women desperate enough to do her bidding with the promise of large sums of money. I asked the private investigator to dig deeper, and it turned out that one of these shelters is managed by a Mrs. Walsh who receives generous donations from you."

A quick pang stabbed Royston's aching chest; it was as if he'd been punched. "It can't be."

Havisham lowered his gaze. "I'm sorry, Wharton, but it's the truth. If you don't believe me, ask Mrs. Walsh."

"I don't know what to say." The pain was real. He could barely speak.

"Mrs. Haywood isn't the good person you believe she is. Think about it." Havisham patted Royston's shoulder. "I'll see you in the archery field. Good luck with the competition," he said before leaving.

Royston needed more than luck to survive the nobility.

He remained still for a few moments, digesting the news. Angeline had never talked about her father, but he'd heard he'd died. If her father had left his family in need, Mrs. Haywood might have become desperate enough to resort to blackmail. He couldn't judge that. He'd resorted to crime, too. But taking advantage of desperate fallen women, who had seen nothing but abuse, was cruel.

He ran a hand through his hair, not sure about what to do. On the one hand, he didn't want to damage Mrs. Haywood, if what Havisham discovered was true, but on the other, he couldn't allow her to hurt fallen women.

Still, recovering Havisham's documents had nothing to do with helping fallen women, but if he could get a bloody seat and increase his political power, he might use it to stop people like Mrs. Haywood.

He released a breath, resuming walking. Too many thoughts crammed his mind. He needed a moment of peace and quiet to think.

To reach the archery field, he took a meandering path through the gardens to avoid Lady Redvers and her daughter on the main path. Perhaps he should leave. He'd made his donation for the fundraising. He wasn't interested in anything else unless he could talk to Angeline, and not because of his doubts about her mother.

Right then, Angeline swept into view when he got closer to the edge of the archery field. Dressed in a lovely bottle-green dress, she stood out like a crown jewel. He smiled for no reason other than he was looking at her. An unusual flutter started in his chest.

She tested the bows set on the rails at the edge of the field.

Other gentlemen were already practising shooting arrows at the hay targets for the upcoming elimination rounds.

"Careful with that arrow, miss," a man said.

"The lady had to pull some strings to be here," another one said, laughing.

More mutters and loud jokes came from a few men. She ignored them though.

Her focused expression caused her delicate eyebrows to draw together. The sunlight glinted off her raven hair; it was so deeply black that it shone with blue hues. He changed his mind about leaving. Thoroughly. With her fiery temperament and determination, she was likely a great archer, and he looked forward to seeing her shoot.

He strode across the field and stopped in front of her. "Angeline. I'm pleased to see you again."

Her frown deepened. "Royston." She dropped the quickest and shallowest curtsy in history. She must have beaten a record in curtsying speed.

"You are going to participate in the archery competition," he said.

"I am. Does that bother you?"

"Not at all. Is something the matter?"

Her frown didn't relax. "No. Everything is fine."

He selected a bow and a set of arrows. "I'm looking forward to competing with you."

A gentleman walked over to them and picked up a bow. He cast a glance at Angeline. "Miss, you should leave now before you get hurt."

"I was about to say the same thing to you, sir," she said to the man.

Royston chuckled. The gentleman had to lack a sense of humour because he strode away.

A heated glint flashed in her gaze. Perhaps she was more

competitive than he thought. Never mind. It was actually better that way. He loved a fierce competitor and a passionate lady.

As the crowd gathered around the field for the competition, he watched Angeline choose her bow. She selected a relatively small one, surely perfect for her height and arm's length. She tried it, acquiring a good shooting pose.

He chose a recurve bow made of walnut wood. "I see I'm going to have a serious competitor."

She flushed. "What makes you think that?"

"You obviously know how to handle a bow."

"I do." Staring at him, she plucked out her gloves.

His gaze dipped to the scar marring her creamy skin. The scar tissue was lighter than the surrounding skin and with bumps like large blisters and indentations. Her stare dared him to make a comment, but if she feared that, he ought to reassure her.

He offered her his hand. "May I?"

Her confident expression wavered, and her breathing quickened when she slid her scarred hand into his.

He lowered his head and kissed her knuckles, which was a big mistake in retrospect. Not because the marred skin repulsed him, but because he didn't want to let her hand go. And because everyone must have seen what he'd done. So much for being more careful.

Every time she was close, his logic deserted him. She drew in a breath that could mean anything from outrage to pleasant surprise.

He released her hand quickly. "Apologies."

She muttered, "Don't worry," so low he barely caught it.

Mrs. Haywood stood under the shade of a tree, seemingly not bothered by the fact an unmarried man had kissed her daughter's hand. He wouldn't consider himself an expert in etiquette. , but as a former footman, he'd been around ladies and gentlemen for enough time to understand what behaviours were considered appropriate.

Mrs. Haywood gave him a graceful nod of her head. He reluctantly returned it.

Doubts about Mrs. Haywood bothered him. He still couldn't believe she could be so callous as to exploit unfortunate women. He needed to see Mrs. Walsh.

Havisham strode to the middle of the field and spread out his arms. "Ladies and gentlemen, we're about to begin the first elimination round. Two archers will take turns with one target, so you'll need to swap places. Thank you everyone for being here. Your participation is much appreciated."

Royston gave Angeline an encouraging smile for no particular reason. She returned it this time, but it was strained.

"May I ask why you're so upset today?" he asked. "I saw North at the rowing race. Did he bother you again? If he did, tell me what I can do to help you."

"It's not Mr. North." She rolled her plump bottom lip between her teeth, which was distracting. "I have to say that—"

"Let the best archer win!" Havisham flourished a handkerchief and left the field while the referees entered.

"We'll talk later," Angeline said.

The giggles and chatter from the crowd behind Royston made it difficult to focus, but there wasn't a gust of wind and the air was crystal clear. Perfect conditions.

"Good luck, Miss Haywood."

Another sad smile. "Good luck, Lord Wharton."

"After you." He stretched out an arm towards the target.

"Please start. I need to warm up my fingers. They need time."

"Fine." He wished he could help her feel better.

Other competitors lined up in front of the row of targets. He nocked the arrow, took aim, and released the string.

The arrow hit the centre of the target with a hiss renting the air. A round of applause rose from the audience, with Lady Redvers clapping quite loudly.

"Miss." Royston stepped aside to give Angeline room.

Before nocking the arrow, she angled towards her mother who replied with a slight nod. Angeline lifted the bow and set her shoulders in an elegant position.

And that was pretty much the last thing he understood about what she was doing. Her movements became a blur of activity. She shot three arrows, one after the other. Two hit the centre, knocking off his arrow. The third missed the centre by half an inch, but her precision was still impressive.

"I say!" He let out a whistle. "That was— Angeline."

She put her bow back on the rail and stormed off of the field.

"Miss Haywood?" Havisham said. "Why are you leaving? You hit the mark three times."

"Angeline, wait." Royston put his bow back on the rail and chased her.

She was fast even when walking.

"Angeline." He overtook her and stopped in front of her.

She was a storm bottled in a pretty gown, and he had no idea why she was so upset.

"What happened? Why did you leave? You didn't give me the chance to reply to your great shots." He meant it as a joke, but a moment of anxiety made his words sound strained and pretentious.

"I'm sorry..." She gazed everywhere but him. "I didn't mean to leave like that."

"You seem furious. Was it something I did?"

She didn't reply.

"Should I apologise? Well, just in case. I'm sorry. I didn't mean it."

Her angry expression softened. "Oh, no. It wasn't you."

He offered her his arm. "Care for a walk? We can talk if you like."

She slid her hand tentatively over his as if worried he might yell at her.

They promenaded along the path among romping children and stalls of food and flowers.

"You'll think my predicament is silly," she whispered.

"Can't you tell me first what it is?"

She released a long breath. "It's not a secret that I'm a spinster."

He didn't see what her marital status had to do with archery, but anyway.

"My mother and... another lady started bickering about the fact a proper lady shouldn't shoot arrows. The lady claimed I wouldn't be able to find a husband if I showed everyone I used a bow. Mama defended me in her own way, but I got angry and..." She waved a hand. "I'm sorry. Telling the story out loud makes me realise how silly the whole affair is."

He disagreed. "I wouldn't consider myself an expert in how people get married or when a lady should be considered a spinster, but it seems obvious you've had enough of hearing about your chances of finding a husband. The conversation between your mother and the lady was the last straw."

She gave him a genuine, bright smile that lit her whole face. "I shouldn't have stormed out of the field."

"I really liked your energy." He mimicked her shooting an arrow. "Your precision when shooting is commendable. Your speed is astonishing. You made quite a scene and left the other competitors stunned. Well done."

Her smile vanished. "I'm not sure it's a good thing. See, deep down, I think the lady is right. I've never had a suitor, and today's performance won't help."

"Do you want to marry?"

It was astonishing that she didn't have a queue of suitors at her door. Not that he complained. Thinking about Angeline married to someone like North was no small source of anxiety.

A blush the colour of dawn crept over her cheeks. "Yes, but I want to find someone who really loves me, someone I can build a family with. I want children and dogs, too." She chuckled nervously. "I don't want to marry just to marry. It's a simple dream, but it's all mine."

"Simple but powerful. You want to be happy. Who doesn't?"

"And you? Are you looking for a wife?" Her big obsidian eyes became larger, perhaps with interest.

"I don't know."

He stroked the fluffy seed of a dandelion carried by the wind. It soared over Angeline's shoulder and caressed her cheek before drifting off towards the trees.

She laughed at the feather-like seed, and the sound was like that of blown-glass bells. He acted on pure instinct and caressed the gentle curve of her cheek with a finger.

She froze, her eyes growing even larger.

He lowered his hand. "Sorry. It was the blowball." Well, not his finest explanation.

She touched her cheek. "It was nice," she whispered. "I would say... thank you."

"I would say you're welcome."

They burst out laughing, and the tension between them dissolved.

She leant closer to him as they walked onwards through other promenading couples and vendors.

"Why don't you know if you're looking for a wife?" she said.

"Growing up in a brothel showed me the worst of our society. My mother was always miserable. Her jockeys didn't help her feel better. It's a dark past I don't know how to leave behind. A burden I'm not sure I should share. And I'm focusing on my business at the moment."

The whole speech sounded like a pile of rubbish to his own ears although he was scared of sharing his past with a wife. But, a voice inside him argued, the right person would understand, and he wouldn't have anything to fear. No judgement, only love.

"But…" She trapped her bottom lip between her teeth. "Forgive me."

"Please, go on. What did you want to say?"

"If your father hadn't left your mother but had married her, her life would have been different. Your life would have been different. Happy families are quite common."

"That's true, but married men are the largest part of a brothel's clientele, which makes me think about how depressing marriages could be. Frustrated wives, bored husbands, everyone lies to everyone. I'm sorry. My words don't make any sense."

"No, I think I understand. You don't believe you can build a happy family." She stared at him solemnly. "You would never lie to your wife, though. You have a kind heart."

A pang of guilt bit him. If he decided to go along with Havisham's plan, he was going to steal from her mother. She couldn't be involved in her mother's scheme, could she? She wasn't a blackmailer. If she was, she was the best actress he'd ever met, and he might be her next victim.

No, he refused to believe that. Her voice never wavered. Her expressions were genuine. She didn't play a part.

"Angeline, my past isn't that of a kind man." He didn't know if she was lying to him or not, but he wanted to be honest about his past. "I did things I'm ashamed of, and the worst thing is that I'm not sure I've changed."

She stopped under the shadow of a tree. "Trust me, I understand the need to survive against all odds. I don't judge you for your past, but I think I know your heart. You saved me from certain death. No one forced you to enter the blazing theatre over and over to save people you didn't know. I don't care what you did in the past, but I trust your present."

That was likely the best compliment he'd ever received.

He got lost in her gaze and the deep pink of her lips. He wondered if they were as velvety as her cheek. Once again, she chased away his dark thoughts with the ease of a zephyr blowing away the clouds. And that was the best gift he'd ever received.

"Besides." She lowered her gaze. "I have my share of sins, too. There are things I did that made me feel ashamed of myself. Well, not exactly things *I* did, but I helped someone else do those things." She shook her head. "I'm sorry. Now my words don't make any sense."

No, he got a good hunch of what she meant. A part of him wanted to blurt out what Havisham had told him and demand an explanation. Another part advised caution. He needed to know more about Mrs. Haywood's blackmail scheme and to see Mrs. Walsh.

"I didn't have a good example of a happy family either," she said in a low tone. "I don't remember anything about my father. He abandoned my mother when I was a child. But exactly for that reason, I want to build my own happy family. It would be like breaking a curse."

So yes, dire circumstances had driven Mrs. Haywood to crime. People got easily lost in a life of crime.

"I understand. If you need to talk, I'll always be here for you," he said.

"If I could tell you everything, I would." She opened her mouth to say something else, but whatever she meant to say was cut off by her mother walking towards them.

He stepped away from Angeline, aware he'd spent too much time alone with her. But Mrs. Haywood didn't show the angry face of an outraged mama. She smiled when she stopped next to them.

"Darling, are you all right? You ran away." Mrs. Haywood bowed her head at him. "Thank you for taking care of my daughter, my lord."

"My pleasure, madam."

Angeline gazed around. "I needed a moment, Mama."

"It's all right," Mrs. Haywood said. "I'm glad Lord Wharton

kept you company. Mr. Wright is giving a piano concert to end the event. Would you care to join us, my lord?"

"I'll be delighted." Anything to spend more time with Angeline.

"It's decided then. Shall we?" Mrs. Haywood's happiness reminded him of that of those mobsters in the rookery after they'd collected protection money.

Definitely, he had to understand what she was doing.

twelve

A NGELINE'S CHEEK TINGLED pleasantly when she sat next to Royston to listen to the piano concert. The soft brush of his fingers had left a path of pleasant shivers on her skin, but his words had left a path of happiness and tenderness in her heart.

The gazebo where a grand piano sat was adorned with pink roses, and the rows of seats around it had pretty matching ribbons. Mama sat on Angeline's other side, a smug expression on her face.

If anything, Angeline had proved her wrong because Royston had been impressed with her archery skills. She still glowed about his praise. It didn't mean anything though. He wouldn't court her only because she was good with a bow. Oh, well, she didn't care. He wasn't interested in marriage anyway, and she enjoyed his company.

Lady Redvers and her daughter took the seats in front of her, chatting in whispers. Mr. Wright, a tall and thin man, bowed to the audience. His rich auburn hair and sparkling green eyes gave him a youthful look. He sat on the piano bench and began playing a beautiful, sweet piece.

"Which piece is this?" she whispered to Royston.

"Liszt, *Liebestraum* number three. It means love dream."

There wasn't a more fitting title for the beautiful music, and the piano player added a ridiculous amount of ache to it.

Now she understood why Mr. Wright was the best pianist at the moment. He had the uncanny power to capture those who listened and never let them go. She raised her gaze from the talented pianist and was surprised to find Royston staring at her with intense hazel eyes.

He smiled, long bronzed eyelashes fluttering. His harsh lines softened, and his boyish beauty shone. When he smiled like that, he didn't look harsh at all.

She couldn't help but smile back. With the music caressing them and the blowballs floating around, she could easily believe they lived in a fairy tale. She should feel uncomfortable about sharing such a long stare with a man, but instead, a sense of calm washed over her. In that quiet moment between them, the world seemed perfect.

She returned her attention to the pianist when the music ended and clapped with the rest of the audience.

"Beautiful, isn't it?" she said.

"One can't help but fall in love." He sounded so serious she wondered if he meant... no, of course he didn't.

Lady Redvers stood up, clapping. "Thank you, Mr. Wright, for your performance. Now my daughter Georgiana will play a Chopin's sonata."

Judging by how Miss Taylor turned the colour of turnips, she wasn't ready.

"Mother," Miss Taylor said.

"Don't be shy. Lord Wharton loves music, don't you, my lord?" Lady Redvers asked, half-turning around to see Royston.

Angeline held back a comment. What did Royston have to do with Miss Taylor's playing?

Royston rose as well. "I do, my lady."

"Go, darling." Lady Redvers almost shoved her daughter towards the gazebo.

Miss Taylor shuffled towards the piano. She exchanged a few words with Mr. Wright, who flushed a deep red, before she sat on the piano bench. She and Mr. Wright went through a stack of music sheets, talking in whispers.

"You'll see, my lord," Lady Redvers said. "Some young women like my daughter are skilled in delicate, tasteful forms of art. Other not-so-young women instead, alas, find pleasure in unladylike activities."

Like archery? Angeline clenched her fists in her lap.

"It's not a surprise if such women can't find a good match or any match at all," Lady Redvers continued, sitting down.

"I believe that every skill has its merit." Royston sat as well. "Especially if it comes from hard work and dedication."

Angeline mouthed, "Thank you."

"Does your daughter play the piano, Havisham?" Lady Redvers asked.

"Not really," the earl said. "But she loves cricket. Who knows, perhaps one day she'll be as skilled as Miss Haywood is with a bow." He gave her a polite nod.

"Thank you, my lord," Angeline said.

Lady Redvers straightened. "I guess cricket is better than archery."

Mama pressed her lips in a hard line. "I have to say—"

Oh, heavens. Angeline gave her mother the slightest shake of her head. No arguing.

Mama cleared her throat. "Being good at something like archery doesn't exclude being good at other, more delicate activities."

"Besides, Lady Redvers," Lord Havisham said, "now that I think about it, Miss Haywood is an excellent piano player."

"What?" she said at the same time as Mama said, "Excuse me?"

Lord Havisham didn't flinch at the surprised tones. "I heard her playing. She sounds like an angel, true to her name. A professional."

Royston frowned.

"Oh, really? I'm eager to hear her play then." Lady Redvers sounded livid.

What in the blazes was happening? Angeline exchanged a glance with her mother who was speechless. Royston kept frowning.

"I'm sure Mrs. Haywood will be happy to organise a piano concert for us only." Lord Havisham angled towards Mama. "What do you say, Mrs. Haywood?"

It was the first time Angeline had seen her mother astonished.

When Mama swallowed and said, "Of course," Angeline knew she was doomed.

~

AFTER THE FESTIVAL ended and Angeline had left in a hurry with her mother, Royston headed to the women's shelter. A jumble of different thoughts and feelings crammed his mind. The moments spent with Angeline had been the best, not only of the day but of the year. The worry about what her mother might be doing poisoned his happiness.

He paced in front of Mrs. Walsh's door, waiting for the lady to open. He'd always considered himself a good judge of people, but if what Havisham had told him was true, Royston had been wrong about Mrs. Haywood. Very wrong.

Blackmailing rich men who were unfaithful to their wives, as wrong as it was, was one thing, especially if Mrs. Haywood might not have had many choices in her life. But taking advantage of the misfortune of poor women was quite another.

"Lord Wharton." Mrs. Walsh curtsied. "Sorry to have made you wait. I didn't expect anyone."

"Madam, do not worry." He handed her another envelope filled with banknotes he'd hastily put together before coming.

Mrs. Walsh hesitated before taking it. "Thank you, my lord. A second donation so soon."

"Actually, I came here mostly to ask you something." And he hadn't wanted to come empty-handed.

"Anything, my lord."

"Did a Mrs. Haywood come here, asking to see the girls?"

Mrs. Walsh's peaceful expression hardened. "Oh, what a nasty visit, my lord. Yes, a woman came and introduced herself as Mrs. Haywood. Quite a refined lady. Dark hair, dark eyes. Very well-spoken and very pretty."

Royston's heart gave a solid kick of disappointment. "What did she want?"

"Honestly." Mrs. Walsh shook her head. "She wanted to recruit a few women who live in the house. She said she could pay well if the girls did a good job by..." She averted her gaze. "Well, Mrs. Haywood wanted to use the girls to meet some gentlemen in an intimate rendezvous. She was quite insistent about the idea of taking photographs of the girls with the gentlemen."

He passed a hand over his face. "Unbelievable. What did you say to her?"

Mrs. Walsh lifted her chin. "I told her to leave immediately. My guests have seen enough violence and abuse. They don't need more."

"Bless you, madam."

Mrs. Walsh wasn't finished. "When I asked her why she came here and not to a brothel, she had the audacity to say that she didn't want to recruit women from the trade because she'd need to share the income with the madam of the brothel." Her voice broke. "She said the girls here were cheaper since they didn't work for anyone."

"That's horrible. I apologise."

She smiled. "For what, my lord? You didn't do anything."

"I don't know, for the cruelty people are capable of." He almost jolted when she put a bony hand on his cheek in a maternal gesture.

She withdrew her hand. "We're lucky there are people like you who balance the unkindness."

No, he wasn't the damn hero everyone thought he was. "Thank you, madam. Please, should Mrs. Haywood return, send for me."

"My lord." She curtsied.

Royston bowed and dragged his sorry self towards Havisham's house. Mrs. Haywood was such a disappointment, and since he hadn't been sharp enough to understand how conniving she was, perhaps Angeline was the same.

No. His heart screamed she was innocent. Still, she had to know of her mother's activities. He wondered why she didn't protest against the recruitment of abused women.

He shoved his hands in his pockets and braved the cold wind blowing from the north and carrying a chilly drizzle. The day had started with bright sunlight, but it'd changed quickly, just like his mood.

Icy raindrops slid down his neck, causing his skin to pebble. By the time he arrived at Havisham's house, he was cold and drenched, and he didn't care. He could have hailed a cab, but he needed the air to clear his head. Not that it worked. His feelings were all over the place.

Havisham welcomed him into his warm and dry drawing room, eyeing him with suspicion. "Good Lord, what happened to you?"

"I went to see Mrs. Walsh." He brushed a wet curl of hair from his face.

"I see." The earl poured him a glass of brandy. "Here. You seem to need it."

He took the glass. "Mrs. Haywood... I can't believe it."

"She's a clever woman who would deceive the most skilled

criminal." Havisham took a sip. "The private detective informed me Mrs. Haywood keeps a list with the names of those women whom she employs. They're at her beck and call, constantly threatened by her."

"How did he discover that?"

Havisham plopped down on the armchair. "Because he talked with a girl who was blackmailed by Mrs. Haywood. That woman is a menace."

Royston nursed his drink. "Bloody hell."

"I've been in Mrs. Haywood's house a few times when she was alone. I noticed a filing cabinet in her personal study. I've seen her myself stashing important papers in there. I hate being insistent, but if you search her study, you won't simply recover the material she has on me and give me back my life. You'll have the opportunity to search for Mrs. Haywood's list of girls, those girls she exploits for her games because surely, you aren't naïve enough to think she tried to recruit only Mrs. Walsh's women."

He couldn't swallow the brandy.

Havisham took Royston's arm. "You could save them all. You could help them get away from their miserable lives and find a proper job. I don't need to tell you how many of those women die every month from starvation and diseases."

A sickening lump crawled into Royston's throat. Mrs. Haywood had to be stopped.

"What's the plan?"

"Remember the little scene at the festival when I mentioned an event where Miss Haywood could exhibit her skill at playing the piano?"

"Yes?"

"That event is going to help us. I'm going to talk to Mrs. Haywood immediately." Havisham smiled. "I have an idea."

thirteen

ANGELINE WAS FUMING. She was so angry she couldn't express her frustration with words, only with scoffs.

Closing and opening her fists, she paced in the sitting room. Lord Havisham needed to hear her opinion. Oh, as soon as she was capable again of producing a speech that made sense, she'd give the earl a piece of her mind. Every time she started to say something, her anger blocked her, and a string of gibberish came out.

"Honestly," Mama said, drinking her tea as if the world weren't ending. "I don't understand why you're so upset."

"Why?" She skidded to a stop in the middle of the hessian carpet, creasing it. "I don't know how to play the piano. That's why. You agreed to invite a bunch of people to listen to me playing an instrument I know nothing about, and I don't even know why."

"*Pff.*" Mama rolled her eyes. "After all these years, after everything we've been through, you still doubt me. It hurts. Really."

"I can't become a skilled piano player in a matter of hours."

"Of course you can't, you silly. Nevertheless, you're going to play exquisitely and leave the audience in awe. Listen, I was shocked as well when Lord Havisham intervened with his preposterous claim, but while you stormed off, the earl and I talked after the concert. He explained to me he didn't like how Lady Redvers talked to you, so he wanted to teach her a lesson and said you were a great pianist. He admitted the affair went out of control. Never mind. Apparently, your success with the bow impressed him, and I have no problem admitting I was wrong and you were right about archery. Who would have thought? But I digress. Lord Havisham and I came up with the perfect plan." She grinned. "I would've never thought the earl could be so protective of you. His behaviour astonished me. Such a nice behaviour, after all."

Enough. Angeline gave up. She had to accept the fact her mother wasn't of sound mind any longer.

"Do you trust me?" Mama asked.

"No." She stomped a foot on the floor.

Mama glowered. "I truly am hurt."

"I'm sure you'll recover soon."

"Lord Havisham told me Lord Wharton is an excellent piano player," Mama said as if that clarified the confusion.

Not even a great piano player could speed up time and turn Angeline into a skilled musician in a matter of hours.

"He'll play on your behalf." Mama gave a wink.

"I don't understand."

"Let me explain." She walked over to the piano— the piano that Angeline had never touched, not even to dust it —at the end of the room. "We'll put some thick tea towels here." She opened the piano panel, revealing all the strings and hammers. "When properly placed, the tea towels will block the hammers, silencing the piano. While in the next room, hidden from view, we'll set up a proper piano, which His Lordship is going to play." Mama sat in front of the piano and pretended to play it. "You'll simply move your fingers as if you were playing while the actual sound will come from Lord Wharton's piano, and it'll be a beautiful sound." She wasn't finished. "We'll open this vent here." She pointed at a vent underneath the piano. "And add a horn bell like that of a phonograph, I'll disguise it, of course, and voila! You've become a pianist."

"Ah..."

Angeline didn't know if Mama had a stroke of genius, or if the whole idea was the most ridiculous thing ever produced after swan-shaped candlesticks because the wax dripped everywhere and the swan looked grotesque... goodness, she was losing her mind.

"We can't call the whole thing off. Lord Havisham will be humiliated, and Lady Redvers needs to think more carefully before she disparages you."

Actually, Angeline didn't care about what Lady Redvers did or said. "I don't want to do this."

"I know what you're thinking," Mama said.

"I seriously doubt that."

Mama pretended to play again. "You and Lord Wharton need to be coordinated, otherwise your fingers will keep moving when there's no music or vice versa, which would be a problem."

No, she hadn't thought about that at all. "Mama, this is..." There again. She was at a loss. No word came out. Anger caused her tongue to trip on the words.

"The baron will come here to practise with you." Mama touched her hand. "As I told you, I've thought of everything. I'm not going to let the viscountess win."

Well, two could play that game. "If I have to do this then I want something in return." Angeline jutted out her chin. "If I find a man I wish to marry, you won't do anything to stop me."

Mama's expression froze. "I'll certainly voice my opinion."

"But you won't do *anything* else."

Mama sighed. "Fine."

~

SITTING on the piano bench next to Angeline, Royston couldn't completely remove the sense of guilt gnawing at him.

The only reason Havisham had concocted this absurd plan was to allow Royston to be in Mrs. Haywood's house and search her study undisturbed.

He'd perform on the piano in the study, hidden from Mrs. Haywood's guests, and after that, while the guests enjoyed tea, he would search the room.

He kept going back and forth with his decision, but he had to admit he wouldn't have a better opportunity to find those documents since his solitary presence in the study was part of the plan. No need for breaking and entering.

"And those are the movements of this piece," Royston said, finishing Strauss's Emperor Waltz.

Angeline focused and repeated the hand movements. They were only vaguely correct.

"I'm really sorry for this situation. I can't believe Mama agreed to this madness."

No, he was sorry. "Don't worry. I don't mind helping you, and I agree with the fact Lady Redvers shouldn't have disparaged you. Miss Taylor is a fine player, but what you do with a bow isn't easy either. You have talent. Lady Redvers shouldn't insult people."

"You're saving me. Again. I have a seriously enormous debt with you."

"No, you don't." He took her hand but released it immediately before he did something inappropriate.

"But your being here to help me proves I was right. You have a kind heart." She gave him one of her devastatingly beautiful smiles.

"You think too highly of me." He would have helped her anyway, but instead, he needed to get something from her mother.

She gently put her hand over his. "You're too modest." She glanced at her scarred hand, her brow furrowing. "You kissed my hand," she whispered.

"Because I don't care about the scar. Your scar has a story to tell. A story of survival and pain. No one should make fun of you because of it."

She stared at him with too much awe. "I'm happy to..."

"Yes?" he prompted when she didn't continue.

She laughed. "I don't know. I guess I'm just happy to be here with you. That's all. Your presence calms me. Your closeness makes me more confident." She seemed about to say something else but remained silent.

When she smiled, her lips became more inviting, stretching and curving up. His heartbeat stuttered when she tilted her head and a sable curl of her hair fell to her slender neck. Something was happening to him because he couldn't remove his gaze from her lips, her rosy cheek, or her inky eyes that took him prisoner, and he was a willing captive.

They were still sharing the piano bench, so their shoulders touched, and she was a breath away from him. So close. So tempting.

He inched closer. She parted her lips and inhaled deeply. They met midway. Or rather, their lips did. He pressed a kiss gently to her soft lips. His mouth captured her little moan. He wanted to do more, taste her with his tongue, but at the same time, he didn't want to ruin the precious moment.

Growing up in a brothel, he'd seen all sorts of kisses, some too savage for a proper lady like Angeline. He'd seen love-making positions that defied the law of physics. Hell, he'd performed some of those. But when it came to being gentle, he wasn't sure he could do it. Better to do less than too much.

Breaking the kiss required a ridiculously big effort. "Are you all right?"

Her cheeks were the colour of peaches, and her eyes shone like black diamonds. "Never been better." Her gaze dipped to his mouth.

He ought to remember that he might be a baron, but she was above his status. He came from the gutter. The title didn't count.

She moved closer again, her breathing speeding up. His pulse spiked, hammering in his ears and urging him to devour her pretty lips.

He was so afraid of being too rough that he shuddered. "Angeline..."

The door swung inwards, and Mrs. Haywood entered. Damn. He straightened, finding it hard to say anything. Oh, right. He should stand up when a lady was standing. He scraped back the bench with too much energy, causing Angeline to fall backwards. He caught her by the waist and sat her back on the bench.

"Sorry," they said together.

"I moved too quickly." He released her, but the brief contact caused him to shiver all over again as if it were the first time he touched a woman.

"Is everything going all right?" Mrs. Haywood said.

"Yes, madam. Your daughter learnt the sequence rather quick-ly." He pretended to be busy straightening his jacket.

"I had no doubts. Angeline has always been brilliant."

Angeline stood up as well. Her flush was still there. "Excuse me. My lord." She curtsied.

He watched her leave in a hurry. Perhaps he'd troubled her. Well, the bench hadn't been his peak moment.

"Many thanks for your help, my lord."

The maid entered the room and bobbed a curtsy. "My lord." She turned to her mistress. "Sorry to disturb you, madam, but..." The woman pointed a finger in the direction of the rear of the house. "There's someone asking to see you very urgently. Very urgently."

"My lord." Mrs. Haywood dropped a quick curtsy before she left in a flutter of skirts.

The urgency with which she left teased his curiosity. He opened the French window at the end of the room and quietly stepped outside, searching the garden. Once he rounded the corner, he paused.

Mr. Wright paced nervously in front of the back door, running a hand through his hair. The noise of the door being opened came.

"Madam," Mr. Wright said in an agitated tone.

"What are you doing here?" Mrs. Haywood hissed. "You can't come here whenever it pleases you."

"It's about the money. You must understand. I can't pay it." Mr. Wright lowered his voice to an inaudible sound.

Royston couldn't hear anything else, though, since Mrs. Haywood must have let him inside. He returned to the sitting room and closed the French window, cursing under his breath.

fourteen

ANGELINE COULDN'T STOP pacing moments before her ridiculous debut as a pianist. If the situation hadn't terrified her, she'd laugh.

She mentally rehearsed her hand movements. Not that she needed to be extremely precise. The piano had been turned to an angle from where the audience wouldn't see her hands. But if she moved her hands at the wrong moments, like during a pause in the music, she'd look like an idiot. Or worse, the fraud she was.

"Angeline." Royston entered the sitting room where the silent piano was.

Her gaze dropped unbidden to his sculpted lips. Goodness. She'd kissed him. She wanted to kiss him again. But not now. The whole absurd affair of her playing the piano hadn't allowed her to think of Royston.

"I'm nervous," she said.

"No need to be." He stopped next to her. His warmth stroked her cheek. "We practised. You can do it."

"Will you kiss me again?" Dash it. She clamped a hand over her mouth. "Sorry. I blurt things out when I'm nervous."

He laughed, his hazel eyes shining. "Then you should be nervous more often, and yes, I'll kiss you again. Gladly."

Mama entered the room, fixing a wayward curl. "It's time. My lord, please go to the other room. Darling, you look lovely. You'll be great. I'm so proud of you."

Angeline scowled. "For what possible reason? I'm not doing anything but fooling people."

Royston gave her an encouraging smile before disappearing into the study.

At least a kiss would be her reward. And Mama had promised not to interfere with her choice of a husband.

Let the farce begin.

FROM THE STUDY, Royston could hear the sounds of footfalls and the voices of Mrs. Haywood's guests— Havisham, Lady Redvers, and her daughter.

He'd wait until the end of the performance to search the room when he was sure no one would disturb him, but he couldn't deny a nervous thrill going through him. It was like the old times when he'd snuck inside a house to steal money and jewels. Guilt was giving him a headache, but if he wanted that bloody seat in the House of Lords, he had to be a thief one last time.

Even through the wall, Angeline's voice sounded forced and strained. If anything, the ruse proved she wasn't a good liar or comfortable deceiving others. She'd been truly upset and nervous earlier. She couldn't be involved in her mother's business. He refused to consider that option.

Mrs. Haywood's voice instead burst with joy. "I'm thrilled to have you all here today. It was about time that Angeline's incredible talent was recognised."

"What are you going to play for us, Miss Haywood?" Lady Redvers said.

"A waltz from..." Angeline hesitated. "Strauss's Emperor Waltz, my lady."

There were shuffling and whispering noises.

"Well, we're ready," Angeline said in a too-cheerful voice.

That was the signal. He counted to ten and started. He did his best to follow the music in the way he and Angeline had planned it. The notes drifted from his piano, loud and clear.

The music brought back good memories of when he'd played for his mother, and some not so pleasant memories of when she'd died. Sometimes her pale face, contorted with pain, filled his vision; the image was so vivid he believed he could touch her. Certainly, the pain he felt was real.

He finished the piece with a bitter-sweet feeling in his chest. If Angeline had done her part well, their ruse would work.

"Wonderful, Miss Haywood," Havisham said. "I believe that the piano is your true calling. Forget archery. You have a future as a pianist. Don't you agree, Lady Redvers?"

"Thank you, my lord." That was Angeline.

"Well, I had no idea Miss Haywood was such a talent." Lady Redvers's bitter tone betrayed her annoyance.

"Miss Haywood has real talent," Miss Taylor said. "I would love to hear about your tricks for performing the most difficult passages."

"I... well..." Angeline coughed. "Hard work."

Royston smiled. Good answer.

"Bassett will serve tea now," Mrs. Haywood said.

"Actually," Lady Redvers said. "I'd love to listen to something else."

"Excuse me?" Angeline sounded panicked.

"Chopin, please," Lady Redvers said.

"But I haven't rehearsed anything else."

"A nocturne? A skilled musician as you won't find it difficult."

Lady Redvers had a point. If there was one composer pianists obsessed with, it was Chopin. The bread and butter of every musician.

"Please, Miss Haywood," Lady Redvers insisted. "We'd be delighted."

He ought to intervene. If he improvised a sudden visit, Angeline wouldn't need to play. The search would wait. He started to stand up when Havisham talked.

"Don't be angry with me, Miss Haywood," Havisham said. "But I need a nice cup of tea. Perhaps we might continue another day."

"I agree," Angeline and her mother said together.

As the sounds of porcelain cups and saucers clinking together came, Royston rose from the bench gingerly. The voices and music carried through the vent so well he ought to be careful, or the guests would realise someone was in the adjoining room.

At least, the thick carpet muffled his footsteps.

He gave a quick search to the oak desk that took up a corner of the room. Mrs. Haywood kept everything in perfect order—pencils sharpened and straightened, documents neatly stacked, and books precisely set away. The drawer contained spare pieces of paper. The cabinets were locked, unsurprisingly.

But he'd come prepared. He hadn't picked a lock in years, but criminal skills were like riding a bicycle— once learnt, they couldn't be forgotten. Perhaps it was true that once a thief, always a thief.

It took him a few tweaks and attempts to unlock the cabinet. He inched the drawer open, revealing a stack of documents.

"Bloody hell," he whispered.

A long file of folders filled the cabinet. The labels showed the names of gentlemen in alphabetical order. There had to be a few dozen of them. Some names were struck out, maybe indicating the relationship with the gentleman had been terminated.

He skimmed through the labels and stopped when he reached the letter 'H.' There it was.

Havisham's folder wasn't particularly thick, but to make sure Royston was taking the right batch of documents, he went through the content. The earl hadn't lied. Paid bills in fancy hotels, paid dinners, and some explicit photographs illustrated Havisham's infidelity in all its gory details.

There were even passionate letters in which the earl declared his undying love for her and his unhappiness with his wife. To his credit, the bills and letters didn't show any recent dates, so it looked like he was telling the truth about having stopped seeing her.

In another document, a series of numbers were recorded. One hundred pounds, fifty pounds, two hundred pounds... no doubt. Mrs. Haywood had blackmailed Havisham for a while, asking for money regularly. Angeline's mother did this. All true. She had blackmailed at least fifty gentlemen.

Mrs. Haywood wouldn't need to blackmail anyone again if she agreed to stop exploiting fallen women and receive an allowance from him. He had the means to provide for Angeline and her mother.

Shaking his head, he emptied the folder and slid the documents under his jacket. After putting the folder back in the cabinet, he searched the other drawers for the infamous list of fallen women. More folders on men, expenses, and bills, but no list of women. More photographs, some rather old. There was a list of addresses and flats around London, and another list of drug suppliers and smugglers at the black market— who knew for what reason? But that was it.

His search turned frantic as he went through as many folders as possible. Nothing else. Plenty of incriminating material, but not a single piece of paper on fallen women.

Footsteps sounded closer. He carefully locked the cabinet, wondering where the bloody list of women could be.

He had barely time to sit back on the piano bench when the door opened.

Angeline swept into view, lovely with her hair twisted in a gentle chignon and a few curls framing her cheeks. Just looking at her calmed his ragged heartbeat. She beckoned him to follow her.

He left the study as the chatter came from the sitting room and followed her to the back of the house.

She unlocked the rear door. "Thank you. Everything went perfectly."

Yes, it did. More or less.

When Mrs. Haywood realised Havisham's documents were gone, it wouldn't take long to guess who had removed them. But she might not check the folder soon, and since Havisham wasn't seeing her anymore, chances were Mrs. Haywood might not realise her documents were missing.

But Angeline... she wouldn't be happy to know what he'd done. Although if she learnt he'd taken those documents, she would also learn what her mother did, but she had to know that already. Hell. He needed to tell her what he was doing and find out the truth.

"Angeline..." Maybe it wasn't the right moment. "May I see you later? I need to talk to you."

The rest of what he wanted to say was cut off by her kiss. She rose on her tiptoes and kissed him hard on the mouth. He closed his eyes to savour the softness of her lips and the delicious curves of her body against his as she kissed him with desperation.

The kiss had a lot of passion but was also a little messy. She bit his lips and clashed her teeth against his more than once. Not that her technique mattered, but it was a further reminder that she was innocent, more fragile than he was, that he could hurt her in more ways than one.

She lowered her heels and dragged her hands down from his neck to his chest. "Thank you."

He held her by the waist, wishing to tell her everything. All of it. From what he'd discovered about her mother to the warm feeling for her in his chest. Her large, trusting eyes were like daggers to his heart.

"The best kiss I've ever received," he said, caressing her cheek.

"Angeline?" Mrs. Haywood called from the other side of the corridor.

She sighed. "I have to go. Sorry." She held the door open. "Will you come later?"

"When?" He stepped closer to her until she leant against the wall and he stood a mere inch from her.

She was all breathy and deliciously flushed. "Midnight. Come here and I'll open the door for you."

He dipped his head to meet her gaze. "I'll be here."

She took in a deep breath, parting her lovely lips.

He kissed her hand and left the house, wondering if he was doing the right thing.

ROYSTON PACED in the parlour at Haversham House as he waited for the earl to return home from the Haywood recital.

The earl's butler had shown him in, and Royston looked forward to emptying his pockets and putting the whole, awful story behind him. Although the women's list was still missing.

What tormented him the most wasn't having stolen documents from Mrs. Haywood but having promised Angeline to return to her. He wanted to. Hell, he did. He wanted to tell her the truth. But he didn't want to ruin their friendship or worse, hurt her.

No, it wasn't friendship. He wouldn't feel as if he were about to burst with desire if a friend kissed him.

"Wharton." Havisham entered the parlour and shut the door behind him. "Is it done?"

Royston emptied his pockets on the table. "There was a whole folder with your name."

The earl rushed to the table and examined the wrinkled pieces of paper and photographs.

He exhaled once he finished, closing his eyes briefly. "Thank you, Wharton. You saved my life."

How many times had Royston heard that?

"Finally. My freedom." Havisham smiled. "The nightmare is over."

"I couldn't find the list though."

Havisham frowned. "It has to be in the study. Perhaps your time was cut short."

"Yes, I couldn't search thoroughly." Still...

"I'll ask my private detective to dig deeper. I'll tell you what he discovers. She's a careful woman. She must have put it somewhere safe."

Royston couldn't say he was pleased. "You promised not to do anything to Mrs. Haywood."

"By Jove." The earl put a hand on his chest. "I always keep my word. She doesn't suspect anything, and I plan to keep my relationship friendly with her. Nothing will happen to her. No need to worry."

"The seat?"

"I'll start my request with the House of Lords immediately."

Good news, finally. Royston stretched out his arm. "Thank you, Havisham."

The earl shook his hand. "My pleasure. You have no idea of the service you did for me. My family and my happiness are safe, thanks to you." His voice shook.

"You're welcome." Royston just hoped Angeline would understand.

He left Havisham's house with a riot of feelings in his chest. He wanted to see Angeline and tell her the truth. Yes, he'd go to her to talk about her mother. No kisses until he laid out the truth.

He shoved his hands into his pockets and braved the chilly wind. Walking helped him think. Angeline had to understand. Her mother blackmailed people and abused fallen women, and he needed the seat in the House of Lords, or London would keep producing women like his mother. He couldn't allow that.

But despite firmly believing those reasons, he couldn't help the sensation of a cold blade in his chest whenever he thought of Angeline. She might tell him to go to hell after he confessed. He would lose her before he had the chance to be with her.

But nothing else could have been done. Talking to her before taking the documents would have been a mistake. If she was ignorant of her mother's activity, she wouldn't have believed him. She would have certainly talked to her mother, who would have removed the documents and stashed them somewhere else.

And he would have lost Angeline.

It seemed that every possible outcome led to the same depressing result.

The damage was already done. He ought to take responsibility for his actions and choices and face the consequences. From Westminster, Big Ben chimed midnight. Each gong made him shudder. It sounded as if Big Ben urged him on.

The back gate to Angeline's garden was open. He slipped inside and waited in a dark corner next to the rear entrance, half-wishing she didn't come out.

The door inched inwards, and she came into view in all her dark beauty. Her long hair was twisted in a long braid that reached her waist, and her blue dressing gown made her look like a fairy princess. The moonlight turned her skin into a glowing beacon.

He hitched a breath. For a moment, he forgot about Mrs. Haywood, Havisham, and the whole sodding world. She was so beautiful he could spend the whole night watching her.

"Royston?" she whispered.

He couldn't refuse her call. Removing his hat, he came out of the shadows. "I'm here."

She let out a muffled gasp and laughed. "You came."

"Of course I did. Angeline, before anything else, I need to talk to you."

She wrapped her arms around him and hugged him. "Of course. What is it? You sound so serious."

Since she wore only her dressing gown, he appreciated all the softness and warmth of her body. Her breasts pressed against his chest.

He held her by the waist. "I have something to tell you, something that won't make you happy."

Her lips were deliciously close. "I know. I'm a terrible kisser. But with a bit of practice, I'll improve."

"No, it's not about that." He caressed her hair. "Your kisses are perfect. It's something else."

"Come." She took his hand and pulled him into the hallway. "My mother is asleep, and Bassett left hours ago. But I can't stay long. Mama is a light sleeper."

He didn't walk in further but remained close to the door. He guessed the conversation would be quite short. "I have done something you're going to hate."

She rose on her tiptoes to give him a quick peck on the lips. "I'm sure you're exaggerating." She scattered kisses on his face. Stopping her physically hurt him.

"Listen." He swallowed hard as his mouth grew suddenly dry. "While I was in the study, I did something."

"What? If you broke that awful vase Mama keeps on the windowsill, I forgive you."

He ought to be quick. "Lord Havisham asked me to search the study for some documents."

She drew in a breath and unwrapped her arms from his neck. "What?"

"Let me finish." He forced his voice down. "Your mother has been blackmailing Lord Havisham for months. While she was his mistress, she collected compromising material to use to blackmail him. Lord Havisham asked me to retrieve those documents to save his marriage and family."

She clamped a hand over her mouth. "No."

"I'm sorry. At first, I didn't believe him, but when I saw those photographs, bills, and letters, I knew he told the truth, and I... I took those documents for him."

"No, no, no. This is a disaster." She wrung her hands, pacing.

Her eyes showed too much white, but she didn't have the outraged reaction he'd foreseen. She didn't deny the fact her mother was a blackmailer.

"Did you know about this?"

She stopped pacing and sank her teeth into her bottom lip. "That's irrelevant."

"I beg to differ. Did you know?"

Silence.

"You did." He couldn't completely remove the shock in his tone.

"She's my mother. What am I supposed to do? I tried to convince her to stop, but she didn't listen." She drew in a shaky breath. "What did Lord Havisham give you to search the study?"

He closed the distance between them with one stride. "He promised to help me get a seat in the House of Lords because I want to create better shelters and relief, proper jobs for women like my mother. Unless I'm in Parliament and fight for change, nothing will happen, and my title will remain nothing but a pretty award."

"So you started this journey towards a more equal and just society with a criminal act. You said you'd left your past behind. It doesn't seem like you have."

All the breath was punched out of him as if she'd hit him in the stomach. "It's not like that."

Or maybe it was. Once a thief, always a thief. Perhaps he was the wrong man to invoke change. He couldn't change anything if he couldn't change himself.

Also, Angeline knew what her mother did. That was another blow.

She wrapped her arms around herself. "Were the kisses and the kindness to me part of your plan to get close to me? Did you laugh at my expense because I was such a naïve woman?"

"No." He put all his care for her into his voice. "I swear what happened between us is real, is visceral, is pure. I didn't lie or use you. You have to believe that."

A moment of charged silence thickened between them like an invisible barrier.

"Leave." She lowered her gaze.

"I really like you, Angeline. You're perfect. I didn't lie about the way I feel. I couldn't."

"Please, leave."

He put his hat back on and opened the door. "I didn't wish to cause you harm, and I didn't mean to lie to you. Lord Havisham is an adulterer, but your mother is blackmailing him, and you're her accomplice."

Her black eyes seemed to turn shiny with unshed tears while her cheeks paled. A shiver went through her. "I've never black-mailed anyone. But she's my mother. She isn't as evil as it seems." Her voice sounded small.

"There's more. I learnt your mother—"

"Please leave. I need to be alone."

Her tear-welled eyes were the last thing he saw before leaving.

fifteen

ANGELINE HAD REGRETTED her words the moment Royston had disappeared into the night.

She rolled in the bed, but sleep wouldn't touch her with a barge pole.

Royston had stolen something from her mother, and who knew what Lord Havisham would do to her mama now. But Angeline had hurt Royston. Badly.

On the other hand, Mama was indeed a blackmailer, and of course Lord Havisham wanted the blackmail to stop, but Royston should have talked to her first. And he was right about her. She was her mother's accomplice. Worse, she benefitted from Mama's enterprise. In fact, she owed her education to Mama's money, which meant dirty money.

That was enough to keep her awake at night on any given day.

And she'd thought that being scorned for her scar was humiliating? A man finally showed interest in her, accepting her for who she was, and he'd learnt the truth about her family before she had the opportunity to tell him.

He'd told her the truth. He could have kept kissing her and

pretended not to have a clue about Mama's crimes while taking advantage of her. Instead, he'd confessed.

Still, she'd be lying if she said his behaviour didn't hurt. He'd used her only to get those stupid documents. Maybe he didn't even like her. Although he'd sounded so sincere when he'd told her he liked her.

Her head and heart were going to break from the thoughts and emotions going through her.

"What's going on?" Carrying a lit oil lamp, Mama entered Angeline's bedroom.

"What? How?" Angeline bolted upright.

"You keep tossing and turning. You woke me up." She put the lamp on the nightstand. "Are you sick? Should I call the physician?"

"No. I'm all right."

"Tosh." Mama put a hand on Angeline's forehead. "You're hot and shivering. What is it?"

The combination of sadness, anger, and confusion burst out in the form of a sob. After the first sob came out, she couldn't stop a second one.

"Darling." Mama hugged her and caressed her head. "What is it? You can tell me anything." She didn't prompt Angeline further but held her and stroked her head.

"It's Royston."

"What did he do?" Mama's tone turned icy and dangerous. "Did he hurt you?"

"No. Not in the way you think." She wiped her face and took a deep breath. Staying silent could be potentially dangerous. She didn't know what Lord Havisham would do now. Mama needed to know the truth to protect herself from the earl. "While he was in your study, he took Lord Havisham's documents from your cabinet."

"What?" Mama sounded breathless.

"Royston came here tonight." Angeline gazed up at her mother, waiting for her to be shocked.

Mama looked more furious than shocked. "Why did he come here?"

"We agreed to meet at midnight, but anyway, Royston told me what he'd done and then left. Lord Havisham has his incriminating documents now."

"That sneaky, traitorous bastard." Mama clenched her fist.

Angeline didn't know if Mama was talking about Lord Havisham or Royston.

"I'm sorry. I'm confused. I don't know if he used our friendship to get the documents or not."

Mama's expression softened. She hugged Angeline again. "Sweetheart, I told you. You can't trust men. They use you and then discard you as if you were nothing. Don't let him hurt you. Don't give him that power. And you have nothing to be sorry for. You have a good heart and trust everyone. Men take advantage of that. It happened to me many times before I hardened myself to their cruelty."

Was Mama right? Was Royston nothing but a scoundrel? But he'd been so kind to her. His kisses had been so gentle, his words so true. A lone whisper from her heart told her Royston cared about her, but her brain screamed he'd only used her for a seat in Parliament.

"What about the stolen documents?" she asked.

Mama kissed her forehead. "Do not worry about that. Lord Havisham isn't my only source of income. I have others."

No, that wasn't what Angeline meant. "He could go to the police."

"And say what? That he's an adulterer who lies to his wife? Lady Havisham is a duke's daughter. Other women might turn a blind eye to their husbands' escapades. Not her. She'd ruin him."

"He could retaliate, though, now that you can't blackmail him anymore. He could hurt you."

Mama flashed a sad smile. "Well, that wouldn't be the first time a man had tried to hurt me. I have survived. I can do it again. I doubt he'll do anything. Yes, I don't have the photographs, the letters, and the bills anymore, but if I go to his wife and have a heart-to-heart conversation with her about her husband, she will believe me. I know intimate things about him only a lover can know. Or I can simply spread a rumour about him. Either way, he's aware I can harm his reputation badly if I want to. He isn't stupid. He won't provoke me."

"I hope you're right." She shivered, and Mama covered her with the quilt.

"That awful baron is another matter though. What do you want me to do? Shall I have a word with him? I can easily find a way to make him pay."

"Oh no, please." She shivered again at the thought of Mama using Royston to test her drugs. "Leave him alone. He saved my life. I can't forget that."

"Who cares? He hurt you, and no one hurts my beautiful daughter without consequences."

"Yes, but I don't want revenge. I want to move on."

She'd take her time to think about what had happened and carry on with her lonely life. Royston had been a lovely dream, but nothing more.

Royston's mood hadn't improved from the night of his confrontation with Angeline three days ago.

If he could write a proper letter to her and explain how he felt, he would, but his writing skills were worse than his speech. He'd changed his mind about what to tell her, how to tell her, and when to tell her a dozen times in the past few days.

He wanted to make her understand how important a seat in the House of Lords was, but at the same time, he couldn't ignore the fact she'd been aware of her mother's crimes and maybe even her accomplice.

Or maybe Angeline was right. He couldn't leave his past behind.

The worst part of the situation was that he couldn't retire to his house to think and stay alone. He had to mingle with London's society and show himself around since he was going to be a member of the House of Lords soon. Havisham claimed that showing oneself in society was vital to having the seat approved, especially since Royston didn't come from the nobility.

So here he was in Lord Fountaine's house for yet another sophisticated event where he didn't belong. With the Season in full swing, the society seemed to do nothing but dance, drink, and eat. Fountaine's grand ballroom sparkled with one year's worth of oil and gas. The chandeliers amplified the glow, bothering his eyes. And the banquet table held enough food to feed a rookery for a month.

He stood in a corner as the young debutantes twirled around in their pretty gowns, smiling. He lowered his gaze and focused on the pattern of the wooden floorboards.

When his mood was as low and troubled as it was now, his bad memories rushed out of the ugly dark corner of his mind where he stashed them. The last thing he needed was an anxiety attack.

A hint of nausea burned the back of his throat. He wished Angeline were here to help him through the darkness. One smile from her, and he'd calm. For someone who was supposed to mingle, he was spending too much time on his own.

He took a tour of the room and scowled when he spotted the infamous North, drinking and laughing with a debutante. Just because Royston had recently had a strained conversation with Angeline, it didn't mean he'd forgotten what North had done to her.

Judging by how North returned the scowl, he hadn't forgotten either. But Royston would rather stare into North's angry face than think about the brothel and his mother or the fact he hadn't recovered the list of fallen women.

Havisham broke the moment, stopping next to him. "I have news. We must talk."

"About what?"

If Havisham answered, Royston didn't hear it; his attention was focused on the set of double doors. Angeline and her mother entered the ballroom, smiling at everyone as the master of ceremonies announced them. Angeline greeted the hosts with a graceful curtsy in a froth of pink silk. When she turned in his direction, their gazes locked. The air between them was charged with energy.

Hot turmoil boiled in his chest. Meeting her was bound to happen sooner or later, but he wasn't ready for the deep unrest her presence caused him. He should talk to her again. Perhaps she would listen.

Her smile vanished, and she averted her gaze.

"For heaven's sake," Havisham muttered. "What is Mrs. Haywood doing here? Will I ever get rid of that woman?"

"You didn't confront her? She must have realised your documents are missing."

Royston wasn't going to inform the earl of his conversation with Angeline. Surely, she'd told her mother.

"What am I supposed to tell her?" Havisham said. "Don't underestimate her. She's quick-witted and resourceful. I got the documents, and she isn't going to extort another penny from me, but I don't want to provoke her further. I'm not that stupid."

Mrs. Haywood, Angeline, Miss Taylor, and Lady Redvers crossed the room towards them. Royston stiffened. He wasn't sure he had the energy to pretend everything was all right. To make things worse, even North joined the happy group.

Royston felt like prey surrounded by predators.

After a quick round of bows, fake, happy greetings, and curtsies, Royston couldn't stand still. Angeline was so close that if he stretched out his fingers he'd touch her.

"What a delight to see you here, Lord Wharton," Mrs. Haywood said. "I heard you didn't leave your house for days. I was worried you were sick." She added three 's' to sick.

He gave her a quick bow of his head. "I'm perfectly well, thank you, madam."

"You remember my daughter Georgiana, don't you, Lord Wharton?" Lady Redvers asked.

Bloody hell. That was likely the fifteenth time he'd been asked that question. Lady Redvers was on the path to beating a record in introductions.

"I do, my lady." He bowed his head again. His neck muscles would grow stiff by the end of the night.

"Georgiana loves dancing," Lady Redvers said. "Don't you, darling? And you, Wharton, haven't danced with her yet, despite what you promised."

Not this again. He started to think Lady Redvers's memory didn't work. "I didn't promise to dance, actually."

Miss Taylor lowered her gaze. "Mother."

Angeline shifted her weight.

"I don't remember you and Lord Wharton dancing together." Lady Redvers frowned.

"My lady." North shot a glare at Royston. "You won't remember having ever seen Lord Wharton dancing at all. There's a reason Lord Wharton never dances."

Royston whipped his head towards North. "What do you mean?"

Angeline whispered something he didn't catch. Havisham coughed politely in his fist.

Mr. North sipped his champagne, seemingly in no hurry to answer. "I happen to know—"

"North, perhaps this conversation isn't apt for tonight," Havisham said, giving North a piercing glare.

North lifted a finger as he took another sip. "Forgive me, my lord. You're absolutely right, but Lady Redvers needs to hear the truth. Rumour has it that Lord Wharton's mother was tortured by a man who forced her to dance until exhaustion. The poor child was so shocked that he hated dancing from that moment. Obviously, he remains troubled to this day."

Lady Redvers gasped. Mrs. Haywood's eyes widened. Miss Taylor opened her mouth.

Angeline blinked, her eyes shining with sorrow. "Is it true?"

Royston didn't have the courage to answer. Fear and sorrow prevented him from saying anything. Earlier, he'd wished for Angeline's presence. But now he regretted his wish. She shouldn't hear about his past. Not like that.

"Are you accusing me of lying, Miss Haywood?" North's voice rose.

"You can't talk to Miss Haywood with that tone, North," Royston said.

The man bared his teeth. "I don't accept reprimands from a man whose mind is definitely troubled."

"So that's the reason why the infamous Baron Wharton doesn't dance." Lady Redvers fanned herself. "I don't understand, though. Why wouldn't you dance, Wharton? Only because of something that happened many years ago."

"A man who can't overcome his fears isn't worthy of holding a title," North chimed in. "The baron isn't of sound mind, I think."

"But anyone who witnesses the death of a loved one would be troubled," Angeline said.

North leant forwards. "That doesn't change the fact the baron is mad. He's unstable. Deranged. Troubled. Pick your definition."

Enough. Royston didn't have to explain himself to these people.

He turned and strode towards the set of double doors only to bump into a maid carrying a tray loaded with champagnes flutes.

Tottering on her feet, she cried out as the flutes smashed on the floor in a splash of champagne and bubbles.

He went to steady her, but his foot slipped on the wet floor, and he ended up shoving her quite hard. The maid fell over backwards with a thud and a groan of pain.

"Shit. I'm sorry." He didn't have time to help her up before a footman intervened, shooting a reproachful glare at him.

"I didn't shove her on purpose," Royston said.

The footman arched his brow but didn't say anything.

The room had gone suddenly quiet. Even the music had stopped.

Sod it. Crunching the pieces of glasses under his shoes, he marched out among whispers, mutters, and laughter.

"Royston, wait," Angeline said behind him, but he didn't stop.

sixteen

NGELINE'S HEART CLENCHED for Royston.

She'd had no idea where his dislike of dancing came from. Now she almost wished she hadn't learnt the truth. The truth hurt too much.

Mr. North was indeed a despicable man.

She watched Royston's broad shoulders as he strode out of the ballroom after the incident with the maid. It'd looked like he'd shoved her, but she hadn't seen him properly because Lady Redvers had blocked her view.

People turned their heads towards him, and ladies whispered behind their fans as the servants cleaned up the floor from the broken glass.

"Mama, please come." She took her mother's hand and pulled her aside to a quiet corner. "Please tell me you have nothing to do with what happened to Royston."

"Excuse me?" Mama put a hand on her chest. Her pearl earrings swung back and forth from her earlobes.

"Mr. North blurted out some details about Royston's life he couldn't have conjured up out of thin air. He must have had help."

Mama's lips parted. "You think it was me?"

"You had the opportunity. I'm sure you know how to dig into someone's life."

A flush crept over Mama's cheeks. "I assure you I did nothing of the sort. Was I tempted to teach a lesson to the baron? Yes. He stole documents. He hurt you, and no one hurts my daughter. But you asked me to leave him be, and that's what I did. Besides, he did a good job at humiliating himself without my help."

"Forgive me if I don't trust you, but you have the tendency to keep secrets from me."

Mama's cheeks flamed further. "It wasn't me. If you don't trust me, I have nothing else to say."

"Mama—" Angeline winced as her mother walked away.

Goodness. Everyone she talked to lately ended up angry with her.

Mama had sounded honest, but if she hadn't found that information about Royston and passed it on to Mr. North, then who? Was it possible that Mr. North had acted alone?

Somehow, she doubted it. He didn't have a reason to attack Royston so viciously. Although Royston had antagonised him. But Mama definitely had a better reason to get revenge on Royston.

"Miss Haywood," Miss Taylor said, close to Angeline.

She hadn't seen the viscountess's daughter coming. "Evening."

Miss Taylor fiddled with her fan. "If you see the baron, will you tell him I'm sorry for what my mother said?"

Angeline softened. "I will." Although it was unlikely she would meet Royston any time soon. "But I think Mr. North did the greatest damage. Did the baron shove that maid?"

"So it seemed. He was in a hurry to leave, though. I feel sorry for Lord Wharton." She lowered her gaze. "He seems rather fond of you if you don't mind my saying it."

Actually, Angeline minded it. Because she wasn't sure it was true. "Do you think so?"

Miss Taylor blushed and lifted a shoulder covered in muslin.

"It's the way he looks at you as if he were lost. It's the same way my Dani—" She coughed in her closed fist. "Excuse me. I think my mother is looking for me."

She hurried away before Angeline could say anything.

Angeline didn't have time to ponder Miss Taylor's words before Mr. North joined her.

"Angeline," he said her name as if making the point of not wanting to address her properly. "Not a dull night. You should thank me."

"Why?"

He nodded in the direction of the door. "I showed you who Wharton really is, a deranged coward. Did you see how he pushed that poor woman?"

"No, I didn't, and I don't believe he did it on purpose." A hot flare of anger surged. "Mr. North, I must speak my mind."

"You're welcome."

"I found the manner in which you behaved towards Lord Wharton very..." She had to take a breath. "...not worthy of a gentleman."

"I only spoke the truth." He gave her a glare. "I hope you made up your mind about my offer. Naturally, you can forget my three thousand pounds. I'll give you one thousand this time."

Never a bow and an arrow when she needed them. But she had a better weapon.

She removed her long glove with one snappy gesture, uncovering the scar in all its ugliness. "What do you—" She couldn't finish the sentence.

Mr. North glanced at her arm and let out a silly squeak that offended her ears. He stepped back from her. "Is it syphilis?"

"How dare you. It's a scar."

He paled, his legs shaking. "It's syphilis."

"No, it's not. Goodness, how ignorant are you."

His jaw clenched. "You can forget our deal."

"Great."

"You won't see me again."

"Good," she said, but he didn't hear her because he hurried away from her.

It was what she wanted, but she didn't expect such a dramatic reaction from him.

Well, who was deranged now?

AFTER THE HORRIBLE scene at Lord Fountaine's ball, the only thing Royston wanted was to be alone and not think about Angeline's face filled with pity.

Pity. There wasn't a more horrifying feeling to face in the world. She shouldn't pity him. He didn't pity himself.

He wondered how North had found out about what happened in the brothel. No one knew about that detail, and the man who had murdered his mother was dead.

Enright, his butler, entered the room, carrying a tray with a steaming pot of tea. On instinct, Royston stood up. Old habits. Although he found it disrespectful to stay seated in front of the older man.

Enright smiled under his beard. "My lord, you don't need to stand up for me."

Bugger. If he apologised, he'd make things worse. If he said, 'I know,' it sounded pretentious. He opted for a non-committal grunt. Great.

Enright put the tray down. "Lord Havisham would like a word, my lord."

"Oh hell." He winced. "Sorry, Enright. Today I'm not myself."

Or maybe he was more himself on days like today than on other days... if that made sense.

"Shall I tell Lord Havisham you're indisposed?"

"No, I'll see him. Thank you, Enright."

"My lord."

Royston poured two cups of tea, hoping whatever Havisham had to say was quick. If he wanted to discuss what had happened, Royston wasn't in the mood.

Havisham entered the drawing room and waited for Enright to close the door before talking. "You shouldn't have stormed out like that, Wharton."

"Good afternoon to you as well." Royston sipped his tea. "North shouldn't have made that comment. Lots of things that shouldn't happen actually happen."

"You're in a philosophical mood." Havisham exhaled. "Allow me to tell you that after the disaster of the other night, your popularity has plummeted. What the hell happened with that maid? It looked like you pushed her out of your way."

"An accident. I slipped."

The earl didn't look impressed. "The key to getting you a seat in Parliament, in the House of Lords, is all about how the other peers see you. If you want to be one of us, really one of us, you must earn respect and sympathy. Right now, North has more chances of getting a seat than you."

"Thank you, Havisham. I feel much better now."

Havisham chuckled. "I didn't come here to discuss your behaviour although you need to think about it. I have some news that may or may not please you."

"I doubt my mood could get worse."

"Do you want to hear the good news or the bad news first?"

"Good news."

The earl sat in an armchair. "I think I know where Mrs. Haywood keeps her other documents."

"What's the bad news?"

"They're probably in a safe in her small parlour. I thought about where she could keep the documents, and I remembered having seen her storing her jewels in a safe behind a mirror. It's worth a try."

"Opening a safe is no small deed."

"How much time would you need to open a safe?"

Royston pressed his fingers to his temples. "An hour, maybe two. It depends on the safe. But I can't search Mrs. Haywood's house again. I'm not welcome there."

Havisham held up a hand. "I understand, and I'm here to help. I'll ask one of my friends to organise a soirée this week, something small. I'll make sure that both Mrs. and Miss Haywood are invited. Their house will be empty, and you'll have the opportunity to search it and plenty of time. I'll make sure they stay out for the whole evening."

He shook his head. "I don't think I can do it."

Havisham inched closer. "I'm going to be honest. I have my documents. You did your part. Helping those girls is your choice. If you need help, I'm more than happy to keep the ladies busy for a few hours. If you don't want to do it, I understand. But no one else is going to help those girls."

That was true. Still, he didn't want to break into Angeline's house, even though his relationship with her was ruined anyway.

"Your choice, Wharton," Havisham said. "Whatever you choose, I'll help you."

It wouldn't be the first time Royston had done something against the law, but he held a title now and had responsibilities towards the people he employed. But the earl was right. No one was going to help those girls. He'd failed his mother. The least he could do was to help those girls, using his criminal skills to do something good.

He nodded. "I'll accept your help."

IN A PLAIN WOOLLEN jacket and brown trousers, Royston left his house from the rear door.

No coachman or footman to accompany him. With the flat hat

pulled down over his face and the scarf up to cover his mouth, he doubted anyone would recognise him.

He hadn't worn plain clothes in a long time. The collar of the shirt chafed his skin, and cold gusts of air somehow found their way through the fabric of the jacket, and through his thoughts. Sitting in front of a blazing log fire and enjoying a nightcap would be wonderful, but he had to finish the damn job and then move on.

When he arrived at Angeline's house, he paused in a dark spot on the street.

Mr. Wright appeared from behind a corner, and since the lights in the house were still glowing, Royston followed his instinct and tailed him. Wright's involvement in Mrs. Haywood's affairs was still unclear. The pianist could be another victim or an accomplice. Or worse, Wright could be another North, annoying Angeline.

Wright walked with his shoulders hunched as if he were sitting at a piano.

"Mr. Wright." Royston sped up.

Wright turned around and glanced at Royston before breaking into a run. What the hell?

"Mr. Wright!" Royston chased him. "It's me, Lord Wharton. I just want to talk to you."

Wright stopped, his breath coming out in hard pants. Wheezing, he put a hand on his side and bent over, panting.

Blimey. The pianist needed to spend some time outdoors and to move more.

"Apologies, my lord. I thought you were someone who wanted to rob me," Wright said among shallow breaths. "I didn't recognise you."

"I opted for more comfortable clothes for an evening walk. I'm sorry to have given you a fright."

Wright straightened, as pale as milk. "I don't feel well."

"Let me help you." Royston led him to a bench and helped him sit. "I must ask you a personal question."

The pianist dabbed his forehead with a handkerchief. "What is it?"

"Does Mrs. Haywood blackmail you?" Straight to the point.

Wright stopped wiping his face. "I beg your pardon."

"By chance, I happen to have heard a conversation between you and Mrs. Haywood about money. If Mrs. Haywood is causing you trouble, I can be of help."

Wright chuckled, but the chuckle turned into a coughing fit that caused him to shake hard. "You misunderstood, my lord. Mrs. Haywood is helping me."

Royston found it hard to believe that.

"Pianists, even pianists as famous as I am, don't earn much. I live in a small room above a tailor shop in Bloomsbury. I have barely enough money to pay for food and coal." Wright fiddled with the handkerchief. "I love playing. Music is my life. I wouldn't need the money if not for the fact I wish to marry the woman I love. She's the daughter of a viscount, and I can't afford to give her the type of life she's used to. Mrs. Haywood is generous enough to help me."

Miss Georgiana Taylor, as Royston had suspected.

Wright took a few more deep breaths. "I hope to marry her and move to Paris where musicians receive better salaries, and thanks to Mrs. Haywood, I'm putting aside a decent sum."

That fit the frantic conversation between Mrs. Haywood and Mr. Wright Royston had witnessed.

"What does Mrs. Haywood ask in exchange for her help?" He couldn't believe Mrs. Haywood helped Wright out of her good heart.

Wright shrugged. "Nothing really. Small favours. She asks me to bring her pouches of herbs from the market. She gives me a list, and I buy the items."

"Why doesn't she get them herself?"

"I haven't the foggiest. To be honest, I'm happy to receive her help without asking questions."

Royston helped him up. "Thank you."

AFTER ATTENDING an endless stream of parties and balls, for the first time, Angeline was glad she'd never had a Season.

It wasn't only about the money spent on gowns, shoes, and accessories, but all the energy and effort put into chatting and being pleasant with everyone, even when her mood was forlorn.

Also, if she was completely honest, after what happened at Lord Fountaine's ball, she wasn't so keen to mix with the upper echelons of society again. Her last conversation with Royston had left her shaken, but he didn't deserve to be mocked for his past.

She was ashamed of how others had reacted to Mr. North's accusations. Miss Taylor had been the only decent person.

If anything, she should think of how to talk to Royston. Maybe she should write a letter. His face had been absolutely dejected; her heart had broken.

"Are you sure you don't want to come with me?" Mama asked as Bassett helped her slide into her evening cloak.

Angeline handed her the bag. "Yes, don't worry about me. A soirée is the last thing I'm interested in tonight."

Bassett draped Mama's cloak nicely over the bustle. "If your shoulder is still sore, you should apply that numbing poultice your mother prepared. I tried on my aching fingers. It worked."

Angeline shook her head. "I'm fine."

"Sore shoulder?" Mama's tone turned sharp. "Have you practised with the bow again?"

"You've never had problems with my bow training. In fact, you've always encouraged it, saying you never know when you need to shoot someone."

"I encouraged you when you didn't have to attract the attention of sophisticated gentlemen. I don't care how you amuse your-self, but I do care about what people say. Did you see what happened to Lord Wharton? He's almost an outcast now. He went from being London's darling to London's imbecile in a second. That poor maid is traumatised."

"It was an accident."

"For the moment being, you must renounce any public, unla-dylike activities until further notice. After all, *you* asked me for advice on finding a husband."

That was true.

Angeline leant against the newel post. "May I ride?"

"You must. Ladies meet the best gentlemen when riding in Hyde Park." Mama tugged her gloves on. "Pick someone you like. As long as he's rich, I will approve."

"You're angry because of the conversation we had the other day," Angeline said.

Mama pressed her lips hard. "No, I'm not angry. Any man will fall at your feet if you use the right technique."

"What technique? Oh, forget it." She waved a hand.

The conversation was a useless exercise.

"Would you like me to stay here until your mother has returned?" Bassett asked.

"No, thank you. I'll go to sleep early."

Angeline exhaled when finally Mama and Bassett were gone and the house was all for her. Her shoulder throbbed, and she winced as she went upstairs to her bedroom.

No, she didn't want to go to another soirée with potential targets for Mama's drugs.

She wanted a quiet, nice evening by the warm hearth with a good book. A scary story was the maximum level of excitement she wished for tonight.

What could a girl want more?

seventeen

ROYSTON COULDN'T DENY a hint of excitement before breaking into Angeline's house.

He'd always loved that part of the job— the waiting, sneaking, and planning.

He walked around Angeline's house to the rear, keeping his pace casual not to attract the attention of a patrolling peeler.

An eight-foot-tall brick wall enclosed the back garden. Not a problem though. Back in the days when he'd lived on the streets, he'd climbed walls that high every other day.

He chose the darkest spot in the alleyway to start the climb. The uneven bricks and the thick stems of the English ivy offered enough grip to make the ascent easy. Being over six feet tall helped.

With a push, he hauled himself up and grabbed the top of the wall. Then it was a matter of sheer muscle strength and gravity before he straddled the top and jumped down on the other side. Cup of tea. He wasn't sure if he should be proud or ashamed of his skills. Right now, he didn't give a bloody damn.

The garden didn't offer many hiding places. Only a couple of trees grew in the middle, but at least there weren't any lamps.

He crept on the grass to avoid making noise on the gravel. Opening the set of double French doors was another cup of tea. The lock was nothing special, a cheap thing he could buy at the market for a penny.

He slipped inside and closed the door behind him. Angeline's scent lingering in the air was like a punch in the stomach. It was as if she stood next to him.

A warm glow shone from the corridor. A forgotten lamp, perhaps. No one should be home. He paused again. No sound could be heard.

Keeping his scarf over his face and his flat hat low, he stole along the corridor, heading towards the front of the house. The parlour was tucked in a corner between the study and the dining room, almost hidden.

The tools in his satchel made a metallic clink as he went on. He had no intention of ever breaking and entering Mrs. Haywood's house again, so he'd carried everything he might need to open a safe.

He stopped next to the door to the parlour when the sound of light footfalls came. His pulse spiked. He didn't have time to search for a place to hide when a voice stopped him.

"Don't move." It was Angeline. A scared Angeline, judging by her tone. "Don't turn around. I warn you. I have an arrow aimed at your back, and I'm an excellent archer. Raise your hands above your head. Do what I say, and you won't get hurt."

He believed every word she said.

He raised his hands slowly. His only chance to leave the house with all his limbs and pride intact was to run past her and make a dash for the front door. She wouldn't actually shoot him, would she? She wasn't a violent woman.

A swish of fabric came closer. "I don't want trouble. If you leave quietly, I won't call the police."

Every thief would agree just to leave the house with all his limbs attached. He slowly turned around inch by inch, but she got startled and jolted.

"I said don't move!"

She jerked and released the arrow that shot towards him with a snake-like hiss.

He cried out when the sharp arrowhead sliced his upper arm before stabbing the door behind him. Blood soaked his shirtsleeve, and an instant burning throbbed through his flesh.

"Bloody hell!" He clamped a hand on the cut.

He'd been stabbed once, and the pain had been fairly close to this one.

"Oh, my goodness. I didn't mean to shoot. You gave me a fright, and I told you not to turn around..." She lowered the damn bow. "Royston?"

Great. He gritted his teeth and pressed the hand on the wound harder. "What were you thinking? You could have killed me."

"What are you doing here?" She pulled the lapels of her dressing gown closer.

Long story. "Can we discuss the matter another time? I'd rather go home and send for my physician because, you know, I'm bleeding!"

She frowned. "Well, you wouldn't bleed if you hadn't sneaked inside my house or if you'd followed my instructions not to move. What were you doing? Don't make me ask again."

"Or what? Are you going to shoot me again? Kill me this time? Go ahead." He pointed to his chest. "Straight to the heart. Break it."

She parted her lips. "I would never do that."

He was about to protest that his heart was already broken when a loud banging thudded from the front door.

"Hello? Anyone in the house? Open immediately. Police!"

"What?" he and Angeline said together.

"How did you get word to the police?" he whispered.

"How, when? I didn't have time. I was too busy shooting you."

"Yes, very funny."

"Police." Another loud knock caused the door to shake.

Royston nodded towards the door. "You'd better answer before they bring the door down."

She exhaled and threw a hand up. "Bother." She put the bow aside and snatched the arrow from the door. It took her a couple of attempts.

"Police!"

After hiding the bow and the arrow in a closet, she hurried down the corridor towards the front door. From the hook on the wall, she took an afternoon cloak and wrapped it around her shoulders.

"Police!" Another loud banging.

"Give me one moment," she said, lighting a gas lamp in the entry hallway.

Royston slid inside the parlour, leaving the door ajar to keep an eye on the corridor. A mirror hanging on the opposite wall offered a clear view of the entrance hall.

If she wanted, she could have him arrested in a moment. He should have told her not to say anything. He'd implicitly trusted her although she might not be as trustworthy as he thought. Now he'd find out if it was a good or a bad assumption.

She inched the door open. "What is the meaning of this?"

"Madam." The peeler removed his hat. "I'm Police Constable Davis, madam. I'm sorry to disturb you, but a man came to the police station, saying this house was being robbed. I came here to make sure everything was all right."

Angeline let out a nervous chuckle. "Good gracious, there must be a mistake."

Royston sagged in relief. A smile fought its way through his grimace of pain.

She waved a hand around. "There's no robbery going on here."

Police Constable Davis craned his neck to look past her. "Do you mind if I have a look around?"

"Actually, I do."

So did Royston.

"Madam, it's possible the thief is hiding in the house and you aren't aware of that. The man who warned us saw a thief breaking through your front window. My presence might have alerted him, forcing him to hide."

No, that wasn't true or possible. No one could have seen Royston breaking in through the front window because he hadn't. Besides, he would never use the front window. He stifled a groan as the wound pulsated.

"My window is intact." Angeline held the door open. "Do you want to take a look?"

Police Constable Davis gripped his baton as he entered the house. Royston inched back into the shadows.

"Everything is in order in the sitting room." Angeline lit more lamps; their warm glow flooded the entry hall. "Nothing amiss."

The constable stuck his head into the sitting room. "I should check the other rooms."

"There's no one in the other rooms. I wasn't asleep. I was reading in my bedroom and didn't hear anything." Her tone sounded high-pitched.

"Madam, I must make sure the thief isn't here."

"Police Constable Davis, I appreciate your concern, but I think the whole robbery thing was a practical joke. No one is here. If a thief had broken into my house, I would have noticed it."

Davis loitered, gazing around.

"And I'm alone with you. Honestly." She held the front door open. "I must ask you to leave, constable, before my mother returns."

"Very well, madam." Davis touched his hat and finally dragged his sorry arse out of the house.

Bugger. Royston exhaled, closing his eyes.

Angeline locked the door and, shedding the cloak on the bannister, hurried to the parlour. "I don't understand. What's happening tonight? You come here and then a police constable shows up."

"The warning about a robbery is a set up. I mean, I'm sure what Davis said is true. Someone went to the police to report a robbery. But no one saw me. I didn't use the front window. No thief worth his salt would ever use the front window under the street lamps."

"This lesson in thievery is fascinating, but I'm afraid I'm more interested in understanding what you're doing here." She pointed to the other side of the corridor. "To the kitchen. I'll clean your wound, and you'll give me answers."

"Fine," he croaked out.

"And don't stain the floor with blood, please. The floorboards get stained easily. Cleaning them is a chore. Be careful on the carpet as well."

"I'll do my best to bleed only where it's appropriate."

She stopped. "I don't particularly like your attitude."

"I don't particularly like being shot."

"You broke into my house and gave me a fright. I've been generous to you. I could have told the constable you were here. I could have shot you again."

He worked his jaw. "Shall we carry on? I'm bleeding. You keep forgetting that."

"By all means." She lit a few lamps in the small kitchen, which smelled of garlic and spices, and offered him a chair.

He sat down on it, wincing as the wound burned.

The cut might need stitches. The bloody arrow had cut through his jacket and shirt and opened a wide gash on his biceps. Even closing his fist hurt.

He unbuttoned his jacket and shirt as she rummaged through the cabinets, which contained a ridiculous amount of labelled jars and pots. Shelves loaded with more glass jars took up an entire corner. It looked like a dispensary.

He groaned when he shrugged off his jacket.

"What are you doing?" Her high-pitched tone startled him.

"Undressing myself."

"But..." She clenched a pot for dear life.

"How can you clean my wound if you can't see it?" He removed his bloodstained shirt by grabbing it from his back and pulling it over his head.

Even in the dim light, her fierce blush was evident. "It's just that... oh, fine."

She dragged a chair next to him and focused on the wound, pressing a clean cloth to it.

Her sweet rose scent teased his senses. The soft glow from the lamps suited her. The golden light kissed her cheek and profile, making the tips of her long eyelashes glitter and enhancing her plush lips. Lips he'd kissed. Lips he wanted to kiss again.

She caught him staring and blushed again. "Is that it? All this fuss for a shallow cut?"

He arched his brow. "Shallow? It's half an inch deep."

"Tosh. I get more serious wounds with a paper cut."

He grimaced as she applied a cloth soaked in some stinky liquid. "Blood hell! It bloody hurts."

"I didn't mean to shoot you. The arrow just went off." She cleaned the wound that throbbed and burned like the flames of hell.

"What the hell is in that cloth?"

She tossed him a glare. "A tincture my mother prepared. She's quite skilled with medicinal herbs. Trust me, the wound won't get infected and will heal quickly."

That would explain Mrs. Haywood's interested in drugs, but not why she needed to pay Mr. Wright to buy them. He couldn't hold back a shout as she applied more bloody potion to the wound.

"Dammit."

She clicked her tongue. "The bigger they are, the harder they cry."

A little shiver went down his back when she brushed his skin, and the stinging pain had nothing to do with it.

"I'll admit it was a lucky shot," he said, exhaling, "you could have killed me."

She thankfully removed the stinging gauze. "I will ask again. What are you doing here?" She wrapped a bandage around his arm with snappy gestures.

His guilt soared. "I'm sorry. Coming here was a terrible decision on my part. I made it in a moment of weakness."

He pushed down another curse, not sure about what he should tell her.

Oddly enough, all the good reasons he'd had about breaking into her house seemed hollow now.

"A moment of weakness? You chose this night of all nights, the night when the house was supposed to be empty." She tied the bandage around his arm with surprising kindness.

He pushed down another grunt of pain.

She paused, bringing a finger to her chin and looking quite lovely. Also, she had a nice, pointed chin. "The other time, you ransacked my mother's cabinet—"

"I didn't ransack it."

"— to take Lord Havisham's documents. Did he send you here? Oh. *He* sent you here, didn't he?"

Fantastic. He exhaled and rubbed his forehead. "It was my decision."

"Why?"

"Your mother exploits young fallen women for her schemes, and you know that." He huffed. "Are we really going to play the 'who's the criminal' game?"

She stiffened. "I assure you my mother doesn't exploit any fallen women. That's ridiculous."

He jabbed a finger on the table. "I asked Mrs. Walsh, the woman who runs the women's shelter I finance. She confirmed your mother went there to recruit girls."

"This is absurd. I'm sure my mother would never do that." She tossed a kitchen towel on the counter. "Yes, my mother blackmails her lovers. Yes, it's illegal, but she's never, ever used poor women for her own gain. She isn't that despicable. Believe it or not, she has principles." She gathered her medical supplies, avoiding meeting his gaze.

"I have a witness," he said.

She shook her head. "This story is poppycock. Mama has strong opinions about men, but she would never hurt other women. If anything, you should ask yourself who called the police because it wasn't me, obviously."

Yes, that was a valid point. "Only Lord Havisham knew about my nocturnal excursion. He planned it, actually."

"Excursion. What a nice way to talk about robbery."

"You aren't your mother's accomplice?"

"No, I'm a victim, too." Her voice lowered.

"How?" He was genuinely curious because the possibilities scared him.

She closed a fist on the table. "Do you remember that night in Lady Redvers's house when Mr. North chased me? Well, my mother had made a deal with him for me to spend a night with him. Three thousand pounds for my first night with a man. Mr. North believed you wanted to make an offer on me. Of course, after I poured the content of the vase over him, he decided to lower the offer. One thousand pounds for my virginity."

The shock made him speechless. He went through his memories of that night in Lady Redvers's sitting room when Angeline had barged inside, followed by North. Now his words about the offer made sense.

A surge of sheer, undiluted anger flared up in his chest. "Did you... is the deal... Did he touch you?"

"No."

He exhaled. "He didn't hurt you."

"No, he didn't. But If I'd agreed to the deal with him, I wouldn't have needed to lie with him."

"What do you mean by that?"

She hesitated before answering. "Mama developed a drug that confuses people and fabricates false memories. She planned to give it to Mr. North so I wouldn't need to actually lie with him. He would have only believed he'd spent the night with me."

The pots of drug and Mrs. Haywood's deal with Wright made sense now. "And you believe she isn't capable of exploit fallen women? She drugs people, for crying out loud."

She rubbed her forehead. "I know, but she drugs men, not women. Men are expendable for her. Women aren't."

He cocked an eyebrow. "Did she want to drug me as well?"

"Mama found your two hundred-thousand-pound asset interesting," she said in a low voice, like a confession. "She had plans for you before you stole her file on the earl."

He didn't know what to say. Silence filled the kitchen. Only the soft sizzling of the flames in the lamps could be heard.

She let out a nervous chuckle. "My mother has plans for everyone."

"You must not be happy about her plots," he said in a low tone, sorry that she had to endure men like North because of her mother's plots.

"It's awful. I don't want to be forced into doing anything. All I want is to find a husband and have a family, but Mama disagrees. She says that marriage is a trap and that I can have everything I want without shackling myself to a man. Although I've never had any suitors. None. Especially after the theatre fire." She paused, stroking her scar. "I'm not getting any younger."

"Don't say that."

"It's true. Soon, my chances of finding a husband and having children will be gone. I want to marry for love. I wish to find someone whom I like and have many things in common with, but I'm growing a little desperate."

Her sadness hurt him physically.

"Angeline, you're lovely and kind. You'll find happiness." He tried to touch her hand, but she scraped her chair backwards and rose.

"I talked too much. Let's get back to you. Who told you that my mother uses fallen women?"

Right. He guessed he deserved her mistrust. "Lord Havisham hired a private detective to investigate your mother."

"What?" She folded her arms over her chest.

"That has nothing to do with me." He held up a hand. "Anyway, the detective followed your mother to Mrs. Walsh's shelter. Later, Lord Havisham told me the list of the women your mother used could be in the safe in her parlour. That's where I was going."

A crease appeared between her eyebrows. "My mother is very organised and tidy. She keeps everything in the cabinet in her study. And I'm sorry, but I don't believe Lord Havisham hired anyone to follow her. She would've noticed it."

"How does Havisham know about the safe then? Is there's a safe in her parlour?"

She worried at her bottom lip. "Yes, there's a safe. As for the infamous list, we'll find out immediately if it exists. Come with me."

After hastily putting his shirt and jacket on, he followed her to the parlour, patting his throbbing wound. She moved a mirror aside, revealing a safe in the wall, just as Havisham had said.

Angeline turned the handle right and left a few times and opened the safe.

He peered from over her shoulder. There were stacks of banknotes, a pearl necklace, and other pieces of jewellery, but no papers. No documents at all. Angeline shuffled the boxes and velvet pouches around. Nothing.

"See? I seriously doubt she exploits women." She shut the door. "I might be naïve. I didn't realise my mother was the mistress of many gentlemen for years, but I'm absolutely sure she would never stoop as low as taking advantage of fallen women."

He scratched his chin. The fact the list wasn't there didn't mean Mrs. Haywood was innocent. "What about Mrs. Walsh? She's an honest woman who cares about fallen women."

She shrugged. "I have no explanation for that. Also, maybe the earl genuinely believes Mama has that list."

Possible, but unlikely. "Something is going on. Tonight was a trap. He sent me here on a wild goose chase to get me arrested."

"But why? Isn't he helping you get a seat in Parliament?"

"Yes. I don't understand." A new wave of worry washed over him. "Unless Havisham was never going to get me any seat."

Her black eyes became two midnight pools. "I think you could be right. He used your compassion for fallen women as leverage. He built a cock-and-bull story about my mother exploiting fallen women, and you fell for it. Then he warned the police with the hope they'd arrest you."

Possible. Or perhaps Angeline just refused to see her mother for who she really was. Havisham had told him Mrs. Haywood was conniving and clever. He wouldn't be surprised if she'd warned the police that night, knowing he would come. Perhaps she'd orchestrated the whole thing.

Her expression softened. "You care about those women, don't you?"

"I do."

She gave him a few shy glances. "What happened to your mother was a shock."

"I don't usually talk about her."

She closed a gentle hand around his, sending a jolt of sensations through his body. "If you want to talk about it, I'm here."

"Despite my breaking and entering into your house?"

"Yes, even though you used me to get the documents. I'm not sure I'm ready to forgive you for that yet."

He gripped her hand. "I would never, ever use you. You must

believe me. The moments we shared were only ours. They're genuine."

She furrowed her brow.

"I can prove it," he said, inching closer to her.

"How?"

"From the moment you kissed me, I can't stop thinking about you." He took her hand and placed it right over his heart. Her soft palm warmed his skin. "I want to kiss you right now. I always want to kiss you. I know I didn't behave like a gentleman to you and that I made mistakes, but do not doubt, not for a moment, how much I want you."

Her eyes widened. "Your heart is beating faster."

"I'm not lying. That's the truth." He took a deep breath. "You want to know what happened to my mother?"

"Yes."

"The night my mother was murdered..." A familiar choking sensation crawled into his throat. "I've never talked about that night with anyone."

"Take your time." Too much honesty and compassion shone in her eyes.

He sucked in a few deep breaths. "There was this jockey who was particularly violent. My mother had been poorly for a while, complaining about chest pain." He swallowed past the lump in his throat. "One night, he forced my mother to dance. When she stopped, he'd use a whip to make her start again, until she collapsed on the floor and didn't move."

"Oh, Royston." Her voice cracked.

"The doctor said she had a heart condition, and the forced activity had caused her heart to stop. He said it wasn't murder, but I disagreed." He pushed down the memory of the sweet music, a stark contrast with the scene flashing through his mind.

Unshed tears shone in her eyes. "What happened to the jockey?"

He huffed. "One night, he left a brothel so drunk he fell into the Thames and drowned. I didn't shed a tear when I learnt the news."

"And what happened to you?"

"After I was kicked out of the brothel, I did everything to survive. I'm not the gentleman you think I am." He let out a bitter chuckle. "Look at me. I'm a thief, no matter how polished I am."

"I beg to differ." She cupped his cheek. "I understand why helping those women is so important to you."

"I feel so powerless, just as I was when my mother was killed in front of me. I couldn't do anything. I couldn't save her, and she died because no one protected her. I should have protected her."

She held him, and he buried his face in the crook of her neck. He wrapped his arms around her to push aside the onslaught of horrible memories assaulting him.

"This is why you don't dance," she whispered, caressing his nape.

"I feel sick just thinking about dancing. I shiver, and nausea torments me. I can't do it. Her pale face will forever be impressed in my mind."

"Royston, stop torturing yourself. You were a scared child, and she was ill. There was nothing you could do to save her."

He inhaled her rose scent. "Why can I believe my life will be better when I'm with you? Why do you make me feel better? When I'm holding you, my fears stay in a dark corner of my soul and don't dare to bother me. You scare them away, bringing a ray of sunshine into my darkness."

He didn't know for how long they held each other, but his dark thoughts vanished, at least for now. Only the pure happiness of holding her remained.

She took his face and pressed her mouth against his, shocking him. When she parted her lips and invited him in, he nearly shook with disbelief. He gently inched his tongue into her mouth and explored it. A soft moan escaped from her as he grazed her bottom lip lightly.

He held her closer until her body was flush with his. She arched her back, thrusting her breasts out. Slowly, he moved his hand up the flare of her hips, the curve of her waist to her breast. She released a breath when he brushed her nipple with a thumb until the tip became hard.

Her breathy moan fanned on his neck. He had to stop himself from ripping her dressing gown open and kissing her everywhere he pleased. He slowly circled the hardened tip of her breast until she sagged against him.

"Enjoying it?" he asked.

"Oh, yes. I feel all tingly and hot." She squeezed her thighs. "Achy."

"I can't allow that." He kissed her temple. "Let me help."

He bunched up the fabric of her dressing gown, uncovering her exquisite leg and thigh. Her skin was like velvet. They both sucked in a breath when he slipped his hand between her thighs. She was wet and warm.

"Do you want me to stop?" he whispered against her lips.

"No." No hesitation.

At the first stroke of his fingers, she gripped his shoulders hard. The fact he didn't feel any pain was a testament to how eager to please her he was.

He drew circles to rub her, inching a finger inside now and then. She was as tight as a fist. Another reminder he ought to be careful. He stroked her until she muffled a scream against his chest and closed her fists.

Little pulses beat against his fingers, and his trousers became painfully tight.

His arm was the only thing holding her up because she sagged against him completely, soft and warm. The deep, intense need to protect her burst within him. But above all, the need to become a better person made him shiver.

"Are you all right?" He adjusted her dressing gown, reluctantly covering her lovely legs.

She said something that was silenced by his chest since her mouth pressed against it.

"What?" He caressed the top of her head.

She lifted her head, and her face was the most beautiful sight. Her cheeks and lips were flushed, and her eyes glowed from within. "It was wonderful. Can we do it again?"

He kissed her forehead as a crazy idea formed in his mind. "I have a better idea. Marry me."

eighteen

E NGAGEMENT. SPECIAL LICENSE. Eloping. Marriage. All those words came out of Royston's mouth, and Angeline couldn't believe she listened without dismissing his idea. Maybe it was the overwhelming pleasure she'd just experienced.

"On a practical level, if we get married," Royston said in a serious tone that didn't leave room for jokes. "Your mother will stop making deals with dubious gentlemen on your behalf, and I'll finally have some peace of mind. Lady Redvers will stop introducing her daughter to me, and married gentlemen are held in higher esteem than bachelors. Marriage could help me get a seat in the House of Lords. And your mother won't need to blackmail anyone. I'll provide for her as well. She won't lack anything."

"I understand the practical aspect of a marriage between us, but what about us? A marriage is forever. Do you really want to spend the rest of your life with me?" She didn't know what she wished he'd say.

He stared straight into her eyes. "Yes, I do. We know each other well, especially after tonight." A wicked smile flashed over his sculpted lips, and a tingle started pulsing between her legs. "I respect and admire you. Your fierce spirit and sharp mind are qualities I'll always appreciate. You give me strength and calm. You make me smile even when I'm sad. Today, many marriages are based on less than that. If you do me the honour of becoming my wife, I'll do everything I can to make you happy. If you can forgive me for the fright I gave you tonight."

"Well, I shot you. I think we're even." Right now, she wasn't thinking straight though. She ought to take time to ponder a reply. "I feel better when I'm with you as well."

He showed another lopsided smile that transformed his handsome face into a mischievous one. "I know different ways to make you feel good."

Her cheeks warmed. All her body did. "There's something else. I want children." She had to make things clear. "Do you?"

He squeezed her hands. "Absolutely. I'm going to enjoy making them."

She laughed again. "I think—" The rest of her sentence was cut off by the sound of a carriage stopping at her front door. "Mama," she whispered. "She's early."

Before he could say anything, she grabbed his arm and led him upstairs to her bedroom. "Quick."

"Why am I hiding?" he said once she'd locked them in.

"Do you really want my mother to know you went through her things again? We don't have to tell her anything."

"I don't think lying to her will make things better." He looked out of the window. "I can't leave from this window. It's too high."

"I didn't think about letting you out of the back door." She looked around. "Just hide somewhere until she goes to bed."

"Angeline?" Mama's voice sounded closer.

"Under the bed. Quick."

Muttering a curse under his breath, he squeezed himself under the bed. But his bulk didn't fit.

Mama knocked on the door. "Darling?"

"I don't fit," he whispered.

"The wardrobe." She waited for him to be inside her wardrobe among his scoffs and puffs before opening the door. "Mama."

"I was worried. The lights are on. Are you all right?" Mama put a hand on Angeline's forehead. "Are you sick?"

"No. I'm fine."

Mama furrowed her brow. "You're all flushed and hot."

Yes, that was how Angeline felt. "You're home early."

"Oh, what an odd evening." Mama walked inside the room and sat on the bed, pulling off her gloves. "Lord Havisham came, unfortunately. I wouldn't have gone if I'd known he would be present. He was rather upset by your absence. He asked me a few times if I wanted to send a cab to fetch you. I told him you didn't feel well and needed to rest, but he insisted that you should have come. After a while, the host called the evening off, claiming he was suddenly indisposed, and the earl said I should be with you since you were ill. Such an unusual behaviour. I didn't even try the dessert."

The door of the wardrobe inched open. Dash it. Likely, Royston's bulk was too large for her wardrobe as well. She shut the door with nonchalance.

"Maybe Lord Havisham was only worried about me."

Although his behaviour was further proof that he'd planned the whole evening. He'd known the police would have come.

"Since when does he care? He's never shown any affection towards you aside from the bizarre piano affair. No, something bothered him, and he wanted me to go home, which made two of us. He also told me he had something urgent to tell me, but he then changed his mind and didn't say anything else."

"Does Lord Havisham know about the safe in your parlour?" she asked.

Mama looked taken aback. "What an odd question. But as a matter of fact, yes." She laughed. "He paid for the safe. Ridiculously expensive. It was one of his gifts for me. Why?"

"Well—"

A soft groan came from the wardrobe, and the door swung outwards again. She slammed it shut, but grimaced when another noise came. She must have hurt his injured arm.

"Angeline." Mama shot up, her rouged lips parting. "Is there a man hiding in your wardrobe?"

"No, no, what an idea." She leant against the door to keep it shut.

Mama's smile held too much excitement. "Well done, darling. Who is it? Mr. North? He wasn't at the dinner tonight."

"No. Mama, there isn't anyone in the wardrobe, and *if* there were someone, it wouldn't be Mr. North."

"You don't fool me." Mama craned her neck to look past her. "I really want to know."

"Please."

"Come on." Mama took Angeline's hand and tugged.

At the same time, the door was pushed open, revealing a crumpled and not-at-all pleased Royston.

He closed his eyes for a moment and muttered something she didn't understand.

"You!" Mama shifted her gaze from Royston to Angeline. "What is Baron Wharton doing here?"

Royston uncoiled his massive body out of the wardrobe. Now that he was out, it seemed incredible he'd fit in it to start with. Thank goodness his jacket covered the bandage, although the fabric was ripped, or Mama would ask more questions.

"I'm not here against your daughter's will, madam," he said with a strained note.

Mama's eyes widened as she turned towards Angeline. "This is why you didn't come to tonight's dinner. You had an assignation with the baron after everything he did to you. To me."

Oh, bother. Angeline was going to get a headache. "It's not like that."

"Why is your jacket ripped?" Mama pointed a finger at the ripped sleeve.

"A little incident." Royston straightened his jacket.

"You should probably go," Angeline said.

He nodded. "Ladies, I bid you goodnight. Madam, I wish to tell you that nothing happened here tonight."

Angeline shook her head. That was the wrong thing to say.

"I'm glad I interrupted you." Mama didn't look as shocked as a mother should be.

"No, we weren't doing anything," Royston said.

"What do you mean by that? Then why are you here?" Mama said at the same time as Angeline said, "Can we let him go, please?"

"But I don't understand. Why would you stay home and invite him without telling me if you didn't have any debauchery in mind? Why him? He made you cry."

"Did I?" Royston asked, furrowing his brow.

"Please." Angeline held up her hands. "We should discuss this tomorrow. Or never."

"No." Mama crossed her arms over her chest. "I demand to know what's happening."

"I want to marry your daughter. That's what's happening." Royston's tone sounded a bit too sharp.

Silence dropped. Even Angeline didn't know what to say.

"Good Lord." Mama paled and tottered on her feet. Her breath came out in uneven pants.

"Sit down." Angeline helped her to the bed.

Her bottom lip quivered. "How can you do this to me? Me, your mother, the woman who spent thirteen hours labouring to give birth to you."

Royston straightened. "What? A tryst is better than marriage?"

"Yes!" Mama said.

"That doesn't make any sense," he said.

"It's complicated." Angeline waved dismissively.

"When did everything start to go wrong?" Mama gripped the bedpost. "I raised you with solid principles, and instead, this happened."

"You're exaggerating." Angeline poured a glass of water from the pitcher and handed it to her mother. "There's no need for this dramatic scene."

"No need?" Mama's face reddened. "You don't have to marry this man and be his slave. If you want to have a tumble with him, then do it, but you don't have to shackle yourself to him and do his bidding for the rest of your life."

Royston came forwards. "Madam, I assure you I have no intention of turning Angeline into a slave."

Mama scoffed. "Don't listen to him. They all say the same things, and then everything changes once they marry you, and before you know it, you're his maid, housekeeper, cook, sex slave, and mother all rolled up together. That's the future waiting for you if you marry him. He'll expect you to do everything he asks, inside and outside of the bed. He'll expect you to do the housework, cooking, and everything else."

"That's absurd." Even Royston reddened. "I have enough money to hire a cook, a maid, and a housekeeper."

Mama jabbed a finger at him. "You're missing the point. It doesn't matter how much money you have. You'll still treat her like a slave. She'll never be enough for you. You'll resent her wish to be independent until you crush the very flame of life within her, and she'll no longer exist. You'll murder her."

"Goodness, this can't be possible," Angeline said.

"You're very much mistaken, madam," Royston said. "And I'm sorry for the pain someone you cared about caused you."

Mama swallowed the water with one gulp, staring at Angeline as if Royston hadn't talked. "What do you know about marriage and men? Nothing."

"Madam." Royston's tone sounded more strained by the minute. "I'm sorry for what happened to you, but I'm not one of those men who considers his wife a slave or a servant. I don't know what I have to do to prove it."

Mama stood up with surprising energy. "There's nothing you

can do that will change my mind. This marriage will never happen. Especially after you came here and searched my study.”

“I understand your rage.” Royston arched his brow. “But you blackmail people, madam.”

“Out of my house, Lord Wharton.”

“Madam—”

“Now!” She stretched out an arm towards the door.

“This conversation doesn’t end here. I want to marry Angeline and—”

“Out,” Mama ordered.

Angeline gave him a nod. “Please.”

He bowed. “Good night, ladies.” He strode out of the bedroom and down the stairs.

“Mama.” Angeline clenched her fists. The more Mama ranted against Royston, the more she wanted to marry him. “You shouldn’t have treated him so cruelly. He’s an honourable gentleman.”

“There’s no such thing as an honourable gentleman. It’s a contradiction. They’re all the same, ready to use you. He used you.”

“Royston and I talked about that. He had some convincing arguments.” Perhaps that wasn’t the right time to mention Lord Havisham’s lies about Mama abusing fallen women. “The fact you had a terrible, awful experience doesn’t mean all men are the same.”

“Oh, really?” She folded her arms over her chest. “Let’s put your white knight to the test.”

“How?”

“Have a tumble with him and see what happens next. I bet my diamond bracelet he’ll walk away from his marriage proposal and will call you a harlot faster than I can say, ‘I told you so’.”

“He would never do that.”

“If you’re so sure, then do it.” She touched a rather large ring with a big ruby on its top. “Go on. Seduce him.”

Angeline copied her mother's stance and crossed her arms. "I will not seduce him only to prove to you he's honourable."

"Fine. We can give him my special poly potion. I've laced it with almond wine. My men say it's delicious. He'll believe he tupped you—"

"Your language!"

"—and after that, after he thinks he had you in his bed, he'll forget about you. You won't hear from him ever again."

"It's wrong. I forbid you to drug him."

"I can use my Lucrezia Borgia's ring, if you prefer." She showed her the large ring.

Angeline shook her head. "I don't even want to know what that thing is."

Mama tilted her head. "Scared that your white knight will behave like a scoundrel?"

"Mama." Angeline took Mama's shoulders. "Stop it. I know you were hurt. I know you had one horrible experience after another with men, but Royston is different. Leave him alone."

"The fact he pulled you out of that burning theatre doesn't mean you owe him anything."

"I certainly owe him my respect, and your plan is disrespectful. So no almond wine. And that's final."

nineteen

ROYSTON WASN'T A politician.

He aspired to hold a seat in the House of Lords, but he preferred taking action to negotiating with only his oratorical skill, which wasn't great. Last night's unfortunate incident with Mrs. Haywood was proof of that.

He should have handled the situation better, made his argument stronger. Instead, Mrs. Haywood had been furious with him, and Angeline hadn't agreed to marry him. Understandable. Instead of talking about how achingly he cared about Angeline, he'd discussed with her the practical aspects of being married.

Havisham's behaviour left him perplexed. If he'd set up the break-in and the police, Royston couldn't understand why. His motive was missing. The evidence pointed at Mrs. Haywood, but the list was nowhere to be found, and he didn't trust her. Angeline instead loved her mother too much to be objective.

Royston was in his sitting room, pondering his next move, when the butler announced the earl had just arrived. Speaking of the devil.

"Shall I let Lord Havisham in, my lord?" Enright asked. "Or shall I tell him you aren't receiving anyone today?"

Tempting. But if he wanted to understand what Havisham had in mind, he should pretend not to have figured out anything.

"Let him in, Enright, and please bring tea."

Havisham walked into the room with tentative steps, his face pale. His hair was dishevelled, and the handkerchief in his breast pocket seemed to have been stuffed without regard for the fabric.

"Wharton, thank you for seeing me without notice."

As usual. "Havisham. It's becoming a habit. Please take a seat."

The earl didn't talk until Enright had served the tea and left the room.

"What upsets you?" Royston asked. *Your plan didn't go as you wanted, did it?*

"How did last night go? You didn't send me any messages."

"A fiasco, I'd dare to say. I didn't find anything else in the safe." He watched Havisham for any reaction.

The earl ignored his tea. "Did you break into the house?"

"I did. Everything went well."

The earl frowned. "Miss Haywood was at home though. She didn't come to the soirée."

He huffed as if it didn't matter. "She was sound asleep. She didn't rouse, and I'm quite silent."

The frown deepened. "I see."

"Do you have any idea where Mrs. Haywood might keep the infamous list?"

"No. Perhaps you could try again. Search other rooms. I'll organise something else to keep Mrs. and Miss Haywood busy."

No, enough. Royston wouldn't play that game again. Mrs. Haywood wasn't a saint, but Havisham wasn't innocent either. Royston had followed enough pieces of advice from the earl.

"Havisham, I don't intend to break into Mrs. Haywood's house again."

"Well, if you don't want to help those women, it's up to you. I thought you cared."

Royston straightened. No, the guilt trick wouldn't work. "I

can't keep breaking the law." He stared at the earl. "Sooner or later, someone might notice and warn the police."

Havisham lost his concerned expression, his facial muscles tightening.

"Besides, I can have a simple chat with Mrs. Haywood about her illegal activities." Something he should have done a while ago. "Once I'm a member of the House of Lords, things will be different."

"Of course." He lifted his cup and put it down without drinking. "Well, I hope you'll be present at the next ball. Lady Redvers will be delighted to have your appointment as a member of the House of Lords announced at her event. If she agrees to invite you, of course."

"Of course." Yes, Royston had every intention of talking with Lady Redvers, or rather, with her husband.

As the earl left, Royston wondered who the liar was.

After Havisham left as quickly as he'd arrived, Royston sipped his tea.

He both winced and smiled when he rubbed his arm. Winced because the wound bloody hurt, and smiled because it made him think of Angeline. She could have killed him. She knew how to take care of herself. He shouldn't find her so adorable.

Hell, he wanted to marry her. His marriage proposal had shocked her, and not in a good way. He'd expected her to say yes immediately. There was a lesson for him to learn.

He leant back in the armchair in his drawing room. The warm hearth spread a nice glow that soothed his nerves as he read the latest issue of the *Weekly Information Bulletin* from the House of Commons.

In the past two years, he'd studied everything about the law, but he still had problems understanding all the nuances of the legal publications. If he wanted a seat in Parliament, he needed to become fluent in law.

A dull thud came from the window. He bolted upright. A blob

of gum was splattered on the glass, attached to an arrow. Angeline. He opened the window and snatched the arrow from the glass. A piece of paper was wrapped around the shaft.

I'm here. May I see you? A.

He stuck his head out of the window but didn't see anyone. Grinning, he walked down to the kitchen. The voices of his butler and housekeeper came. They were always the last servants to retire to their rooms.

He entered the kitchen, feeling uncomfortable because, years ago, he'd spent a lot of time in a kitchen, but now he didn't have many reasons to.

"Enright, Mrs. Lawerence."

They stood up from the chairs around the table in a flutter of action.

"My lord." Enright bowed, and Mrs. Lawerence curtsied. "Do you need anything?"

"You may retire for the night. I have everything I need. Thank you." It was the first time he'd asked them to leave the kitchen early. He wasn't fooling anyone.

"What about your nightcap, my lord?" Mrs. Lawrence asked.

"I'm not in the mood tonight."

"Would you like me to check the windows?" Enright asked.

Bugger. He appreciated his employees' efficiency, but as a former thief, he knew how to keep his house safe.

He waved a dismissive hand. "No, it's fine."

Mrs. Lawrence fought a smile. She might have understood his eagerness to be alone. "Then we'll retire, my lord, and see you in the morning."

"Excellent. I'll be in the drawing room, reading for a while."

Enright frowned. Mrs. Lawrence offered a polite nod. Royston returned to the drawing room with a vague sense of guilt.

He paced, worried Angeline would leave before he had the chance to let her in. He exhaled when the sound of doors shutting came, a sign that his butler and housekeeper were in their bedrooms. Finally. The things a grown man had to do for a bit of privacy.

As he walked towards the rear door, he felt like a lad, scared of being caught red-handed by his parents, doing something he shouldn't. He inched the door open and muttered a curse when the hinges let out a screeching noise that left a trail of goosebumps on his skin.

He paused, waiting for one of his servants to come. Either Enright and Mrs. Lawrence were the two fastest people to fall asleep, or they were pretending not to hear. Anyway. The important thing was that Angeline's reputation remained intact.

"Angeline?" he whispered. "You can come out."

A soft rustle of dry leaves being crunched rose from the shadows, and Angeline emerged, wrapped in a long cloak. A hood hid her features. Her bow was slung on a shoulder.

"I wasn't sure."

He let her inside and closed the darn screeching door. Pressing a finger to his lips, he guided her along the dimly lit corridor and up the stairs. He was an adult man, owned the house where he lived, and paid the salaries of the people who worked in the house, yet he was sneaking into his room. Being a footman was easier.

He shut the door to his bedroom and lit the gas lamps. "Why are you here?" He couldn't remove the concern in his voice.

She pulled the hood down. "I wanted to apologise for what my mother said and the horrible way she treated you."

Oh, that. He'd hoped she'd come to tell him she wanted to marry him.

He shoved his hands in his pockets. "It's all right. She's your mother. I understand. You needn't come to apologise, although the sticky arrow idea was great."

She put down the bow. "I didn't come here only to apologise." She walked over to him, tugging at the strings fastening the cloak on the front. The fabric swished down her body to end on the floor. "I want…"

She must have had second thoughts about whatever she wanted to do because she stopped and gazed everywhere but at him.

"What do you want? A cup of tea? Are you hungry? I have the finest quality ham in the pantry. A nice slice with some mature cheddar is excellent. A cure-all."

She laughed, throwing her head back. "No, I'm not hungry. But it's something similar to hunger."

"I see. You want to indulge in something sweet. Pudding?"

She smiled. "I certainly want something sweet."

"I'm not good with riddles."

Her steps towards him were small and tentative. She seemed ready to bolt out of the room if he sneezed.

When she was close enough, he caressed her cheek. "What is it?"

She rolled her bottom lip between her teeth. "I'd like to be with you. In bed. Without clothes."

"What?" he raised his voice and regretted it.

"I'm too bold, am I not?" She stepped back. "I shouldn't have come. I'll leave immediately."

"Wait." He took her slender wrist and tugged gently. "It wasn't too bold. I was surprised. That's all."

She smiled, and the trust in her gaze almost broke him. "So we're going to get in bed together."

Oh, hell. "Let's start slowly."

Her happy expression faltered. "What do you mean?"

"It's like learning something new. You learn step by step without skipping ahead."

"All right." She tugged at her gown. "Shall I undress?"

"No." Damn. His tone rose again. "Let me do the undressing."

"If you don't want to be with me, you have only to say it." A quiver rang in her voice.

He closed his eyes for a moment. "Of course, I want you here. I want you more than anything. But see, I grew up in a bordello. I saw and did things not appropriate for a fine lady as you are. I have to learn as well."

"Learn what?"

"To be gentle. The women I've known so far were very well experienced without a shred of discomfort, and I knew what they wanted from me. With you, everything is different."

She drew her eyebrows together. "What do I have to do then?"

"Just be honest and tell me what you like and what you don't." He cupped her cheeks. She was so beautiful he wanted to weep.

"Fine. I'll be honest. Now what?"

So impatient. "What do you want me to do?"

"Kiss me." She tilted her head back.

He didn't need to be told twice.

She wrapped her arms around his neck and pressed her sweet mouth to his. Immediate desire shot to his groin. His thoughts became a jumble of incoherent voices.

He forgot to ask her again if she wanted to marry him. Later, later, later.

He deepened the kiss, exploring her mouth with slow lashes of his tongue. She wilted in his arms, running her hands over his chest.

Holding her by the waist, he lifted her and laid her on the edge of the bed. She breathed hard already, and he hadn't done anything yet.

"I like kissing you," she said, her lips glistening.

"I like kissing you, too." He unbuttoned her shirt. "Lie down."

He took his time uncovering her creamy skin although the corset and chemise didn't reveal much. The hooks on the corset were little buggers, hard to unfasten, but he won the battle with patience, kissing her now and then. He discarded her corset and shirt, leaving her chemise on. Her cheeks were a riot of colours.

"Embarrassed?" he asked.

"No, no. A little. May I keep the chemise?"

He took her chin and kissed her. "Your chemise will stay. For now."

The skirt and petticoats joined the shirt quickly. The boots needed to go as well. She lay on his bed in only her chemise, drawers, and stockings— the most beautiful vision he'd ever seen.

She moaned when he caressed her lovely legs, feeling her warm skin through the fabric of her stockings. He ran his hand up, following the curve of her waist to her breasts. Their dark tips were visible underneath the flimsy fabric of her chemise. A few strings tied it on the front, and he pulled at them slowly, watching her reaction.

Her eyes were glowing, and her chest rose and fell quickly. A shiver went through him when he lowered the straps and tugged the chemise down until her breasts were bared. Her drawers were next.

Bugger. He'd promised her the chemise would have stayed. His ability to focus was seriously compromised by her beauty. He went to pull the chemise up again, but she stopped him.

"No. I changed my mind. I like how you look at me," she whispered.

"How do I look at you?"

"As if I were beautiful."

He focused seriously now because he needed to be clear. "You are beautiful. I've never seen a more beautiful woman." He kissed her lips, cheeks, and neck, inhaling her flowery scent.

She laughed but fell silent when he rolled her nipple between his lips. Quick pants came out of her. He forced himself to be delicate. She arched her back and closed her fists in his hair as he tongued her breasts, pinching and sucking at her nipples.

"I like this," she whispered among breaths.

"Good." He kissed his way down, parting her legs to accommodate his bulk.

She propped herself up on her elbows, but plopped down again when he brushed her intimately.

"It's..." She gasped.

"I know." He ignored the aching stirring in his trousers or the wound in his arm throbbing. That moment was for her only.

He lapped at her, smiling when her hips lurched up. He drew circles with the tip of his tongue, tasting her sweetness. She said something unintelligible, and he paused, worried she might have asked him to stop.

"Do you like it?" He gazed up, lingering on the hardened and glistening tips of her breasts.

"Yes, yes." She nodded several times, so he guessed he could continue.

The incoherent words, moans, and lurches started again the moment he kissed her deeply. If she enjoyed it, he could go on all night. He added a finger just because he wanted to feel her velvet squeezing around him.

She writhed and trashed on the bed until she let out a piercing cry that, without a shadow of a doubt, Enright, Mrs. Lawrence, the maid, and the footman must have heard. But who cared? He would never ask her to be quiet. Quite the opposite. He wanted her wild and unrestrained.

He kissed her inner thighs and moved up her body, pausing to suck her nipples again.

She lay on the bed, her arms spread and her eyes shining.

"Did you like it?" He caressed her hair.

A strangled noise came out of her.

"What?" he asked.

She nodded.

He covered her with a quilt and gathered her in his arms. She sagged against him, likely exhausted. His own desire roared with desperation, but he was happy to hold her and give her the comfort she needed now. He rubbed her back.

"You're the most wonderful thing that has ever happened to me. I hope you will marry me, and not simply because it's practical, but because I can't think of anyone better than you to share my life with. No, sorry, that sounded terrible." He chuckled. "I mean, I really want you to be my wife." That was hardly better, but at least he'd been clear. He waited for her to say something, but she remained silent, her head on his chest. "Did I shock you?"

Not a word.

"Angeline?" He craned his neck to see her face.

Her eyes were closed, and her breathing came out softly. His angel had fallen asleep.

twenty

ANGELINE HAD NO idea how she could have experienced the best feeling ever one moment and the next, the worst.

She'd fallen asleep in Royston's arms after he'd taken good care of her. How embarrassing. She hadn't reciprocated his attention, told him how much she'd enjoyed herself, or even kissed him. Instead, she'd collapsed without as much as a 'thank you.'

Sitting on his bed, she finished buttoning her shirt. "I'm so sorry."

"Stop apologising." He knelt in front of her to tie her boot. "You don't need to apologise. Feeling tired is normal."

"But you... I didn't do anything to you." And she had to leave now.

He gave her a radiant smile that stole her breath. "You did a lot of things to me." He kissed her other foot before sliding it into the boot. "I enjoyed every moment I was kissing you, and when you were asleep in my arms, I've never felt happier in my life."

"I'm sure I'm your first lover to fall asleep like that."

"Shush." He adjusted her skirt and stood up. "You're the first lover to make me truly happy." He sounded so sincere she couldn't argue.

She caressed his cheek, and he leant into her palm, his hazel eyes shining from within. The warm, fluttery sensation in her chest couldn't be simple lust.

He kissed her inner wrist. "I'll take you home."

"No need for that."

His expression hardened. "I'm not going to let you leave alone at this hour. There are all sorts of people out there. Trust me, I know that because I was one of them. The only problem is that we must be quiet."

She clamped a hand on her neck. "I screamed so loud my throat hurt. I'm sure your butler wondered if you were murdering someone."

He laughed. "Still, I'm coming with you."

She tiptoed out of his bedroom, holding his hand. They went down the stairs, one step at a time. He paused halfway down to lean over the bannister. A beam of light lit the corridor, and footsteps sounded.

He pulled her back, and she ended up sprawled on his chest, a giggle rising in her throat. The whole situation was exciting. The sound of footsteps faded, but Royston didn't move.

When the light died, they resumed going down the stairs.

The cold air calmed her when they exited the house. "That was exciting."

"Exciting? I don't want my butler to recognise you. I don't think he'll blabber, but I'm not going to take any risk when it comes to you." He hailed a cab and helped her in.

She shamelessly snuggled close to him and rested her cheek on his chest where she could hear his pounding heart. He wrapped an arm around her shoulders in a protective gesture she loved. Goodness, she could get easily used to being held by him and enveloped by his warmth.

"What we did tonight," she said, "is it the first step?"

"Yes." He rubbed her shoulder with his thumb.

"I can't imagine how it progresses from there."

"Only time will tell."

"By the way." She moved away from his chest to look at his face. "I want to marry you."

At first, he remained frozen, and she worried he might have changed his mind. But then a wide smile spread across his lips, and he was kissing her everywhere— her lips, cheeks, chin, eyelids, forehead.

She chuckled as his hair tickled her. "I gather you're happy."

He took her face, his eyes wild with happiness. "More than happy. You've made me ecstatic." Another round of kisses started, and who was she to complain?

"I didn't know you'd be so happy to marry me, especially after I shot you."

"I am. I am." He gave her a crushing hug, squashing her against him with desperation. He quivered. "So happy," he whispered in a trembling voice.

"What is it?" she asked. "Why are you shivering?"

He swallowed hard. "I would have never thought I'd be able to have a normal life. Who is born in the gutter dies in the gutter. That's the rule. Even when I received the title, I didn't think the sense of achievement would last. Deep down, I have always feared I would be alone and despised, always powerless, always a criminal. But marrying you..." He released her and kissed her again. "Being your husband is the best thing I could wish for. I want you to realise your dream as well, give you a family who loves you, and make you as happy as I am now."

Her eyes stung. She blinked to clear her vision. "Thank you."

He hugged her again, and she got lost in his strong arms and warmth.

"This is the beginning of a new life," he whispered.

"For both of us."

They remained in each other's arms until the cab rolled to a stop in front of Angeline's house. He escorted her to the back door and remained on the pavement, raising a hand in farewell, until she was safely inside.

After she closed the door, she leant against it.

How quickly the day had changed. She'd gone from being a thief shooter to being an engaged, happy woman in a matter of hours.

ROYSTON WOULD DO everything by the book.

Angeline had agreed to marry him, and even though the circumstances that had led him to that happy conclusion hadn't been the best, he would give her the finest wedding ever. The preparations for a great wedding that would lead to a great marriage started with a ring.

To think that a few years ago, he'd been about to rob Garrard's Jewellery. Instead, he was there to buy a ring. The irony of life.

"Does anything catch your eye, my lord?" the clerk asked from the other side of the glass display counter.

A few magnificent rings shone against the backdrop of a black velvet cloth. He couldn't decide if the diamond ring was better than the blue one.

"Which stone is the blue one?"

"A topaz. It symbolises love, fidelity, good fortune, and confidence."

"Perfect. The topaz then."

"I'll polish it and put it in a box, my lord."

As the clerk put away the other rings, Royston paced around the glittering shop. Thank goodness he hadn't robbed the place. The situation now would be awkward.

"Wharton." Lord Redvers stopped next to him. "What brings you here?" He shook Royston's hand.

"I'm buying a ring for my engagement." Just saying that warmed his heart. "What about you, my lord?"

"I'm searching for a new pair of cufflinks, and I like to choose them myself. My wife buys me cufflinks I don't like." He glanced at the clerk polishing the ring. "So a marriage is on the horizon. Good on you. Who's the lucky lady?"

"Miss Angeline Haywood," he said with pride.

Lord Redvers's eyebrows rose. "Fine lady. I wish you all the best, Wharton."

The viscount didn't say a word about the incident at the last ball, and Royston was glad for that.

"I meant to ask you something." He lowered his voice.

"I know what you mean to ask." Lord Redvers sighed. "Alas, no luck with that bill in Parliament yet. It's not considered a priority."

He wasn't surprised. "Actually, I meant to talk to you about something else. Lord Havisham is petitioning my candidature for a seat in the House of Lords. Do you think that will make a difference with the approval of the bill?"

Lord Redvers frowned. "I'm sorry, but I don't understand."

"Lord Havisham promised me to help me get a seat."

"I don't think so, Wharton. We were discussing the possible candidates just the other day, and Lord Havisham didn't mention you." He narrowed his gaze. "There must have been a misunderstanding."

Not likely. So there it was. The earl had lied to him. So Mrs. Haywood might not be guilty of exploiting fallen women.

"I see you're disappointed," Lord Redvers said. "Well, I can tell you that, now that you're getting married, your chances to get support from the lords will increase. If only... forgive me." He waved a dismissive hand.

"Please do go on."

Lord Redvers cleared his voice. "Well, it's about the incident from the night at the ball. There are rumours about your state of mind. You know how gossip works. If you danced in public, people would stop making up stories about you."

Royston tilted his head. "What rumours?"

"Rumours about your... er, mental condition have been circulating since the ball. You haven't shown yourself anywhere since. If you want a piece of advice, show yourself around town and dance in front of everyone to quash every possible rumour. The stories about what happened at the last ball became rather exaggerated and outlandish."

"I'm not surprised." Royston shifted his weight as the usual uneasiness surged. "North must have done his level best to smear my reputation and start the rumours."

"What people say is that you don't want to dance because you become unstable when you dance, smashing things and punching people. I myself heard a couple of people claiming to have witnessed wild behaviour, that you punched a maid while dancing."

"Me punching a maid? I would never do such a thing, my lord." Outrage rang out in Royston's voice.

"I didn't believe the rumours, but rumours are snowballs rushing down a slope. All it takes is a little shove. By Jove, I'd support you in Parliament if you danced at the next ball and proved the gossip mongers wrong."

"You would?" Royston asked.

"I would." The viscount raised a closed fist in encouragement. "Show everyone those rumours are ridiculous. Dance in front of everyone, and let's put the gossip to rest, once and for all."

"Yes!" Royston copied the viscount and closed a fist, energy rushing through him.

"You're Baron Wharton, the man who challenged the fire. Dancing is nothing," Lord Redvers continued. "Show everyone what you're made of. You're going to marry a fine lady. Prove to her that she can be proud of you by facing your biggest fear."

"Yes," Royston said again.

A fire started in his veins. The viscount was right! He must dance for Angeline and for his future.

"The world is yours for the taking." Lord Redvers spread out his arm. "Dance, Wharton."

Lord Redvers was right. Royston had to act. He had to do it for Angeline as well.

Royston shook Lord Redvers's hand with energy. "I accept the challenge."

~

WHAT HAD POSSESSED Royston to accept that stupid challenge?

After the heated moment of bizarre energy fuelled by Lord Redvers encouragement had passed, Royston realised what he'd agreed to and he shivered, his teeth chattered, and his heart had pounded so fast he'd believed it wanted to crawl out of his body.

Lord Redvers's words had sounded so simple. But afterwards, the familiar sense of panic had descended upon him, leaving him exhausted and cold.

If he had to be honest, he knew Lord Redvers was right. He should put the rumours to rest and bloody dance in front of everyone, not simply for the seat, but for his bride-to-be as well. And for himself.

He didn't want to spend the rest of his life scared of a ghost. As much as he loved his mother, he wanted to move forward and not live with his fears of the past. He should grab his life and lead it.

The velvet box with Angeline's ring rested in his pocket. She was sitting on the edge of his bed, but he was so agitated he couldn't find the right moment to give the ring to her. The fact they were having another secret night meeting in his bedroom didn't help. He loved to be alone with her, but disliked the secrecy and the subterfuge. They were engaged... well, not yet. But they shouldn't hide.

There was another reason to be agitated. Seeing his bride-to-be on his bed triggered all sorts of beautiful visions of their future together. But since his mind had a dark side, those beautiful visions came with the company of dreadful ones, in which Angeline decided she'd had enough of rumours and gossip about him and wanted to leave him.

"That's what Lord Redvers said," he said, finishing recounting his encounter with the viscount.

"So it's as we thought," Angeline said. "The earl is lying to you."

"I should have realised Havisham had no intention of helping me, but I believed him. He used me to retrieve those damning documents. Then he tried to get rid of me by calling the police." He raked a hand through his hair. "I agreed with Lord Redvers's plan. He made a rather motivating speech about me being brave and quashing the rumours. At that moment, dancing at the next ball sounded like a jolly good idea."

Also, he didn't want to disappoint her. Just the thought of letting her down made him feel sick to his stomach.

She slid off the bed and knelt next to him. His wish to make her proud grew tenfold. "I can help you. I love dancing. I can teach you."

He laced his fingers through hers. "I know the steps. It's the dancing itself that makes me sick and nervous." A shudder went through him.

"We can try. Here, without music." She rose, holding his hand. "Come."

Cold sweat dampened his neck. "Perhaps I should call the challenge off."

She gave him a heated glance. "I'll kiss you if you dance with me."

He sprang up. "What are we waiting for?"

Laughing, she dragged him to the centre of the room. He couldn't change his mind now.

"Let's start with the dance that's all the rage at the moment, the Viennese waltz. Do you know the steps?" she asked.

"I do. I've watched others dance."

She put his hand on her waist and held his other hand. "Just perform to a count of eight."

He didn't move. Not hearing the music was maybe worse because the music of that night played in his head. A funny taste filled his mouth. His knees weakened.

"Royston." Angeline ran a hand over his arm. "It's just you and me. Look at me."

He seemed to choke on air but did as told and stared at her. Her obsidian eyes were filled with compassion and care.

"It's just us."

Her hand caressing his arm soothed some of the tension tightening his chest.

His mouth grew dry and his feet seemed to have turned into lead. "It's very difficult for me."

"I know." She kept caressing him. "But I believe you're strong enough to let the past go. It wouldn't be a lack of respect for your mother. You'll always honour her memory. But this fear is born from a dark moment. A moment you must let go of. This isn't about a seat in Parliament. It's about you as a person. A person who deserves a future of happiness."

"Oh, hell." He reclined his head and released a breath through his teeth. "You're right. Everything you said is very sensible, but I feel torn apart. My mind says to let the past go. My heart is full of fear."

"Let me guide you. Perhaps if I'm leading, you'll feel better."

She moved her feet in the first series of box steps, but even though he wanted to follow her, his legs were two tree trunks.

Since he didn't move, she tripped on her own feet and fell backwards. He snatched her before she could hurt herself. The result was a sensual pose with her leaning back in his arms, and he bending over her. His lips were an inch from hers.

She smiled. "Well, that's a tango pose

"Tango?" He straightened. "What is it?"

"A most scandalous dance from Argentina. I learnt it from a friend who went there." She wrapped her arms around him. "It's performed with outrageous closeness." She pressed her body against his. Not even air stood between them. "Wandering hands." She put a hand on his nape before dragging it down his neck and chest, causing him to shiver with desire. "Almost kisses." She rose on her tiptoes to brush her lips against his. Another shiver left a path of fire on his skin. "And sometimes, the lady hooks a leg around her partner like this." She pulled up her skirts and uncovered her thigh before coiling a leg around his waist.

At this point, his blood was boiling.

He ran a hand over her thigh and slid it under her skirts to cup her firm rear. "I think I like this tango. How's the music?"

She cleared her throat and hummed a fast-paced, accented music. He had to admit she had musicality and a good sense of rhythm.

She burst out laughing. "It sounds terrible."

He stroked her leg, toying with the garter. "No, I think I understand. It's similar to a polka. It has syncopated accents and four beats in each measure, and a quarter note receives one count."

"Are you speaking English?" she asked. "I'm not fond of maths." She snatched her leg out of his grip and stepped back. "For me, tango is all about seduction and the sensual chase." She took another step back. "It's more of a tease than an action."

He could do nothing but follow her. He took her waist again and pulled her closer. But she slid out of his grip again, holding his hand. He chased her because he wanted her leg around him again.

As he gave her hand a tug, she twirled towards him, letting his arm coil around her. She repeated the move a couple of times.

Before he knew it, he was dancing. Surely, his steps had little to do with the tango, but he twirled, following her moves and stepping around the room in a circle.

The more she fled from him, the more he chased her. The steps turned faster. He hardly knew what he was doing, but it didn't matter. She repeated the gesture of caressing his neck, dispelling his last ounce of uneasiness. When she hooked her leg around him, he grabbed it under her knee.

"I want my kiss now."

The intense possessiveness in his voice surprised even himself. He leant closer, but she arched her back.

"If you want a kiss, come and get it." She slipped through his grip faster than he could say 'tango' and twirled across the room.

He chased her again and took her hand. Before pulling her towards him, he let her make a few turns. When she finished, he was too aroused not to kiss her.

The kiss wasn't sweet or gentle but a battle that involved their whole bodies. Her skirts went up and legs went around him, and he held her up. She became demanding, fighting for dominance. He loved every moment of it.

He moved her towards the bed until they both fell in it, still kissing each other. He controlled the fall with his hands so as not to crush her, but after that, he showed no mercy. He unbuttoned her gown in a frenzy.

She fumbled with the buttons of his shirt and the falls of his trousers. Somehow, they were both half-naked in a moment. He scattered kisses on every available inch of her smooth skin, his hand pushing aside her chemise and pulling off her drawers. The promise he'd made to be slow and gentle echoed from a corner of his mind. Yes, he ought to ask before going any further.

"Why did you stop?" she asked before he could say anything.

"Are you sure you want this now?" He panted so hard his words were broken.

"Do I look like a woman who has doubts?" She slipped a hand between them and wrapped it around him.

The shock silenced him.

"I have no doubts. And to be honest, I'm tired of waiting and always wanting." She spread her legs. "I begin to think you don't want me, that you're making excuses not to bed me because you don't find me very attractive."

"What?" he roared.

The kiss he gave her held no kindness. It was sheer passion to dispel all her doubts. She matched his strength as he devoured her mouth. He broke the kiss, only to drag his lips down her neck and draw her nipple into his mouth.

He couldn't get enough of her. He caressed, kissed, and tongued every inch of her he could reach. She kept stroking him with her gentle hand.

The movement was uncertain and at times a little too tight, but he didn't care. They both stilled and drew in a breath when his blunt tip touched her.

"Angeline," he whispered. "Tell me to stop."

"Never." She put her hands on his shoulders and urged him in. "Do it. I need it."

"It's going to hurt."

"I don't care."

He kissed her again before switching places. She straddled him, which he loved because he could cup her breasts.

"And now?" she asked.

He undid her chignon, scattering hairpins anywhere. The black silk cascade of her hair fell over her breasts. Perfection.

"Go at your own pace," he said.

He fondled her breasts before holding her by the hips and helping her over him.

She shifted her hips and inched up and down until she found a comfortable position. The most difficult part for him was to remain still while she lowered herself. If he jerked his hips, he might hurt her. She paused and winced a few times, but she didn't let him go.

"If you change your mind—"

"No." She regarded him from underneath heavy-lidded eyes.

"It stings a little, but it's manageable."

He supported her when she needed it, and inch by inch, she took him in until she was sitting on his hips. It was heaven. The feeling of her tightly wrapped around him was so powerful he nearly found his release.

"Hurt?" he asked, caressing her thighs.

"No. I'm good and well now."

She moved up and down slowly before finding a faster pace. She put her hands on his chest and reclined her head, black hair falling on her back.

He couldn't resist for long. She was too beautiful, and the sensations were too strong. He lifted her off him to spend out of her. Bugger.

"Wait." He gently laid her down on the bed. "I'm sorry. Don't leave."

She smiled. "I'm not going anywhere."

He kissed her lips. "I'll be back in a moment."

He quickly wiped himself with a clean cloth and used a fresh towel to clean her with lukewarm, soapy water. A few drops of blood stained it, worrying him.

"Does it hurt?" He cupped her face.

"No, really."

"I'm sorry. I couldn't last longer. Let me take care of you." He nestled between her legs, already dizzy with her scent. He licked his lips, ready to feast on her.

"I can wait—" She gasped when he dipped his head between her legs to give her a deep kiss. "Royston."

His name, said with that breathy voice, had him hard and tense in a moment.

He smelled the soap on her skin as he deepened the kiss, hoping to soothe the sting. He added a finger and rubbed her with the pad of his thumb.

She made a few noises, rocked her hips, and writhed. The way she whispered his name would be the death of him.

Her wild scream was the best sound for him. Her inner muscles tightened as she moved against his tongue. He shifted and slipped inside her again.

She welcomed him, wrapping her legs around him. Since she had to be sore, he controlled his speed but made sure to rub the right spots.

Their gazes locked as he moved in and out of her with gentle strokes.

Time stopped to have meaning as he laced his fingers through hers and stared at her glowing obsidian eyes. The woman had put a spell on him because every time he stared at her, he would do anything for her, anything she asked. She'd made him dance because darkness couldn't touch him when he was with her. Only love was that powerful.

She breathed hard as he went deeper, taking his time. She closed her eyes and arched her back as another scream of pleasure rocked her body.

He couldn't resist and fondled her breasts, pinching her nipples. She cried out again, saying his name like a prayer. He pulled out of her to spill.

After he wiped her again, he lay next to her, holding her.

"That was..." she said among pants. "Beautiful."

He caressed her head, unable to express his feelings with words. He searched for words could convey the sheer joy and tenderness he felt now as he held her.

She curled up in his embrace and fell asleep before he could tell her he loved her.

twenty-one

ANGELINE COULDN'T BELIEVE she'd fallen asleep again.

Surely, lovers had some kind of etiquette, and falling asleep right after the act had to be frowned upon. Royston had done everything to pleasure her and take care of her, and the moment she'd found her release, she'd collapsed and slept.

She rubbed her eyes and huffed. "Bother."

He was putting on his shirt but turned towards her with a smile. "Hello, beautiful."

"I'm really sorry," she whispered, shifting in the bed because she was a little sore.

"About what?" He crawled over the bed to lie next to her.

"I fell asleep again. I'm sure lovemaking has some rules of etiquette I keep breaking."

He barked out a laugh, full and charming. "I like holding you when you sleep although..." He rummaged through the pocket of his trousers. "You fell asleep, but I... I wanted to give you this."

He handed her a small velvet box with the golden G of Garrad's Jewellery.

She hitched a breath, propping herself up on her elbows. "Royston."

He opened it, revealing a lovely ring with a blue stone. "It's a topaz. Its meaning is about happiness, love, and family. No, it's not family but something else. I don't remember what now. I'm too agitated. But I'm sure about the love and joy. If you prefer a diamond, I'll buy you one. But the topaz has such a pretty colour—"

She shut him up with a kiss. "It's perfect." She gave him her hand, and he grinned as he slipped the ring on her finger, his chest expanding.

He punched the air. "It's official. We're engaged."

The kiss they shared was different from the others. It was slow and sweet. No more battles or struggles to dominate. No more feverish passion.

They kissed with tenderness and the hope of sharing a long, happy life. She moved her hand up his firm thigh to the falls of his trousers. From the moment she'd touched him, she wanted to touch him again and hear that low growl he made deep in his throat. The need to touch him was a combination of curiosity and need.

He sucked in a breath and stopped her hand. "It's not a good idea."

"I won't do anything. Just a caress."

"A caress is already too much." He flashed a boyish smile. "It's late. I have to escort my bride-to-be home."

She wrapped her arms around his neck. "I'm already home."

He beamed so widely, even his eyes brightened. "That's the most beautiful thing you could ever tell me."

She caressed his cheek. "Are you ready to dance at the next ball?"

He kissed her inner wrist. "I guess we aren't going to dance a tango."

"Unfortunately. But Royston..." She waited for him to stare at her. "Whatever is going to happen, I'll be by your side. You aren't alone now. You have a family."

His new smile was less bright but more intense.

He kissed her hand. "Then I'm ready."

THE CUSTOMARY TWENTY-EIGHT balls of the Season were nearly at their end. Thank bloody goodness.

Usually, there were more than that, but twenty-eight was the standard number. Royston was glad the torture of the balls and social events would soon change into more sombre and less dancing gatherings.

He'd been so busy he hadn't had the time to plan a proper engagement party for Angeline. He absolutely didn't want to give the announcement at someone else's house as a passing moment of entertainment. She deserved a night for her only.

Also, her mother hadn't given them her blessing, which posed no small problem. Not that Angeline couldn't get married without her mother's blessing, but he didn't want to start his new life with Angeline with tension in the family.

But no matter. The bloody dancing challenge came first. Getting a seat would also be his score to settle with Havisham.

So here he was, dressed in his best evening suit; his valet had spent a week, choosing the outfit and putting it together. Oddly enough, the shirt, waistcoat, and trousers had been just fine when he'd left the house. Smooth, fresh, and soft. Plenty of space to move. Now that he stood at the edge of the ballroom in Lord Redvers's house, his clothes had turned into instruments of torture, chafing, restricting, and tightening.

He fiddled with his tie to give more room for his throat to work.

"Bloody hell," he muttered under his breath.

Angeline stood next to him. "I'm looking forward to showing

everyone how the baron who never dances has become a great dancing partner."

"I don't share your enthusiasm."

Lord Redvers walked over to them, his face tense as if he were the one who had to dance. "Are you ready, Wharton?"

"More or less. Yes. As ready as I can ever be."

"They're all here," Lord Redvers said.

Yes, Royston could see that. From Mr. North, Miss Taylor, Mr. Wright to Havisham and the other ladies and gentlemen who had attended the ball where he had fled., They were all there. And last but not least, Mrs. Haywood; she shot him daggers with her gaze whenever he glanced at her.

The last thing he needed was to have an argument with her before the dancing started. He'd stay out of her reach for as long as possible.

"I don't mean to worsen the situation," Lord Redvers said, "but North started a round of bets on you. He thinks you aren't going to finish the dance."

Which is likely.

"Very unlikely," Angeline said, seemingly reading his mind. "Lord Wharton will show everyone how elegant and skilled he is."

"Let's not exaggerate." Royston scrubbed the back of his neck.

Murmurs spread when the master of ceremonies announced the dances would start soon. Young couples drifted towards the centre of the room. Sideways and curious glances were thrown in his direction.

"Good luck, Wharton." Lord Redvers gave him a paternal pat on the shoulder.

He was so nervous he couldn't say anything.

"Let's go." Angeline tugged at his hand. "Don't be too anxious. I know you can do it."

He followed her, dragging his feet onwards. The deep breaths he kept taking didn't seem to help, and he became dizzy while the lights were too bright.

"Look at me," Angeline said. "Focus on me only."

He nodded, not trusting his voice.

"Ouch!" She wriggled her fingers. "You're crushing my hand."

"Sorry. I'm nervous."

When he and Angeline found their spot among the other couples, following the social ranks, a combination of mutters and whispers swept the room. Some shook their heads. Others nodded their approval. A few smiled, either in encouragement or mockery. Then the music started.

"Royston," Angeline whispered. "You recognise the type of dance, don't you?"

"F-flat major."

She narrowed her eyes. "I didn't understand a word you said. I mean that this is a polonaise. It starts with a sweeping step, then we form a circle with the other couples. We'll head right while the others... just follow me."

"Yes."

"Let's begin."

"Yes. Don't leave my hand."

She gave him a warm smile. "I have no intention to."

The music of the Polish dance began; it was lively and strong, masterfully played by the orchestra, but a buzzing noise rang in his ears, threatening to drown out the music.

He needed to focus on Angeline's smiling face because Mrs. Haywood and Lady Redvers looked like they wanted to murder him with their fans.

"To the left," Angeline said, guiding him. In fact, she was leading because he might have improved, but he wasn't ready to lead. "Right and backwards."

He stared at her, and slowly his muscles loosened a bit. When the dance reached its climax and the couples at the front of the line formed the circle, he and Angeline kept performing the sweeping steps, and he caught himself having fun.

Maybe *fun* was the wrong word. If he kept his dark memories down, and ignored his crazy heartbeat, he could enjoy Angeline's sweet smile and soft hands.

"We're nearly finished the first round," she said. "We'll make another one. You're doing great."

"I love you, Angeline," he said for no particular reason other than it was true. "I'm looking forward to being your husband, and I hope I'll make you as happy as you make me. You're like the light of a clear dawn after a long winter night. With you, my new days have started."

"Royston—" She tripped.

He caught her by the waist, but they missed a beat, and now they weren't following the music.

"Sorry," they said together before laughing.

She beamed so widely her eyes brightened the whole room. "We need to hurry."

They sped up to catch up with the couple in front of them. From the crowd, Lord Redvers gave him an encouraging nod.

"I love you, too," she said. "I want to marry you because I love you, not because having a family has always been my dream, although I know I'll realise my dream with you and we'll be happy."

He nearly tripped, too. She did her best to hold him up, but the result was that they skipped another beat and were far behind the music again.

They had to nearly run to close the gap with the couple in front. Not the best performance. Still, better than no performance at all.

Angeline and Royston stared at each other as they had to speed up again, and something absurd happened. They burst out laughing at the same time. She laughed so hard she nearly hiccupped.

The weight oppressing his chest lifted, leaving him finally free from the ghosts. His mind got free from the shackles of the past, and he could finally breathe and dance without choking on his memories.

When the polonaise finished, a few people clapped. He'd danced. Danced! The woman he loved was next to him. Life was wonderful.

Angeline leant closer, clapping with the other couples at the end of the dance. "Now Lord Redvers will become your champion."

He'd nearly forgotten about Lord Redvers's promise. He clapped at the orchestra and smiled.

The viscount walked towards them with long strides, a wide smile on his face. "Lord Wharton." Lord Redvers shook Royston's hand vigorously. "Congratulations. You've found your champion."

twenty-two

A FTER HAVING DANCED a gallop, a quadrille, and even a waltz, Royston had had enough.

He'd danced without following the music, tripped a few times, and improvised many times, but overall, he was happy because Angeline had told him she loved him, because holding Angeline in his arms and watching her smile always cheered him up.

The night couldn't be more perfect. So when Mrs. Haywood had approached him at the end of the waltz, asking him to meet her in the parlour, he'd agreed.

He doubted she wanted to make peace with him, but he'd listen to her. Perhaps now that he'd soon become a member of the House of Lords, she'd give her blessings to the marriage.

On his way to the parlour, a footman, carrying a tray, stopped next to him.

"Wine, my lord?"

"Thank you." Royston took the only glass on the tray and took a sip for courage.

The rich taste of the wine filled his mouth. There was honey, cinnamon, almonds, and something else he couldn't place. Something pungent and bitter that stung his throat.

As he paced in the parlour alone, since Angeline was busy in the ladies' room, he pondered what was the best way to offer an allowance to Mrs. Haywood.

She slipped inside and shut the door behind her. "Lord Wharton, thank you for agreeing to see me."

He bowed. "Madam."

There was a moment of silence as she studied him. He didn't know what to say. His body sizzled with nervous energy.

"I'm sorry for my outburst from the other night, Wharton. You caught me off guard with your proposal, and you must understand Angeline is the most precious thing I have."

"I understand. I would never hurt her, madam. I love Angeline." He'd never tire of saying it.

"You love her." Her features hardened.

"I really want to take care of Angeline... and of you," he said.

"Of me?" Her voice rose a notch.

"I can provide for you more than adequately. You won't have to keep your business practices. You can leave behind the unpleasantness and danger of that life forever and live a life of leisure."

Her features tightened further.

"I wouldn't let the mother of my bride risk going to prison for something I could provide," he said.

"What a generous offer."

"We're going to be family soon." He had no intention of letting her blackmail people any longer.

"I'm sure Angeline will want to see you after we talk," she said, pouring herself a glass of wine from the sideboard. "Shall we have a toast first?"

"To what are we toasting?"

"A new beginning."

"A new beginning." He took a sip, and again the sweet aroma teased his taste buds, followed by the bitter flavour.

Mrs. Haywood watched him from over the rim of her glass as she sipped. "How do you feel, Lord Wharton?"

Her face blurred. The whole room blurred, but in a pleasant, comforting way if that made sense. He wasn't panicking. He was calm, if not a little drowsy.

"I'm fine." True. He wasn't nervous or scared.

Tiredness caught him, but at the same time, he didn't have a care in the world. Somehow, he felt more optimistic and happy. If only he could stand without his head spinning.

"Come here." Mrs. Haywood led him to the Chesterfield sofa, seemingly reading his mind.

The colours of the room burst with energy and became bright. The sofa tilted. He feared nausea might catch him, but no. His stomach was all right. The sensation was like flying.

Mrs. Haywood sat next to him. "Now, I want you to follow my voice."

He smiled. What a nice, deep voice she had.

"Everything I say is what's happening now."

Of course, it made perfect sense. He trusted her. Yes, he did. She was his future mother-in-law. He was in no danger.

"You're lying here with Angeline. She's beautiful."

"Yes, she is," he slurred.

"You and she are naked. You desire her so much."

So bloody true. Everything she said was true.

Yes, Angelina lay next to him. Mrs. Haywood vanished. He hadn't noticed her leaving the room, but never mind. Angeline was here.

Her dark hair was loose over her naked shoulders and perfect breasts. He caressed her cheek, feeling her silky skin under his fingers. She smiled. Hell, her smile was devastatingly beautiful. She kissed him, and he smiled against her lips.

"What are you doing?"

That was her voice, but it sounded as if coming from a great distance, and she didn't seem happy at all.

He waved at her. Her long curls of hair floated around her, and her flimsy nightgown caressed her curves, showing everything to him. A breeze coming from somewhere caused the fabric to flutter and plaster against her lovely body. If only her tone of voice matched her ethereal beauty.

"Royston?"

She cupped his face, and for a split second, she didn't appear dressed in her nightgown but in an evening ballgown, which was pretty, but he preferred the diaphanous nightgown that showed everything.

Her hair was different as well, no longer loosened but gathered in a chignon. She looked like that night when he'd danced the mayonnaise. No, it was the lyonnaise. Who cared?

How odd. Her attire kept changing. He blinked, and there she was in all her ethereal beauty, wearing her transparent nightgown.

"Can you hear me?" Her voice sounded high-pitched and hysterical.

Bugger, her evening gown replaced the revealing nightgown again. He wouldn't know how she changed so quickly, hairstyle and all. Anyhow. She'd asked him something, but he didn't remember what.

Distant voices reached his ears. It seemed that two women were arguing about something.

"Royston. Your skin is purple." Angeline took his face again, her dark eyes large with worry. "I'll be back with a physician. Don't fear."

Fear? He wasn't scared. He'd never been better, aside from his face tingling.

But since she looked concerned, he nodded.

A thud, like the sound of a door closing, came. Then Angeline returned with her loose hair and transparent nightgown.

She stretched out next to him. Her sweet scent teased his nostrils. So delicate. She smiled although it wasn't her usual sweet smile. That smile had something wicked in it. She lowered the satin straps of her nightgown and tugged the fabric down until she was half-naked.

He stretched out a hand to caress her beautiful breasts when she vanished in a curl of steam. Gone. Poof. Like a snuffed-out candle.

"What the hell?" he said, although his tongue felt strangely heavy and thick, as if it were swollen, filling his mouth.

"There we are." A face filled his field of vision. And it was a terrifying sight. Lady Redvers stared at him. "Come, Georgiana."

"Mother, we can't. We shouldn't!"

"Right now. Stop snivelling."

Royston gazed around. The lights were still blurring and shining like beacons. His spirits were still high, but Angeline was nowhere to be found, and he'd lost some of his pleasant mood. Lady Redvers and her daughter shouldn't be here, interrupting his lovemaking with Angeline.

"Come on. This is perfect. He's drunk. What a stroke of luck." That was Lady Redvers.

Then a soft body bumped into him. A mop of brown hair came into view. Small hands pressed against his chest. It was Miss Georgiana Taylor, shivering against him. Or maybe he was shivering. He had no idea.

"Go away," he slurred. He wasn't sure she'd heard him.

"I don't care if this idiot becomes a member of the House of Lords," Lady Redvers said, "but compromising you, Georgiana, means Wharton Steel will be ours."

"What?" he slurred.

"I'm sorry," Miss Taylor said.

Either tears filled her eyes or... he wouldn't know what else. But he wanted Angeline, not this trembling lady.

"What's happening here?" someone asked.

"It's not his fault. He didn't do anything." Angeline's voice.

"What a scandal," a woman said.

"No, he didn't do anything," Angeline said.

Hell, his stomach was really upset. Cramps made him gag. A bitter taste filled his mouth, and the sensation of floating and being light disappeared.

Flames filled the room. He had to take Angeline away. The blaze would kill her. Cold sweat soaked his shirt. His body convulsed, but he felt so cold his teeth chattered, which didn't make any sense because the room was on fire.

twenty-three

ANGELINE SHIVERED WITH anger and worry as she put a fresh, damp cloth on Royston's feverish forehead.

Thank goodness he'd stopped casting up his accounts and trembling. Whatever the physician had given him, it was working. Royston was sound asleep in his bedroom, covered by layers of thick quilts and warmed by a hot water bottle.

It had taken three people to carry him out of the parlour in Lady Redvers's house, lay him in a cab, and then tuck him in his bed.

After Mama had the horrible idea of drugging him, Angeline had found Royston lying on a sofa in the parlour and her mother whispering to him. Angeline had faced the most intense, albeit brief, argument of her life with her mother. Then Royston had started to convulse, his skin turning purple.

She'd left him for a handful of minutes, desperate to fetch a physician who could help him, only to return to the parlour and find Miss Taylor all over him in a promiscuous attitude.

Lady Redvers must have organised the whole scandalous scene. The viscountess had barged into the parlour with two other matrons and caught her daughter in a compromising situation with Royston. A delirious, almost-dying Royston, that is.

Chaos had ensued. No one had listened to Angeline when she'd said that he had been drugged, and she hadn't cared much at the moment, worried about him. But then again, she couldn't explain what had happened to Royston without exposing Mama and raising questions that might reveal she regularly drugged gentlemen to blackmail them later.

Royston casting up his accounts on Lady Redvers hadn't helped his case.

But no matter. The most important thing was that he was all right now and asleep.

"Miss Haywood." Enright, the butler, entered the bedroom, carrying a tray with a steaming cup of tea. The man had been a godsend, helping Angeline take care of Royston. "Your mother is here."

"I don't want to see her." She wrung the cloth in the basin before wiping Royston's forehead again.

"I apologise, but she's quite insistent. She won't leave until you see her."

Angeline sighed and sagged in the stuffed chair. "All right. Thank you, Enright."

He cast a worried glance at Royston before leaving.

Mama walked inside without her usual cockiness. Her cheeks were pale, and her capelet was askew.

She paused next to the bed. "How's Lord Wharton?"

"As if you cared about him."

"I'm sorry. I really am. I had no idea he would have that... what did the physician call it?"

Angeline placed a fresh cloth on Royston's forehead. "Adverse reaction. No, actually, the physician said that Royston had a *severe* adverse reaction, life-threatening. It's a miracle he's alive. If he hadn't cast up his accounts, he would have died from poisoning."

Mama shivered. "I tried the potion on many men, and none of them became so sick. It has always worked."

Angeline checked Royston's pulse. The physician had told her to check that his pulse remained strong and steady. "You almost killed him, and for what? To prove to me that he isn't a good man after I expressly told you not to give him anything. But did you listen? No, because that's what you do. You only do as you please without listening to anyone."

Mama had the decency to lower her gaze. "I apologise. I didn't want any of this. I just wanted to prove to you that he would leave you once he took you to bed."

"Well, you were late." She breathed hard. "I've already given myself to him, and he still wants to marry me."

Mama blushed. Angeline hoped it was shame.

"On top of that," Angeline said, "Lady Redvers demands he marry her daughter because she claimed he ruined her."

Mama held up a hand. "That wasn't my doing. I had no idea that awful woman had planned to throw Miss Taylor at Lord Wharton, only to force him to marry her. That was an unfortunate event."

"Unfortunate?" She tossed the cloth into the basin. "Lady Redvers acted desperately because she knew Royston meant to marry me. Someone must have told her the news, and you were the only one who knew about his proposal. You drug him and leave and she comes in with her daughter? It's too convenient."

Her eyes flared wide. "It wasn't me. I don't even like the woman. Why would I tell her about Lord Wharton's proposal?"

"Because you disapprove of him. You knew she would have done something reckless, like trapping him in a forced marriage." She barely suppressed her tears. "And now he can't marry me. Congratulations. You ruined everything."

"No, darling. I swear it." Mama took her hands. "I don't trust Lady Redvers. I would never associate with her. I have told her nothing."

Angeline didn't believe her, and she was too angry and upset to forgive her.

Miss Taylor will marry him because he won't allow a lady to be ruined. If he refused to marry her, he'd likely lose the seat in Parliament, and Georgiana would be marked as a trollop. He had no choice but to agree to marry her.

"I have nothing to do with this," Mama said.

"I've had enough." A sob escaped Angeline. "For the past years, I tried to convince you to stop, but I failed. Even worse, I covered your lies, and I shall take my responsibility. If I'd stopped you, Royston would be all right now. But no more. No more."

Mama caressed Angeline's head. "Darling."

"Please leave. I want to be alone."

"I really am sorry." Mama kissed her cheek. "I'll make amends. I promise."

"Go." She waited to be alone to hide her face.

Her betrothed had risked dying, and now he wasn't her betrothed anymore.

She'd barely lived her dream before it was snatched out of her reach.

Mama might not have meant to hurt Royston, but thanks to her, Lady Redvers's plan to force him to marry her daughter had been successful.

ROYSTON MUST HAVE HAD a case of brain fever because a massive headache battered his skull like a hammer, his throat was swollen, a foul taste filled his mouth, and his muscles were aching and sore.

He opened his heavy eyes, which required a ridiculous amount of strength. The sunlight glared at him, filtering through the window of his bedroom. At least he was home.

He groaned when he propped himself up on his elbows. The

last thing he remembered was having a glass of wine with Mrs. Haywood. Then... confusion and fragments of events.

Angeline had been in the parlour, and there had been someone else. He'd kissed Angeline, but he wasn't sure of that. He wasn't even sure why he felt so sick.

He poured himself a glass of water from the pitcher on the nightstand and, with a tilt of his head, polished it off.

The door swung open and Angeline swept into view. He inhaled deeply, ignoring the burning in his throat.

"Angeline."

"Royston, you're awake." She turned towards the corridor. "He's awake!"

She rushed to him. Her simple afternoon dress was wrinkled in places as if she'd been sitting for hours. A few of her black curls had escaped her bun and whipped her worryingly pale face.

"How do you feel?" she asked.

"What happened to me?"

"You're all right." Her lovely face was too gaunt. "We were so worried."

Enright walked over to him. His clothes were wrinkled, and his hair and beard were unkempt.

Mrs. Lawrence came in, as pale and tired looking like Angeline. "Your Lordship, finally. You've been mostly unconscious for three days."

"Three days?" Royston rubbed his aching forehead. "What happened to me?" he asked again.

Enright exchanged a glance with Angeline. "My lord, I'll have a light lunch prepared for you."

His stomach lurched at the idea of food. "I don't think I can eat anything."

"The physician said it's important that you eat something. I'll bring a fresh pot of tea as well." The butler bowed again and left the room with the housekeeper.

"Thank heavens, you're all right." Angeline held his hand with desperation.

He didn't have the energy to reassure. The headache was splitting his skull in two.

"Oh, Royston. I'm sorry." She brushed his hair from his face. "It was my mother. She put something in your drink, a potion she brews herself from mushroom powder and dried herbs. It is a hallucinogenic."

"Damn." He scrubbed the back of his neck.

He wanted to say something, but Enright entered carrying a tray with a bowl of soup and tea.

"My lord, please eat everything. It's very important you drink a lot of fluids. The physician was very clear." The butler stood there, giving him a pointed look.

"I will. I promise." Royston was so confused.

Enright left the room, casting glances at him as if worried he might collapse.

"Drink some tea." She poured and handed him the cup. "I'll tell you more once you drink the tea."

"I remember having a drink with your mother," he said among sips. "But then I dreamed... or maybe it was real. You came in a beautiful nightgown."

He finished the tea. Admittedly, the hot drink settled his stomach.

"No, darling." She helped him with the soup. "My mother's potion essentially helps fabricate false memories."

"Very vivid memories. I could swear you were real."

"Unfortunately, you reacted badly to the drug, and you were incredibly sick. I called a physician, but in the meantime, something else happened." She paused, lowering her gaze. "More soup."

He took a moment to savour the leek and potato soup, not too salty and with a dollop of soured cream. The more he ate, the better he felt.

"What happened?"

She took her time to answer. "Lady Redvers discovered your marriage proposal to me and decided to take action. She threw her daughter at you while you lay delirious on the sofa. Then she pretended to catch you and her daughter in a compromising situation. A few of her friends witnessed the scene."

He lowered the bowl. "Bloody hell. Now I remember Miss Taylor vaguely."

"Lady Redvers expects you to marry her daughter. I'd say everyone does. News of your supposed shameful behaviour towards Miss Taylor is all over town. You can't avoid a wedding." Her voice broke, and his heart broke as well because of her pain.

"Bollocks."

"It's a huge scandal. Lady Redvers took advantage of your state to trap you in a forced marriage. Miss Taylor claimed you confessed your love for her." She swallowed hard, her bottom lip quivering. "You must marry her. Your reputation and her reputation would be damaged forever. You'll never get that seat. Lord Redvers was horrified as well."

"To hell with that seat. I won't marry her."

Bloody hell. His stomach lurched, and his throat was on fire all over again. A coughing fit caught him. The more he coughed, the more his throat smarted.

No, he wouldn't marry anyone but Angeline. He'd find a way to protect her, too.

"Take deep breaths." Angeline rubbed his back and handed him another glass of water.

He was so angry that dark blotches pulsated in his field of vision. He had a vague memory of Lady Redvers mentioning something about his steel factory. He'd give it to her if that was what it took to be with Angeline. He'd renounce his title. He'd leave London. Anything to be with the woman he loved.

He pinched the bridge of his nose and sagged into the pillow. "Is your mother involved in that incident as well?"

"No, she drugged you because she wanted to prove to me that

you would have abandoned me after we'd shared a tumble. She was convinced that, once you believed we'd been together, you would have left me. The adverse reaction of your body and Lady Redvers's trick weren't part of her plan. She says she didn't tell Lady Redvers about your proposal. I know I shouldn't believe her but I think she was telling the truth."

"I ran into Lord Redvers at Garrard's Jewellery when I bought your ring , and told him I meant to marry you."

"Oh." She stroked the topaz. "Then it wasn't my mother."

"I was so happy I had to tell someone." He shook his head. "I couldn't have imagined a simple conversation would have led to this."

"You did nothing wrong."

Perhaps not, but he had to do something. He couldn't let his life be destroyed by people's machinations. He looked at Angeline, the woman he was meant to marry. Their love was too strong to forsake.

He pushed aside the covers and stood up. A moment of dizziness caught him, and he grabbed the bedpost.

Angeline stretched out her arms to steady him. "What are you doing?"

"I must fix this. I have no intention of marrying Miss Taylor."

"You're too weak. You must rest."

"Not a chance. I won't stay here and do nothing while Lady Redvers ruins my life, our lives. Are you giving up on us without a fight?"

"No, but I don't know what to do."

"Would you help me wash and change? I have a plan."

twenty-four

ANGELINE DIDN'T KNOW if she should be worried or impressed by Royston's behaviour.

He'd been adamant about leaving the house despite the fact his face was gaunt, dark circles clouded his eyes, and coughing fits overwhelmed him whenever his temper rose.

"Why are we going to see Mr. Wright?" she asked as they rode in a carriage. "I thought you would go straight to Lady Redvers."

"If the conversation with Wright goes as I hope, there will be no need for me to talk with Lady Redvers." He straightened his jacket and watched out of the carriage window. "I didn't tell you that Wright and Miss Taylor love each other. They meant to get married, but he doesn't have the money to give a viscount's daughter the type of life she's used to. Your mother pays him money secretly for errands he does for her. He brings her pouches of herbs from the market. When he told me I thought it seemed too simple. Now I understand why. She asks him to be her courier to carry medicinal herbs that are likely illegal, so she won't be seen dealing with smugglers."

Angeline pressed two fingers to her temples. "I keep learning new, horrible things about my mother. I wonder how many more secrets she keeps from me."

"If I were you, I wouldn't want to know. I don't think Miss Taylor cares about Wright's finances, but her parents would never allow her to marry a penniless, albeit famous pianist. Wright would like to move to Paris with the hope of earning more money. Artists receive better salaries in France. I'm sure he's devastated by the news that his beloved has to marry someone else."

"But how can he marry Miss Taylor now? He's penniless."

He grinned, regaining some of his colour. "He won't be penniless for long."

She put her hand over his and smiled. "I see."

The carriage stopped in Bloomsbury, in front of a closed tailor shop.

Angeline tilted her head up. The windows of the upper floors above the shop showed broken shutters, and a few glass panes had been patched with newspapers. The front door was ajar, swinging back and forth on its hinges; it nearly came off them when Royston held it open for her.

He entered the entry hallway and went up the stairs on unsteady legs. She followed him, worried he might collapse.

Rotting wooden doors lined the hallway. Pieces of wallpaper flaked from the walls, and she could swear she saw a rat hurrying away.

He knocked on the door with a plaque reading, 'Mr. Daniel Wright.'

"Wright? It's me, Baron Wharton."

The door was flung open before Royston could knock again, which was great because the door was so thin and tattered she doubted it would survive another knock.

Mr. Wright appeared on the threshold. "You!"

"We need to talk." Royston brushed past him none too gently.

Angeline followed him inside. "Sorry for the intrusion, Mr. Wright."

The pianist lived in a room that was actually a glorified wardrobe. The single window was too small to let any sunlight in, and every time Angeline took a step, the floorboards creaked.

"How could you compromise my Georgiana?" Mr. Wright pointed a finger at Royston. "I told you we were in love. I thought you understood my struggle."

Royston shook his head. "I didn't do anything. I'm here to set the matter straight and—"

Mr. Wright wasn't listening because he tackled Royston as a rugby player would. Royston groaned and hit the wall with his back. The fact he didn't react was a testament to his precarious condition.

"Mr. Wright, stop this instant." Angeline grabbed the man's arm before he hit Royston again and pulled him away. "Let him tell you what happened."

The musician staggered back.

She stepped between Royston and him. "You must listen to what we have to say. We're here to help you and Miss Taylor."

"Mr. Wright shook a fist. "I love her. And she loves me dearly."

"Great. Wonderful. Wish you all the best." Wincing, Royston sat down on the only chair that looked solid. "Apologies, Angeline, but I need to sit."

"Of course, darling."

"Darling?" Mr. Wright said. "How many women are you seducing?"

Royston huffed. "Angeline is my wife-to-be. Now, if you let me talk without yelling or attacking me, I'll explain everything."

As Royston told him about Mama's drugs and then Lady Redvers's scheme, Angeline tried to find a chair that didn't have holes or was rotten. A talented pianist like Mr. Wright should be able to live decently. Never mind marrying a viscount's daughter.

"Good Lord." Mr. Wright put a hand on the table with mismatched legs after Royston finished. The piece of furniture shook, about to collapse. "Poor Georgiana. She must be distraught."

"Excuse me?" Angeline balled her fists. "I'd say poor Lord Wharton. He was drugged, accused of something he hadn't done, forced to be betrothed to a woman he doesn't love, lay three days unconscious in bed and almost died."

Royston gave her a light shake of his head.

Mr. Wright frowned "What do you want from me?"

"Simple. I'll give you enough money to live well in Paris and marry the woman you love," Royston said. "We'll buy a special license and passage to Paris. Now pack your things. You and Miss Taylor will be happy in France, and Lady Redvers's scheme will come to naught. Most importantly, each one of us will marry the person we love. I'll give you enough to start a new life and... " He waved a hand. "Whatever else you need. You have my word."

Mr. Wright narrowed his gaze. "Will you give me enough to make a viscount's daughter happy?"

Royston shrugged. "Making Miss Taylor happy is your duty. I'll merely finance your wedding and help you with expenses until you get established as a musician."

"I can't repay you," Mr. Wright said.

"I don't want anything from you." Royston held Angeline's hand. "I'll marry the woman I love. That's more than enough."

Mr. Wright smiled so widely she could see his uvula. "My lord, do not fear. I'll make sure Georgiana and I leave London as soon as possible. But I want to return the favour."

"No favour needed. We'll be happy to hear you play at the *Opera de Paris*," Royston said.

She disagreed. Mr. Wright had attacked Royston. "I want to hear what Mr. Wright has to offer."

"I offer information." Mr. Wright raked a hand through his dishevelled hair. "As you know, I've been invited throughout the Season to play at balls and dinner parties. They paid me nothing, let me tell you. Many compliments, but little money. During one of these events, I happened to have heard a conversation between Lord Havisham and Mr. North while I was taking my break. Lord Havisham informed Mr. North of your... er, past, about your mother's death, my lord. They then made a plan to perform a little public scene, where the earl pretended to want to stop Mr. North from spilling the story of your past. North promised Lord Havisham to continue to spread rumours about you, my lord."

Angeline turned towards Royston, but he didn't seem surprised.

"Why would Lord Havisham do that?" she asked.

"I wouldn't know, miss. Mr. North seemed eager to help, though."

"Of course he was." Royston rubbed his forehead.

"It wasn't Mama," she whispered. At least Mama hadn't lied about that.

"Well, Wright." Royston winced when he stood up. "We both have a busy day ahead of us, and I need to go to the bank. I'll meet you back here soon."

She wrapped an arm around his waist to help him up.

Mr. Wright held the door open. "Will you let me play at your wedding as a thank you?"

Angeline softened. "Thank you. That would be lovely."

Her wedding was going to happen after all.

AFTER THE VISIT TO WRIGHT, the bank, and Wright again, Royston needed rest. For days, he'd slept, eaten, and done nothing else as if he were an infant.

He hadn't had the strength or desire to read the newspapers. If a scandal had started because Miss Taylor and Wright had eloped, he had no idea.

Officially, he was recovering from a bad case of 'brain fever,' and no one had bothered him.

Angeline entered his bedroom, carrying a newspaper.

"It's done." She dropped onto the bed next to him and opened *The Standard*. "*The scandal of the week sees a Mr. W. and a Miss T. involved in eloping. Mr. W with Lord W. were seen at Doctors Common, one assumes to purchase a special license.*"

"Good." He stroked her knuckles.

"There's more." She resumed reading. "*Miss T. was at the centre of another scandal last week when she was caught in the middle of an assignation with Lord W. That's you, darling. Lord W. and Miss T. were engaged as a result, but it's obvious now that marriage will never happen. Mr. W. must have had a stroke of luck because rumour is he's suddenly an incredibly wealthy man.*" She folded the newspaper. "Congratulations. You're no longer going to get married."

"Uh-uh. Correction." He put the newspaper aside. "I'm going to get married to you." He pulled her down for a kiss.

"Will the scandal affect your candidature at the House of Lords?"

His mood darkened as he toyed with the annoyingly small buttons of her shirt. "I haven't thought about that, to be honest. I'd like to talk to Lord Redvers, but I assume he doesn't want to see me."

"You don't seem distraught."

"I'm upset. Do not doubt. But almost losing you put things into perspective. I want the seat, but I'm glad to be alive and be your husband-to-be." He grinned when he unbuttoned the first little bugger.

She swatted his hand away. "What are you doing?"

"I haven't been with you in a while."

"What are you talking about? We've been together day and night."

"Yes, but I was unconscious, sick, or both. I need you, especially since visions of you in that damn nightgown torment me."

She stopped his wandering again. "It was a hallucination."

"But a very good one although the reality is better." He kissed her again.

"No, you need to recover first. A tumble can wait."

"I need you."

"Please, concentrate." She gave him a quick, depressing peck on his lips. "Miss Taylor, no, Mrs. Wright might not be a problem anymore, but the earl still is. Unless we stop Lord Havisham, he'll keep trying to ruin you for some reason."

"Yes, but not now." He barely started kissing a delicious spot on her neck when a knock came.

"My lord?" Enright said from the other side of the door.

"One moment." He had to release his grip on Angeline.

She stood up and sat on the armchair.

"Come in." Royston sat up.

Enright came with a silver mail tray. "It arrived a moment ago. The footman who delivered it said it was urgent."

"Thank you, Enright." Royston opened the letter.

Angeline sat next to him again when Enright left. "Who's it from?"

"Lord Redvers."

As damn usual. Bad news, bad news, and more bad news.

"What does he say?" Angeline prompted him.

"Lord Redvers has withdrawn his support. I no longer have a champion for the House seat." While disappointed, he forced himself to remember he was alive and well and that he was going to marry Angeline.

"It's because of the scandal, isn't it?"

"Actually, no. Lord Redvers wrote that, before eloping, Georgiana had a chat with him and told him what Lady Redvers had done. It seems that Lord Redvers was reluctant about withdrawing his support, even despite the scandal because he'd given his word and because he wasn't happy about what his wife had done to me, but Lord Havisham convinced him not to help me." He exhaled and leant back on the pillow. Another kick in the teeth. "So I lost Lord Redvers, and Havisham is still causing trouble. Great."

"I'm so sorry." Angeline caressed his cheek. "That man is awful."

"And the worst thing is that I don't know why he is doing this." He rubbed the bridge of his nose. "When I was his footman, he'd always treated me well. When I became a baron, he supported me. We never argued about anything. Our disagreements started recently when he asked me to break into your house."

"He also lied about my mother and made up the lie about that list. And let's not forget Police Constable Davis. Lord Havisham must have held a grudge against you for a while."

"But why? I don't understand." He pulled her closer to hug her, needing her comfort.

She rested her head on his chest.

The tender moment was cut off by Enright's booming voice coming from the corridor.

"Madam, I must protest," Enright said.

"Please do protest as much as you like." Mrs. Haywood's voice rang out. "I'm sure it'll be very entertaining. *The butler doth protest too much, methinks*." She laughed.

Footsteps pounded.

"Mama." Angeline straightened.

Royston sat upright. "What now?"

Mrs. Haywood shoved the door open and hurried into the room, followed by a red-faced Enright.

"Darling, Lord Wharton." Mrs. Haywood curtsied.

"My lord, I'm sorry." Breathless, Enright put a hand on his side. "Mrs. Haywood rushed up the stairs before I could stop her."

"Less sherry and Yorkshire pudding is my advice," Mrs. Haywood said. "It wouldn't harm it if you stopped smoking as well."

"Mama!" Angeline said as Royston said, "Thank you, Enright."

"I'm so happy to see you, sweetheart." Mrs. Haywood tried to kiss Angeline's cheek, but Angeline didn't let her.

"Mama, please. What are you doing here?"

Mrs. Haywood was hurt if the sudden tightening of her lips was any sign. "First, I wanted to apologise in person to the baron."

Royston glanced at Angeline. He didn't want to cause more disagreement between Angeline and her mother. Despite the fact he was still upset about what Mrs. Haywood had done to him, he gave her a nod. *Now, please leave.*

"I want to make amends," Mrs. Haywood said.

"Please, no." Angeline exhaled.

Mrs. Haywood ignored her, making herself comfortable on the edge of the bed. "I'm aware that Lord Redvers withdrew his support of Lord Wharton on the Parliament seat because of Havisham's intrusion."

How did she know that? Royston had just received the letter.

"Yes, and?" Angeline asked.

"Well." Mrs. Haywood jutted out her chin. "Here's what I'd do if I were you. Invite Havisham here for an honest chat. If he refuses to stop blocking Lord Wharton, I'll spill what I know about him to his ducal wife."

"Blackmailing? Again?" Angeline's fierce expression made her look like a warrior. "Haven't you caused enough trouble?"

Mrs. Haywood held up a hand. "I won't say anything. My mere presence here will scare Havisham. He's a coward, trust me. He'll panic and do whatever you ask. I won't need to talk at all."

Not the best of plans, but it was worth a try.

Royston scratched his chin. "I like the idea of having an honest conversation with Havisham. No tricks or lies. Just honesty."

Mrs. Haywood's smile sent a chill down his back. "Excellent. Let me arrange the meeting."

twenty-five

SITTING IN AN armchair in his drawing room, Royston stared at the door, waiting for Havisham to come.

Angeline paced, looking out of the window now and then. Mrs. Haywood instead kept knitting in front of the warm hearth as if she didn't have a care in the world. She wore a big ruby ring that caught the light of the flames, almost in a disturbing way. The flashing colour reminded him of the Theatre Royal.

"How can you be so calm?" Angeline asked her mother.

Mrs. Haywood lifted a shoulder. "We have a strategy. I'm sure everything will go as planned, and if it doesn't, we'll make another plan. That's how you survive."

Angeline's gaze shot towards the ceiling. "I hope you're right."

Enright entered the room. He cast an apprehensive glance at Mrs. Haywood. The woman must still have made him wary. "My lord, Lord Havisham."

"Thank you, Enright. Show him in." Royston stood up although his legs were still like rubber.

Angeline stopped pacing and faced the door. Mrs. Haywood rose as well, dropping her knit work on the armchair.

"What is the meaning of your summoning—" Havisham stopped in the middle of the room when he saw Mrs. Haywood.

A couple of scorching glances were exchanged between them.

"Havisham." Mrs. Haywood curtsied with a gesture that was anything but courteous.

Angeline curtsied as well, but her movement was brusque and short. "Lord Havisham."

"Wharton?" Havisham ignored the ladies. "Why am I here?"

"I'll get straight to the point," Royston said. "I know you persuaded Lord Redvers to withdraw his Parliamentary support for me. I also know that the list Mrs. Haywood was supposed to have doesn't exist, and that Mrs. Haywood has never abused fallen women for her purposes, although Mrs. Walsh said otherwise."

"What?" Mrs. Haywood's voice turned low and dangerous. "What did you say?"

Damn. He'd never mentioned to Mrs. Haywood that particular lie of Havisham.

"Lord Havisham said you abused young women for your blackmailing jobs," Angeline said. "That you had a list of fallen women you exploited."

"How dare you." Mrs. Haywood's nostrils flared. She was so enraged that her ruby ring seemed to flash more brightly. "I would never do such a thing."

"Mrs. Walsh," Royston said, "the woman, who manages the women's shelter I sponsor, claimed that a lady with your name and matching your description visited the shelter with the purpose of recruiting women."

"Utter poppycock." Mrs. Haywood pointed a finger at Havisham. "He must have sent a woman who looked like me to the shelter to use the information against you."

Havisham huffed as if bored although a light tremor in his hand belied his true feelings.

Royston continued. "I also know it was you who called the police that night I entered Miss Haywood's house."

Mrs. Haywood widened her eyes. Oops. Another thing she wasn't aware of.

Royston continued, "But I need to hear from you the reason you did all these things. There is no private detective. It was all a lie to convince me to steal those damning documents. Why?"

Havisham surveyed the room before answering. "Do you really think I want to see my former footman rise as my equal in the House of Lords? You were a good servant, and I admit you have a talent for business, but we're talking about a title, politics, and fortune. About being part of Parliament, about creating this nation's laws. These are responsibilities and privileges you have no right to receive. All your opinions about saving those fallen women. Oh, please. They're just harlots. The work we do in the House of Lords is above you and your little charities. Money is one thing. Blood nobility is quite another, and you'll never be one of us."

Royston forced himself to remain calm although Havisham's words hurt him deeply. "I see. Well, now that we're laying our cards on the table, I guess we can start a proper battle between us. I will fight for a seat. I will be in the House of Lords."

"You'll never have a seat in Parliament," Havisham said. "And I'm through with all of you. I don't want to be threatened or blackmailed ever again." He turned towards Mrs. Haywood. "Have I made myself clear? Or I swear I'll have you arrested."

Mrs. Haywood folded her hands in the small of her back in a neat, calm pose. "Very clear. No more blackmailing if you promise to leave Angeline alone."

"I don't care about your daughter," Havisham said.

"Mama." Angeline's cheek reddened.

"Then we have a deal." Mrs. Haywood stretched out her hand towards Havisham. "Angeline and I will be out of your life if you stay out of ours."

Havisham shook her hand. "Finally, you little, insufferable whore."

Royston strode towards him. "I can't tolerate such language towards Mrs. Haywood."

Mrs. Haywood smiled. A sweet, warm smile that caught him off guard. The resemblance to Angeline became striking.

"Thank you for being so gallant, my lord," she said. "Five, four, three..."

"You're welcome. Why are you counting?" Royston had barely time to ask before Havisham slumped into his arms.

"Two, one." Mrs. Haywood looked ten years younger. "Voila'."

"Goodness." Angeline clamped a hand over her mouth. "Mama?"

"He's heavy." Royston slumped the earl on the sofa and bent over him. "Havisham?" He shook his shoulder. When the earl didn't reply, Royston slapped his cheek. "Hullo? Angeline, send for the physician."

"Oh, don't worry. Stay here, Angeline." Mrs. Haywood waved him away. "I just drugged him."

"What?" Angeline and Royston said together.

Mrs. Haywood waved a hand, showing a needle coming out of the ruby of her ring. "Injection. This is my Lucrezia Borgia's ring. Did you know Lucrezia was the governor of a city called Spoleto? First woman to hold that position."

"Mama!" Angeline said.

Mrs. Haywood sighed. "I digress. An injection is more effective than a glass of wine. Do not fret. I can guarantee there won't be any... what was the word again? Right, adverse reactions. I've used this potion on Havisham a few times, and the version I gave him is a diluted one as a precaution. He's going to be perfectly fine."

Angeline put a hand on her heaving chest. "Mama, you must stop drugging people."

"I need to sit." Royston sat on the armchair, staring at Havisham's stunned face.

Wide eyes, mouth open, and eyebrows up to the hairline. The

look would be comical if not for Royston's fear the earl might feel sick.

"I had no intention of drugging him. I swear it." Mrs. Haywood pouted. "I wanted a peaceful resolution to this mess that I, admittedly, started. But he tossed lies about me harming fallen women. I couldn't let the insult go. After this one time, I promise I'll retire from my blackmail activity."

Royston gazed from Mrs. Haywood to the half-unconscious earl and wasn't able to produce a single thought.

"I agree to receive that allowance, Wharton, or shall I call you Royston? Roy, perhaps. It sounds more charming to me. That means you and Angeline have my blessing. See, I was too proud to accept your financial help, but the recent events made me change my mind. Anyway. Let's get back to work."

He remained silent. Perhaps it was all a bad dream. "Mrs. Haywood..." He tried again.

"Later, Roy. I'm busy." She cleared her voice. "Now, since we're here and the damage has been done, we'd better take advantage of the situation. I need you two to be very quiet."

ROYSTON'S HEALTH had improved since his poisoning.

Mrs. Haywood's special healing tonic, made with herbs he couldn't pronounce, had been more effective than his physician's pills. He had to admit Mrs. Haywood possessed a ridiculously vast knowledge of medicinal herbs, which was commendable when applied to good deeds. The fact that she wasn't against his marriage with Angeline anymore also helped.

Last but not least, his new candidature in the House of Lords by none other than the Earl of Havisham and Lord Redvers was just the icing on the cake.

"Congratulations." Angeline kissed his cheek. "You're a member of the House of Lords."

"I still can't believe it." He read the official statement with the Parliamentary seal again. "Drugging Havisham isn't something I approve of, but your mother was right."

The poly potion hadn't had any adverse effects on Havisham. Quite the opposite. Mrs. Haywood had convinced him that championing Royston's seat was in his and his family's best interest and that he should enlist Lord Redvers to also champion Royston.

Havisham hadn't wasted time. He'd made a passionate speech to the other members of the House of Lords, and soon it was done. Royston was one of them.

"We cheated, though." He folded the letter, a bitter-sweet taste in his mouth.

"It was the earl and my mother who did the cheating."

"Yes, I suppose that's true. And the important thing is that I can fight to have the women's welfare bill approved."

Angeline reclined on the bed in his bedroom.

He lay next to her and slipped a hand under her skirts. "I'm fully recovered. I hold a seat in Parliament, and we're going to get married soon. I think this is the perfect time to be together."

"I'm afraid you'll have to wait a little longer." She jumped off the bed.

"What? No."

"Yes. Wait."

Royston scoffed when she locked herself in his private water closet.

A few long minutes later, she poked her head outside. "Close your eyes."

"Done." He did as she asked.

There was a swishing of fabric and other sounds.

"Are you all right?" he asked.

"Yes. Keep your eyes closed."

"I will." How sad.

But then again, he ought to woo her again. He was aware that he hadn't wooed her at all. Everything between them had happened without a proper courtship. He would change that.

"I have a surprise for you."

He frowned. "Is it an object?"

"Er… no. It's alive." More fabric swishing.

"I'd love a dog."

She chuckled. "You can open your eyes now."

"I was thinking— bloody hell!" He couldn't say anything else. He was shocked.

She wore only a flimsy nightgown that softly caressed her curves. Her dark-pink nipples puckered under the fabric, and her glorious hair was loose, falling in glossy curls to her waist.

"Is this like your hallucination?" she asked.

He licked his dry lips. "It's better." He didn't even realise he'd jumped off the bed. "The nightgown looks fantastic. You look fantastic."

He stretched out a hand to touch her, but she stepped back.

"Not yet."

"Angeline," he growled. "Please."

She shook her head. "Lie on the bed."

Scoffing and puffing, he did as told. Or tried to. He walked towards the bed while looking at her, and he didn't see the ottoman. He tripped and plopped down unceremoniously on the bed.

"Goodness, Royston." She rushed to him, which was the most spectacular view he'd ever been lucky enough to see.

As she ran, the diaphanous fabric clung to her body, and her hair floated around, making her look like a forest nymph.

"Are you all right?" She put a hand on his chest.

"Yes… I mean, ouch."

"Where are you hurt?"

He pointed at his lips. "A kiss to make it better?"

She smiled. "You scoundrel."

The moment she leant closer to kiss him, he captured her nape and pressed his mouth against hers. Finally.

As he devoured her mouth, all his need for her burst out. He couldn't keep his hands to himself and stroked her. The fabric created a delicious, silky friction. Her warmth reached his eager palms through the fabric. He rolled her nipples until she moaned and pinched them hard to hear her moaning louder.

He drew one into his mouth with the fabric and all, smiling as it hardened and lengthened further.

"Royston." She reclined her head and fell back on the bed.

He took advantage of that by stretching on top of her. The delicate straps of her nightgown didn't oppose any resistance when he slid them off her shoulders. He gently pulled down the fabric to reveal her lovely breasts.

As he tongued her again, this time without barriers, he slid a hand between her thighs to find her wet and ready.

Her response was immediate. She spread her legs wide. He rubbed her but lifted his head from her breast to stare at her. She was a glorious sight, all flushed, lips glistening, and eyes half-closed. Her scream was as loud as ever when she found her release.

"Please." She urged him on.

Despite his raging desire, he went slowly because he wanted to savour every moment with her. This time he didn't rush. He inched inside her, watching her reactions. He paused to kiss her and brush a curl from her face. He took his time.

When they found their release together, it wasn't simply a temporary pleasure. It was a soul-binding moment, a solemn oath shared between them.

epilogue

BEING A BARONESS was a rather complicated affair.

After the beautiful but simple wedding with white roses, a lovely cake, Royston handsome in his dark suit, and her mother crying buckets—who knew for whatever reason?—Angeline had found herself inundated with invitations to afternoon teas, parties, and dinners, but not because people were interested in her.

Most were prying into what had happened with Georgiana Taylor and Mr. Wright's sudden fortune, asking if it was true that Mr. Wright had played at their wedding. But she didn't mind. As long as Royston's reputation remained intact and no one made comments on his sanity or his past, she was happy.

Mama had channelled her passion for medicinal herbs and remedies in a new direction. She now worked with Mrs. Walsh at the women's shelter, taking care of the girls who escaped from brothels.

Angeline couldn't be more proud of her. Not that Mama had stopped cheating whenever she could; cheating was in her nature.

Royston was sitting at his desk in his study as he often did as of late. From the moment he'd started to work at the House of Lords, he'd been so busy Angeline had seen very little of him.

"May I?" she asked.

"Of course, my love." He opened his arms, and she ran to sit on his lap. "I'm sorry I've been busy."

"How are you faring?"

"It's harder than I thought. All I ask is for the government to guarantee help and support to women who have a child out of wedlock, are sick, or are incapable of providing for themselves. They need help not to be shunned. Putting the law to work is complicated."

"The shelter has received dozens of donations though. Your work is bearing fruit."

"Too slowly, and I suspect your mother is behind half of those donations." He shook his head. "She must have used her Lucrezia Borgia's ring to force many a lord to donate to the cause."

"Perhaps we can use Mama's potions to speed things up in Parliament."

He laughed. "No, it's all right. I cheated to obtain Havisham's support. I won't cheat again. I learnt my lesson. I have left my past as a thief well behind me. Besides, we're going to be busy." He frowned, reading a letter with a golden frame and several stamps and signets. "You won't believe it, but we're waiting for the visit of a Russian grand duke."

She tensed. "Excuse me?"

He read from the letter. "His Grace Dimitri Gruzinsky, Grand Duke of all the Russias, sent me a letter announcing his arrival in London and his request, although it sounds like an order, to meet me. I have no idea why." He scratched his chin. "It seems he has some unfinished business here."

"Oh, no." She covered her mouth.

He narrowed his gaze. "What is it? Do you know of him?"

She swallowed hard. "Royston, there's something I need to tell you..."

about the author

Love stories have always captured my imagination. What's better than two people falling in love with each other? I write steamy romance, usually with a paranormal twist in an historical setting. Add a touch of suspense and mystery and a pinch of darkness. I love stories with  strong, sexy heroes and mischievous heroines who pull no punches.

I live in the City of Sails, New Zealand, drinking tea (coffee gives me anxiety) and devouring books.

Join my newsletter for exclusive content and the chance to receive an ARC copy of my books. Just copy and paste this link into your browser:

Barbara's Newsletter

also by barbara russell

If you love steamy paranormal romance set in Victorian London, my Royal Occult Bureau series is for you:

<u>The Royal Occult Bureau Series</u>

Are you into shape-shifter romance? Check out my da Vinci's Beasts series, set in WW2:

<u>da Vinci's Beasts Series</u>

For more Victorian paranormal romance with witches and sexy warriors, see the Knights of the White Blade series:

<u>The White Order Series</u>

Love steampunk? Check out my Auckland Steampunk series:

<u>Auckland Steampunk Series</u>

www.ingramcontent.com/pod-product-compliance
Lightning Source LLC
Chambersburg PA
CBHW050304110726
47899CB00007B/2111